Once Ghosted, Twice Shy

JESSICA ARDEN

Ebook ISBN: 978-1-946188-11-3

Print ISBN: 978-1946188-12-0

For Abby, Marissa, and Michele, my very own partners in crime. XOXO

"Sometimes when opportunity knocks, it's with a polite hello. Other times, it's a sledgehammer through a wall leading to a secret passageway."
-Matilda Mayhew, girl detective
in *The Mystery of the Nine Hedgehogs*

"You *sure* this is for me?" I scrunched my eyebrows at the massive cardboard box on the delivery guy's hand truck.

He glanced at the manifest. "If you're Paige Harrington." His New Orleans accent was as thick as the bald cypress trunks in the bayou.

"That's me," I said. Paige Magnolia Harrington. Ghost tour gift shop manager, devoted friend, newly 25 and still with no idea what I wanted to do with my life.

"I actually have specific instructions that you're the only one who can sign for it," he said.

My eyebrow rose, and I sized up the enormous box currently blocking the main aisle of the Deveauxs' Historical Haunts gift shop. I briefly entertained the idea that my parents had sent a present — something to atone for the last-minute cancellation of their trip to visit me this weekend—but quickly discarded it. Their newest scientific breakthrough at work had come up unexpectedly. They'd hardly have planned ahead for an apology gift.

Not to mention that whatever the package contained was big enough to be a refrigerator or an arcade game. Anything like that they would've sent to my house.

"Hmmm," I said. I tried to shake it, then leaned my ear against the box. Heavy. Solid. No chirping. Phew.

The delivery guy adjusted his hat and looked at me like I was a few specters short of a ghost tour.

"The last unexpected package I accepted was a bulk delivery of live crickets," I explained. "It was supposed to go to a reptile exhibition in town. Only when I was calling to have it picked up, my co-worker peeked inside and accidentally unleashed a plague of biblical proportions on our little shop here." I wasn't exactly eager to repeat that experience.

Norman, ghost tour operator, friend, and unleasher of the aforementioned cricket plague leaped from the next aisle. His top hat slanted over his flop of wavy brown hair and pale face. "Don't accept it! It's a Trojan horse."

A smile tugged at my lips. Norman was an odd bird with a penchant for conspiracy theories and vampire novels, but a good sort otherwise. "I'm pretty sure we're safe from invading armies."

Norman lowered his voice melodramatically. "Or are we?"

The delivery guy looked at us like dealing with us was above his pay grade. "Nothing live in here or it'd have a special sticker. Where do you want it?"

"Storeroom, I guess." It was the only place in the shop big enough to hold whatever this was.

Once I'd signed for the package, I pulled off the tape, but struggled with the flaps of the awkward box. Norman appeared a few minutes later, slapped a box cutter into my hand and saluted. "I'll watch the shop while you uncover the secrets." He disappeared back into the shop with something that sounded like, "Godspeed."

After wrestling the cardboard off and removing the foam pieces packed around it, I regarded the hulking thing with even more questions than answers.

A large carnival-style fortune telling machine stared back at me. But instead of Zoltar inside the glass, wearing a chintzy wrap and looking crafty, this fortune teller resembled Madame Sophia, the famous NOLA psychic wrongly accused of murder and recently exonerated.

I got on the phone with Julie, one of my bosses, who also happened to be Sophia's granddaughter-in-law. "Hey, did you guys order a fortune telling machine for the shop with Madame Sophia inside?"

"No. Why?"

"Because there's one sitting here, and it came addressed to me, of all people."

"That's odd. Maybe it's from one of your admirers," Julie teased.

I snorted. "This is a pretty unusual gift to come from a stranger. Should I take her to dinner or buy her a fortune telling machine?" I balanced my hands like scales. "Fortune telling machine."

"Really makes a statement, I'll give it that."

"Maybe we can put it out front to attract more walk-by traffic."

"Sure. Hey, I gotta run. Text me a picture of it and let me know if you find out any more about the mysterious origins."

"Oh. My. Stars." Norman peeked in again and took in the fortune teller in all of her purple, gauzy glory. He covered his mouth. "Have you tried it yet?"

"Already abandoned your Trojan horse theory?"

Apparently so, because he was unwinding the cord from the back of the machine. The bare bulbs around the glass casing flashed to life, and an envelope fluttered to the ground.

I had to admit, the odd wonder of it all gave me a little thrill. There is nothing I loved more in the world than a mystery. Besides, I could use something to focus on other than my traffic jam of a life.

I lunged for the fallen envelope. Maybe it would hold the answers I sought.

On the outside, in vaguely familiar handwriting I couldn't place, someone had scrawled *Paige Magnolia Harrington.* Hmmm. Whoever had gifted this to me knew my middle name. Not that it wasn't public record somewhere. Probably. Inside, a thick cream paper merely said *welcome.* I squinted at the tiny cartoon drawing of a ghost at the bottom of the paper.

"Welcome to what?" Norman read over my shoulder.

I frowned. "That's the question, isn't it?"

Mannequin Sophia's heavily glittered eyelids blinked, and her plastic jaw opened and closed. "Pull the lever and make a wish," a mystical voice said.

Another thrill zipped down my spine. Something about this felt oddly inevitable. And right, somehow.

I pulled the lever.

A ball rolled through a metal maze behind Sophia.

OK, Paige Magnolia, make your wish. I sucked in a breath and thought of the way I'd felt growing up with parents who were passionate, so young, and were currently literally working on a cure for cancer. About how my friend Ines lit up at anything that involved planning or hacking into complex systems. About seeing how so many of my sorority sisters had found their "it" thing in life when I'd attended our alumnae luncheon last month.

And then there was me. Twenty-five, working in a ghost tour gift shop, and going home to my hedgehog for company. Granted, I had a lot of treasured friendships and positive things going for me. And I was *good* at managing the gift shop. My meticulous eye for details most people missed came in handy here. But it wasn't that thing that lit me up, not how my parents had their research. It ached sometimes, that hole inside of me where my phantom calling, a way I could help change the world for the better, should go.

Mannequin Sophia's arm swept across the space, and lights chased each other around the cabinet. Just a silly machine. Not a real fortune teller with the power to grant me a calling, I reminded myself.

A card dropped into the slot at the bottom of the machine. My fingers trembled when I snatched it up.

TWO

Instead of a fortune, the machine spit out a tarot card. I retrieved it from the slot and squinted at the dismal-looking illustration. The Tower, this one read. Lightning flashed across the card. The requisite tower loomed in the background, flames gouting from its windows. In the foreground, people fell from the sky to their demise.

I shuddered. "Well, aren't you the worst fortune telling machine that ever was?"

Despite carrying the cards and other sorts of divination items in the shop, I was no expert on their meanings. However, it didn't take a genius to see this wasn't a warm and fuzzy portent. If the card's scenario foretold "my thing," that was a firm "no, thank you" from me.

I sighed. Maybe I'd just double down on being the best darn gift shop manager ever.

I handed Norman the card. "Know anything about tarot?"

He shook his head. "Dude, whatever you wished for, I don't think you're going to get it."

I mulled over where the mysterious machine could've come from for the remaining fifteen minutes of my shift. Wendy

Deveaux, one of the owners of Deveauxs' Historical Haunts, blustered in with a flurry of long red hair and stompy boots.

"All ready for your awards gala this weekend?" I asked.

Wendy groaned. "Don't remind me. I'm only going to that ceremony to humor Alec." They were both being honored at the Crescent City Forty Under Forty gala for an app she and her husband had developed together. It was sort of like *Pokemon Go* for French Quarter ghosts.

Wendy could be grumpy and snarky at times, but was also competent and would do absolutely anything for her family and long-time staff, which now included me. She'd seemed perpetually annoyed with me for the first three months I'd worked here, but I had a hunch from the start there was a squishy marshmallow center inside her cactus exterior. Turns out I was right.

Her, "What the hell is this monstrosity?" from the back room told me she wasn't behind the delivery either.

Could it be a prank? A custom-made machine like this made for a pretty expensive prank.

"I wouldn't try that thing unless you like your forecast cloudy with a chance of apocalypse," I said.

Wendy pushed the lever anyway, but nothing happened. She shrugged. "Guess it only gives fortunes if there's bad news. You heading out?"

"Yeah, I'm meeting my old professor, Liz, at Crumbles around 5:30."

Liz was my favorite professor from college and had become my mentor and something like my cool aunt. We had a standing puzzle night every other week at the cafe she opened a few years back with her late sister.

After poking and prodding at the wooden cabinet for any hidden compartments or more clues to its origin, I went to text Liz I was on my way.

A notification I didn't recognize popped up.

You have a match, it said next to an icon of a ghost.

I cocked my head and clicked the notification. My screen flashed purple, and an icon of a cartoon ghost wearing a Sherlock Holmes hat and sporting a magnifying glass for a mouth appeared.

Weird. Did one of my old apps get rebranded? With the "matched" language, I wondered if this was a revamped dating app for people on New Orleans ghost tours. That was actually not a bad idea.

Clicking on the waiting matches notification took me to a screen with two buttons to choose from: *Fresh* and *Cold.*

My nose wrinkled. *I'll take my dates fresh, please.*

Swipe up to accept. Swipe down to reject, the directions said.

The screen populated with tiny pictures, some in black and white and others in color. I squinted. In one photo I recognized the cute, if a little too surfer dude-esque guy who worked at the daiquiri bar down the street. He always waved to me as I walked by. Sometimes we exchanged flirtatious banter, but we'd never formally introduced ourselves.

I clicked on his picture, which had a purple star in the top right corner. The bartender looked back at me with his floppy sun-kissed hair, tan-bronzed white skin, and lazy grin. Austin Des Jardins, the caption read. Occupation: bartender.

That was it. No profile about how he loved baby sharks and fast cars and wanted someone who wouldn't play games.

Wait, one more thing remained when I scrolled down further: DOD: yesterday. What the heck was DOD in this context? Duke of Daiquiris? Director of Denial? Date of Death?

I laughed a little at that, but shifted in my chair to fight the unease that accompanied the thought.

After a second, a message bubble popped up with a heart and a ghost emoji.

You and Austin are a match! Austin would like to communicate with you. Swipe up to accept.

Without thinking it through, I swiped up. Any caution I'd retained from my southern upbringing had long been thwarted by years at boarding school, being left to my own devices and following my curiosity, sometimes to unpleasant ends.

Aww, son of a stroopwafel, had I just downloaded the mother of all malware on my phone?

Three dots bounced on the screen. Anticipation pinged around my insides like the balls in the vampire pin-ball machine next door.

Austin: *Hey*

I rolled my eyes. Really?

The three dots bounced again.

Austin: *Sorry. New at this. Hit send before I finished my message. It's nice to see a familiar face on here.*

I had no idea u did this sort of thing. But then again, you work at a ghost tour place, so maybe I should have suspected.

What was *that* supposed to mean?

Austin: *So, anyway. You're the only one on here who doesn't look intimidating and might be friendly enough to give me a chance. Plus, I've always thought you seemed tough. I like that.*

Tough. Huh. That was a new one. I sat up straighter. Most people took one look at me: white, blonde-haired, blue eyed with brightly colored clothes and wrote me off as sweet, compliant, and harmless. At least until they knew me better.

Austin: *What do you say, want to team up?*

Okay, clearly I was missing something here. This was light years from Austin's smooth flirty charms. He sounded hesitant, almost backed into a corner to find someone. I highly doubted he was hurting for dates.

But before I could give it further thought, a scream pierced the air.

THREE

I fumbled the phone, my thumb swiping up the screen, and ran outside after Wendy to see about the commotion.

Norman lay sprawled in the street, one of his legs bent at an odd angle.

I crouched next to him, jostling his fallen top hat adorned with ribbon and skeleton hands. A few feet away, the wheels of an upside-down skateboard still spun.

"Are you okay? What the heck happened?" My gaze swept over him, landing on—oh no, was that bone?—peeking out from a tear in his black jeans. I swallowed and looked away to keep from losing my lunch all over him.

Dozens of bystanders on our heart-of-the-French-Quarter street waiting for their tour to start looked on under the street lamps, murmuring and chattering to each other.

"Someone lent me their skateboard. Wiped out warming up the crowd."

Wendy already had the paramedics on the phone.

"Next time, maybe just stick to the vampire jokes," I said.

He grinned and tried to stand. I caught his leg before he pushed too far and caused even more damage. "Easy."

"Speaking of next time, think you could take over my tour for tonight?"

✦▲✦▲✦▲✦

AND THAT'S how I ended up leading a ghost tour down Chartres St. that Friday night. Even though I'd hardly dressed for the occasion. Most of my coworkers rocked a sort of goth chic look, lots of black lace, top hats, and skull accessories. And here I was in my cheery pink sundress and strappy heels. I pinned a black lace fascinator with a pink skull in my hair to look a bit more the part.

I'd lament the heels part of filling in for Norman after our mile and a half trek through the Quarter, though.

Still, I carried on, until we arrived across from the old Ursuline convent with its white French-colonial facade. In the early evening light, the shadows played on the gray shutters and manicured hedges.

We stopped across the street under the purple and cream awning of Crumbles bakery where I should've been having coffee with Liz right now. I peeked into the window and waved to her. She delivered coffees to a table full of customers and tucked a lock of her shiny black hair with its single streak of gray behind her ear. She wiped her hands on her apron and gave me a warm smile and wave. I felt bad all over again for bailing on her tonight. Since her sister had passed away earlier this year, she'd tucked into herself and did little besides work.

But as much as I'd like to be in there having puzzle night, I turned back to my tour group.

"So, the Ursuline convent that you see across the street is one of the oldest buildings in New Orleans. And one filled with the most secrets." I paused for dramatic effect. I could be a performer too if the occasion called for it. "If you're into vampire lore, you may already know the story of the Casket Girls."

I told the story of the young women who'd arrived from Quebec in 1728 with nothing but coffin-shaped caskets of belongings, set to stay with the nuns in the Ursuline convent until they were married off and were later rumored to be vampires.

"But there are legends of even more secrets buried under the oldest standing building in the city," I said. I mentally rubbed my hands together, getting to my favorite part. "Has anyone ever heard of the Enclave?"

"That's the secret society, right?" A mustached gentleman who looked distinctly like a math teacher asked.

"A splinter of the Illuminati or something," said another tourist.

"That's right. There have been whispers about the Enclave running the power structure in New Orleans for hundreds of years. Secret underground meetings. A deal with the devil. Ritual sacrifices in exchange for power and riches beyond their wildest imaginings."

"Where do I sign up?" a guy in a Red Sox jersey asked, drawing laughter from the rest of the group.

"You don't go to the Enclave. The Enclave comes to you," I said. "Rumors abound of secret invitations, lavish vetting parties, and for the chosen few who prove worthy of initiation, the granting of their deepest wish."

"You just have to sell your soul, right?" Red Sox guy joked.

"So the stories go," I said.

I'd long wondered how much truth lay behind the shrouds of mystery. Growing up on my great grandmother's mystery novels, I'd been obsessed with the idea of the secret passages under the French Quarter and had spent more than a few nights in college searching for signs of them after a few cocktails.

Just as I was about to get into the fabled network of secret tunnels underfoot and the ghosts of the Enclave that haunted them, something heavy crashed from the balcony to the awning above my head.

I flung my arms out and stepped back to protect my group. Something large thudded at my feet.

No, not something, some*one*.

A person falling from the sky. Or rather, from the upstairs balcony. The similarity to the creepy Tower card wasn't lost on me.

Heart hammering, and breath hitching all over the place, I knelt to check for a pulse and see how much damage had been done.

All my thoughts jumbled, and weird disjointed bits of observation hit my senses before I could process it all. Nice dark washed jeans and a blue button-up shirt. The smell of garlic and cherries overpowering the street smells of red beans and rice. Shrieks from behind me. I was afraid to look at his face. I maneuvered his shoulder, so he lay flat on his back.

I held two fingers to his neck to check for a pulse. Icy cold seeped into my fingers at the touch. Bruising and puffing mottled the surrounding skin like a macabre necklace. I waited and waited, willing his heart to beat, but nothing came.

That's when I finally allowed my attention to shift to his face.

I did a double take. One of his cheeks pressed to the dirty street; the other faced upward. Prickles of dread raised the hairs on my neck as I pushed the hair off of his forehead.

No. No. No.

His left eye had swollen shut. He was missing the flirtatious smile, but this was definitely Austin Des Jardins. The same guy from the daiquiri bar that I'd been mysteriously "matched" with on that Ghosted app.

"Austin?" My voice came out with a squeak, halfway between a statement and a question. He was so young, barely older than me, if I had to guess, with so much life ahead of him. I wondered if he'd had a chance at a calling of his own before his untimely death.

"Hey Paige." Austin's familiar voice answered with a somber note.

I jolted.

My palm flew to my heart, then I held it out in front of his mouth, waiting for breath. Maybe I'd made a mistake before. But none came.

A cool breeze floated over my neck and shoulders, lifting the hair from my nape. A cool that was out of place in the sweltering Louisiana summer.

That's when I realized the voice had actually come from behind me. Goosebumps paraded up my arms again.

Sirens wailed in the distance. Good. Hopefully, someone called 911.

I spun around, standing in the process. Hovering just above me was a perfect copy of the now-dead body on the street. Only this one was bleached of color, and I could see right through him to the tables and cases of muffins and pies in the cafe.

Ghost Austin gave me a sheepish smile and tucked his hands into his incorporeal pockets. "So, thanks for taking my case."

My knees wobbled, and my vision swayed. I pitched backward. The world went black.

FOUR

And that's how I fainted on top of a dead body.

Good times.

When I came to again, I was perched on one of Crumbles' cushioned purple chairs, wrapped in a crinkly reflective blanket. A paramedic shined a bright light in my eyes and checked me over. Meanwhile, Liz fussed over me.

"Should I get her some tea? Or coffee? Will that be bad for her in her condition?" Liz asked the paramedic. My petite former professor frowned in distress as she regarded me. She had a pretty, round face and long eyelashes, and the same no-nonsense features as her sister Laini, who smiled down at us from a photograph of the two of them visiting their grandparents' ancestral home in China. "What do you feed someone in shock? Muffins?"

The paramedic clicked off his flashlight. "Muffins and beverages are fine, ma'am. You're all good, young lady, but take it easy for a bit, and see if someone can drive you home."

"That poor boy," Liz said. "How could this happen?"

I reached over and squeezed her arm. She'd been through

too much death already this year after losing her sister. Adding this was like the cherry on top of an unfortunate sundae.

Liz wrung her hands. "I'm going to get muffins. Blueberry?"

I nodded, still feeling a little unsteady.

An ambulance's lights strobed outside. With notebooks in hand, a group of police officers moved through the crowd talking to witnesses.

"They asked us to stay put until they could question everyone at the scene," Liz said.

She placed a blueberry muffin, towering with her signature secret recipe sugar crumbles in front of me along with one for herself, then went back for two steaming mugs of coffee.

"You okay?" she asked.

I frowned. Was I? My brain was still catching up to my body. A corpse had just fallen at my feet, and I'd hallucinated, or maybe seen, his ghost.

I sipped my coffee. "I'm better off than Austin."

"You knew that guy?" Liz asked.

"Just a little. He worked at a daiquiri bar down the street. You know, the one that does frozen drinks by the yard?"

The image of Austin's ghostly form with that sad, resigned look on his face flitted into my mind. Real or figment of my imagination? The product of reading my great grandmother's mystery novels too many times? Then the acronym DOD from the Ghosted app sprung back to my mind. *Date of death: Yesterday.*

I cast a stealthy glance around the cafe to see if Austin's ghost hung around amongst the brightly colored chairs.

"Looking for someone?" Liz asked.

Okay, maybe my glance was not so surreptitious. I blame the fainting. I shook my head to clear it. "My head's still fuzzy."

"That poor boy," Liz said again, scrubbing her hand over her face. "I wasn't his biggest fan, but still, how could this happen?"

"You knew him too?"

Liz scrubbed her face and looked up at the mural of the French Quarter streets her sister had painted before they opened. "My sister would say he just got on the wrong track for a bit," Liz said. "She was like you that way, always giving everyone the benefit of the doubt."

Though Liz Pickett shared her sister's compassion, she reserved her trust for only a select few. I wondered what Austin had done to make a poor impression on her.

Liz opened her mouth, but before she could say more, two cops and a police photographer walked in, one officer with a sympathetic smile, the other with a scowl.

Scowley Face was a paunchy white man with a receding hairline who looked pissed off as if someone had stolen his punching bag. Smiley was Officer Declan Durocher, grandson of Madam Sophia, my doom and gloom fortune teller's likeness, and brother-in-law of my boss, Julie. He strode over and greeted Liz and me, his brown eyes filled with concern.

"Hey there, Officer Friendly," Liz said, giving him a wan smile. "How are those girls of yours?"

"Real good." Declan's eyes crinkled, and I noted the sunburn reddening the bridge of his nose. He shared my light, freckled complexion, which crisped at the mere mention of sun, courtesy of my Irish and English ancestors.

"They still gobble up your cherry tarts before I can even get a bite in." Declan had such an abundance of confidence, you could shave a bit off and spread it around. But his was the sort that blanketed people and pulled them into the fold rather than taking something away. "You doing okay? I'm sorry all this happened on your doorstep."

"I'm really sorry this happened at all," Liz said.

Declan gave a rueful nod and pushed a wave of dark hair out of his eyes.

"Which of you's the owner of this place?" Scowley broke in. Liz raised a hand, and with zero niceties, he launched into questions about suspicious activity and anyone using the stairs that connected the back of the dining area to the upstairs area that housed the restrooms and had balcony access.

"We need to get statements from all of you to see if we can piece together what led to this," Declan interrupted. "You up for answering some questions?"

The other cop, Officer Crowder, according to his badge, grimaced.

I nodded.

"If you're the one asking the questions." Liz smirked at Declan and seemed to enjoy Officer Crowder's irritation with her. "Let's pull up some chairs. I can get you boys some coffee."

"Thank you, but you don't need to trouble yourself. You've been through enough tonight," Declan said.

Officer Cranky Pants grumbled his disapproval and interrogated Liz.

"Hey, squirt." Declan sat next to me and ruffled my hair. "How come I always find you in the eye of the hurricane?"

He'd stopped by the shop earlier to see his brother and found me kneeling over Norman. And then there were those times in college. One was a drunken night during Greek Week when I'd recovered a stolen llama who'd been painted pink and green. And another when I'd tracked down two douchebags having a contest to see who could roofie the most sorority girls.

"What can I say? I don't go looking for trouble. It comes looking for me."

"I'm not so sure about that." He glanced over at the photographer snapping shots of the back stairwell. "You doing okay? I hear you went down like a Victorian lady without her fainting couch out there."

"I'll be fine." I think. Just seeing ghosts. As you do. My gaze twitched around again for any sign of said ghost. If he was still here, he was lying low. I rubbed the goose egg on the back of my head. "Though a fainting couch would've been nice. Any idea yet of what happened to him?"

"Not yet. But it seems pretty clear he'd been dead for at least a day before someone heaved him off the balcony. Did you see anyone up there before he fell?"

I shook my head. "I was focused on the tour. Did anyone from the tour group see anything?"

"We're still asking around."

As Declan ran through his questions, my mind whirred around the details like I was the protagonist of one of my great grandmother's mystery novels. Austin's injuries: blood matted in his hair, the frigid temperature of his body, the bruises all around his neck. Had someone strangled him? There had definitely been a fight involved. Had he just wandered into the wrong place at the wrong time? I wondered if his wallet was missing.

I frowned. No. If this were a random act of violence, it would have been much easier to leave him in the street. Why take the trouble to keep him on ice, lug him upstairs, and push him off?

I almost wished his ghost would come back and shed some light on all of this. Austin, what did you get yourself into?

I puzzled this over as Declan moved on to question the barista, Carlie, a stylish blonde who'd been working at the counter. I listened in for anything else that might be relevant.

Officer Cranky seemed particularly aggressive with Liz, which put my hackles up. I wondered if the two of them had bad blood or if he just didn't like women who weren't meek and mild. "Do you have a walk-in cooler or freezer?"

"We do, but I think we would've noticed if we had a corpse next to the chocolate cream."

"Or you put him there. No noticing necessary," Cranky clapped back.

"Whoa." Declan shot out a hand, stepping back to the conversation. "We have no evidence to suspect anyone here had anything to do with that young man's death. You have info I don't?"

Crowder met his hard glare with one of his own. "Maybe."

I darted a glance at Liz. Her icy composure faltered the tiniest bit. But enough that a chill snaked down my spine.

Then Declan turned to Carlie, the barista. "Can you corroborate this? Did you go into the walk-in today? Did anyone else?"

Carlie nodded. She usually looked like she'd walked out of a J Crew catalog, with her peaches and cream complexion and just-off-the-yacht wardrobe. Now, though, she looked like a gator lurked in her yacht's headlights. "We're in and out of there all the time. There's no way there was—" Then her face paled.

"What is it?" Declan prompted.

"Actually, I haven't been in there today. I usually work the morning shift, when we do the baking, and I run back and forth a lot, but today, I've been out front the entire time."

"Angelica worked the morning shift. I can get you her contact info. She'll tell you," Liz said, folding her arms over her chest.

"Ms. Pickett, can you describe the nature of your relationship to the deceased?" Crowder continued.

"My *relationship?*" Liz spluttered.

"Where are you going with this?" Declan asked, the irritation plain in his voice.

"I got a tip that the dead guy robbed this place a while back. Could be she had a score to settle with him."

My eyebrows shot up.

"Is that true?" I asked. "The robbery part? I know you wouldn't hurt anyone."

Liz shifted and turned a frosty glare on Crowder. "Yes. I caught him shoving money from the cash register into a sack."

"That must have made you angry," Crowder said.

Liz's nostrils flared. "Of course it made me angry." Her fists clenched, but then her gaze flicked to her sister's mural and she let out a slow breath. "He got into some kind of trouble, I think. He apologized but said he *had* to take it. That if he didn't, things would go very, very bad for him. Then he promised to pay me back the next week if I didn't go to the police."

If his clothes were any indication, Austin didn't strike me as someone hurting for money, despite working in a service industry job like me. I got the impression he might be living off a trust fund, killing time while he figured out what to do with his life. Did he have a gambling problem or get mixed up with the wrong people?

"And did he?" Declan asked. "Pay you back."

"No," Liz answered. She bit at her nail.

"You sound awfully angry about that, Ms. Pickett," Officer Scowley said.

"He tried to steal from us. To hurt the business that my sister and I built with our own two hands. Laini's dream and her legacy. Yes, I was angry."

"So that's motive."

"In what universe? I wanted him out of my cash register, not out of his mortal coil. Even if I wanted to kill someone, I wouldn't do it over a couple hundred dollars."

Another officer leaned through the door and called out to Declan and Crowder, "A handful of bystanders saw a person in all black push the body over and retreat inside. The suspect wore a hoodie pulled all the way up, so no one got a good look at the face."

"Any of you see someone matching that description moving in or out of here?" Declan asked Liz and Carlie.

Both shook their heads.

"Is there a back entry to this place?"

Liz nodded. "I was right next to it when I heard the scream."

Officer Crowder narrowed his eyes at her again and his gaze flickered to her outfit—black pants and black fitted blouse. "Or maybe you were up there, pushed him, ditched the hoodie, and ran back down."

"That's ridiculous," I said. Liz was about five three and made of lean muscle. Austin was at least six feet tall and probably weighed at least double what she did. Granted, she was training for try outs for *American Ninja Warrior* not too long ago before her sister got sick. Even so, it was a stretch.

Liz didn't flinch, just leveled Officer Scowley with a glare that could melt a glacier. "Maybe you should be out there trying to find the actual killer instead of harassing me. You want to search the place for a black hoodie, go for it."

A sound behind the counter had all of us jerking our heads in that direction.

Austin's ghost had chosen that moment to appear again behind the pie case.

FIVE

A plate clattered to the floor behind the counter. Austin's ghost shot me a sheepish look and ducked out of sight.

Officer Crowder drew his weapon, because of course he did, and soundlessly made his way to the end of the pie case.

I sneaked a glance at Liz and Declan with my peripheral vision to see if anyone else had spied a ghostly entity by the espresso machine. But no one seemed to register any life-after-death in the place.

Crowder lowered his weapon. "Just a broken plate. Looks like chocolate cream pie." I guess he couldn't see dead people either.

"I'll get it." I hopped up, shucking my shock blanket, and leaped for the dustbin.

"Thanks, Paige," Liz said.

"No problem."

Once safely out of view of the living, I crouched down beside a forlorn-looking ghost Austin.

"What are you doing here?" I whispered.

Austin sighed and ran a hand through his floppy hair. "I was really hoping ghosts could still eat pie. I'm an emotional eater, you know?"

He reached for the shard of plate with most of the pie on it. His translucent fingers gripped it long enough for the plate to rattle against the floor but then passed right through it.

I gave him a commiserating look and gathered up the broken pieces. The afterlife had to be pretty miserable without pie. Especially Liz's pie.

"I meant, what are you doing *here*?" I gestured to the space between us. "Around me."

He frowned. "You took my case, remember? Isn't that how it usually works?"

Now came my turn to mirror his confusion. "How *what* usually works? And what do you mean by 'your case'?"

Connections formed in my mind but none that made rational sense. Then again, here I was, chatting with a dead guy who was trying to lick chocolate cream off the floor when I looked the other way.

I carried the remains of the plate to the garbage and shot a glance to see if anyone heard what probably sounded like me talking to myself. Luckily, everyone else had continued with questioning.

"On the Ghosted app," Austin said. The broken plate pieces crashed out of my hands. Luckily, I'd been standing over the bin.

Declan shot me a questioning look, and my heart sped up. Had he heard me talking to Austin? I grabbed a rag to clean up the rest of the mess and plastered on a nothing-to-see-here smile.

"In our orientation, they said any of us who were murder victims—" Austin cringed. "That is *really* not on brand for me. But in any case, we were eligible to be matched up with a living partner who specialized in solving cases to bring our killers to justice so we could move on. And you swiped up—thanks by the way—so here we are. Partners."

Partners.

I rubbed my temples. My already-aching head teetered on the verge of a major explosion from all of this.

"Liz didn't do it, by the way. She's not my biggest fan, but it wasn't her," he said.

"I know."

"How do you know?"

I shrugged and picked up a chocolate shaving. "Because I know her. She mentors kids and runs ultra-marathons. At least she did before her sister got sick. She bakes pies and talks about *The Good Place* when she's teaching economics. She's not about to give up her gym membership and her dreams to commit murder."

"You'd be surprised what some people are capable of." His expression darkened.

"Does that mean you know who killed you?"

"I have an idea."

"But you don't know for sure?"

He hesitated and fiddled with the hem of his shirt. "Right before I died, I was sealed in a room with five other people and a bunch of weapons. It could only be one of them who, you know." He drew his index finger across his throat and lolled his tongue. "Or in my case, I guess it would be more like—" He mimed being bashed on the head and strangled.

I grimaced and held up a hand. "Got it."

My legs tingled with pins and needles from crouching so long. And my head still swam from the fall. The loopiness swooped in big time. Was this really my life right now? Maybe I was still unconscious and just imagining all of this.

"So it sounds like you've got some suspects. That's a good start. Now I just have to go talk to five people who are possibly dangerous psychopaths and ask them uncomfortable questions. That's how you start investigating a murder, right?" The last part, I said mostly to myself.

Now that my trauma-addled brain put it that way, this whole thing sounded way less like an adventure out of the pages of one of my great grandmother's mystery novels and much more like a terrible idea. Especially when I was so out of my depth.

Austin regarded me warily and gave a nervous laugh. "You sound like you've never done this before."

"An orientation might have been nice for me too," I said under my breath.

But apparently ghosts have excellent hearing. Because Austin definitely caught that, if his furrowed brow was any sign. "Wait, are you saying you've really never done this before?"

"Guess it's the first time for both of us." Assuming I even wanted to get involved.

Austin blew out a breath and scrubbed a hand through his sun-bleached hair. He floated up to the ceiling and back and forth across the room. Was this the ghost equivalent of pacing?

"This is a bad idea," he said when he finally swooped back down to me. "A bad bad idea. I can't—"

"What's a bad idea?"

"These people who might've killed me—they're part of something dangerous. Well, almost part of it. Under its protection, in any case."

"Are you talking about the mob?" I tried and failed to picture Austin's peers as part of an organized crime syndicate.

"Less concrete shoes and more robes and rituals."

"A secret society?" An ominous tingle skittered down my spine.

Austin's eyes darted around wildly, like someone might be recording his every word. "Look, this was a mistake, getting you involved. I was in shock and desperate and saw a familiar face on the app. Let's just—"

"You don't want my help?" I blinked to ward off the unexpected hot prickle at the back of my eyes. A minute ago, I wasn't even sure *I* wanted to get involved. So what gave?

Austin flashed me a pitying look. Great, just what I needed, ghost pity.

"I thought this was your regular gig. I had no idea you were just trying this out and had no formal training."

"I'm more of a learn-by-doing sort of girl. And I'm a quick study."

"No doubt. But are you willing to gamble your life on that?"

Was I?

Austin studied me for a long moment.

"Look, I've got some things I need to check into." His gaze darted away from mine, and he slipped his hands into his pockets. I recognized a let-her-down-easy dismissal when I saw one. "Thanks for being game to help a dead guy out. I'm sure you'll be amazing at this one day. I'll see you around."

SIX

And that's how I got rejected by destiny and the ghost of an emotional-eater, all in one night.

Go me.

Once all the questioning wrapped up and we got the okay to head home, Declan offered to drive me.

I checked on Liz before I left. Not that she couldn't hold her own, but she'd launched into full-on cleaning mode now, and was more off-kilter than I'd ever seen her, especially with all the grief Officer Crowder had given her.

She pulled a small bakery box with my name on it from the cooler and thrust it at me. "Here. With all the commotion, I almost forgot."

"What's this?" I asked, untying the ribbon around the box.

She shrugged. "I know I missed your birthday a few days ago."

The smell of chocolate ganache wafted up when I opened the box. "Flourless chocolate cupcake?" Nestled into the perfect treat stood a pink candle.

"I know it's your favorite."

"Aww, Liz. You didn't have to do that, but I love it. Thank you."

I held myself back from hugging her because Liz, unlike me, was not a hugger. But her cheeks still reddened, and she waved off my display of emotion.

"Between you and everyone you send here, you probably account for at least a third of our business."

"You are a softie, even if you pretend you aren't," I said.

"Spread that around, and I'll deny it." She gave me a wry smile and squeezed my shoulder, the closest she came to displaying affection.

Tucked into the passenger seat of Declan's police cruiser, I called for reinforcements, texting Bridget and Ines, my best friends and housemates.

I know it's Friday and last minute, but I could really use a Partners in Crime night if you guys are up for it.

Bad day at work? Ines texted back.

If you call a dead bartender falling at your feet and then fainting on said dead body, then yes.

I kept the whole ghost part to myself, seeing as how I didn't think I'd be getting a return visit from ghost Austin.

OMG, are you OK?? You're probably still in shock. I can call Indira and see if she can come check you out, Ines texted back. Indira, one of our fellow sorority sister alumnae, was currently in med school training to be a pediatrician.

The paramedics already checked me over. I could really just use some friend time right now.

Say no more.

Bridget texted back with similar concern and a copious amount of emojis. *I'm filming in my workshop. Knock when you get here, and I'll come right up.*

A few minutes later, she'd texted me at least five hedgehog

GIFs and Ines sent me a picture of mimosas, Red Vines—my favorite—and Scattergories all set up on our dining room table.

This almost took the edge off of the whole murder/ghost/ominous fortune portion of the day.

✦A✦A✦A✦

I THANKED Declan for the ride home and hopped out at my Garden District home. Its white clapboard, calming blue grey shutters, and pink door greeted me from beneath the old gnarled trees that guarded either side. I made my way around back to where each of us had our own entrance that led to a private bedroom and bathroom suite. This major renovation came courtesy of Bridget and Ines' win on *Wheel of Fortune* Best Friends' Week several years ago. Despite missing the final puzzle, they'd still amassed enough winnings to donate a substantial amount to our local homeless shelter and fund the renovations to this place too.

Light glowed from the single window of Bridget's workshop across the back lawn from our entrances. I made my way there, the dewy grass of the lawn crunching underfoot. A sign that read, *Filming. Do not enter under penalty of torture via Nickelback* hung on the door.

A familiar infectious laugh came from inside the workshop/studio. I peeked inside and watched Bridget narrate to the camera, in her natural habitat among her 3D printer, laser cutter, myriad saws, glues, and paints. Full-figured and bubbly, Bridget was a natural in front of the camera. Her shiny brown curls, currently tied back from her creamy complexion with a bandanna, bounced, and I felt a surge of pride for my best friend who'd won over millions of viewers on her YouTube channel where she shared her geeky engineering projects.

She held up her latest, a bookshelf insert containing a miniature Sherlock Holmes' London that she'd been working on for the past few weeks. With the flip of a switch, the LED-wired gas lamps she'd custom cut flickered to life in front of 221b Baker St.

Bridget made the most incredible projects and talked about the relative viscosity of glues with the reverence that my parents talked about their research. She'd even recently quit her fundraising job to do this full time when she started making twice as much from ad revenue. Looking at her in this studio, it was so clear my friend was right where she belonged. Which made me simultaneously thrilled for her and even more lost after Austin's dismissal.

At my knock, Bridget shucked her safety glasses, stopped her recording, and flung her arms around me.

I hugged her back gratefully. "Can I see?" I said after a moment, pointing at her project.

Her face lit up. "I'm almost finished. I just need to add the windows into the storefronts and the signage. But first tell me about you."

"I'll be okay. When we meet up with Ines, I'll tell you everything. I just want to see something happy right now."

Bridget indulged and showed me how the project unfolded into separate sections that laid flat so she could work on each.

I ran a finger over the faux bricks she'd styled out of foam. "This is so cool, Bridge."

"You think so?"

"Of course. Hey, do you still have that tarot book? I want to look something up," I said. Maybe finding out more about the Tower card the fortune telling machine spit out could give me some more insight into what had happened today.

"Sure. I'll grab it when I go up to change. Should I bring the cards too?"

"I don't think I can deal with any more bad fortunes today."

My gaze strayed to another pile of wood in the corner "Ooh, what's that one?"

Bridget stepped in front of my line of sight and wagged a finger. "Don't go snooping into everything now."

I raised an eyebrow.

"That's your belated birthday present. It's taken me longer than I thought, but I still want it to be a surprise."

Bridget locked up, and we headed to the back stairs. Her mention of a birthday present made me think of the cupcake in my hands, and then, of course, of Liz and the way Officer Crowder seemed intent on accusing her of Austin's murder. An ominous wave of premonition rankled me. He couldn't arrest her for this, could he? Not without clear evidence. Which wouldn't exist because she didn't do it. Right?

I inserted my key, and a dark thought floated up.

Evidence couldn't be found unless whoever planted the anonymous tip about Liz's anger at Austin also planted more than that.

SEVEN

Trying to shake the thought of Liz being falsely accused of murder, I took a quick shower. After slipping into my fleece pajama pants and tank top, I collected Auguste, my hedgehog, for a good cuddle.

"Hey sleepyhead."

Auguste tottered out from his favorite hiding place, and I rubbed his tiny head. He leaned into my palm, and I scooped him up, nuzzling him into my neck.

I collapsed on my bed and let my gaze wander to the rows of Magnolia Castile mystery novels on my bookshelf among pictures of friends and family and Nu Omega keepsakes from my college days. The books' cloth-bound covers from the 1940s and 1950s were worn from many readings. These stories had provided exactly what I'd needed at so many junctures in my life. They'd given me solace and delight when my parents had shipped me off to boarding school. They'd given me Matilda Mayhew, a heroine who, like me, veered a little too curious for most, making me feel less like a weirdo. And my senior year of high school, when I'd learned it was my own great grandmother who'd penned them, they'd prompted my journey back to New

Orleans and to Ursuline University, where Magnolia had lived and founded a sorority while dreaming them up.

Could they help me now as well? I grabbed *Matilda Mayhew and the Mystery of the Falling Man* and set it on my nightstand for some late-night reading.

"You up for a trip downstairs for a girls' night? Mimosas and *Scattergories*," I asked Auguste as he burrowed into my clavicle.

A French accented voice answered back, "Seeing as I am not female and cannot indulge in your fizzy drinks, that hardly seems appropriate. Not that this has stopped me before."

I sucked in a sharp breath and blinked several times in rapid succession. Cradling Auguste to me, I swiveled around the room. "Austin, is that you playing a trick on me? Because I swear—"

But no one answered. There was only a sound like my hedgehog clucking his tongue at me. I held him away from my body to look him over.

"Auguste, did you just *talk* to me?"

"Of course. And to expound on my earlier answer, if apple slices are involved, I could be persuaded. Gala slices, mind you. Those Honeycrisps that Bridget favors are too sweet for my delicate palate."

Just when I thought this day couldn't get any more bizarre.

I set Auguste down on the bed and scrubbed my face. He pounced on a fluffy bit of comforter and rolled around. "My snuggle sack, if you please? I do enjoy the comfort of my pouch."

Still reeling, I grabbed said snuggle sack and the cross-body sling it clipped to. "You want to share why you've just decided to talk to me?"

"Paige, my darling, you wound me. I have always talked to you. It is not my fault it has taken you so long to listen."

"Okay. Okaaaaaay." I paced in front of my bookshelves.

"Now I can talk to ghosts and hedgehogs. This is fine. This is all fine."

Auguste cleared his little throat. Because of course he did. "*A* ghost and *a* hedgehog. We do not know if we can extrapolate from there."

"Right. True. Still weird."

"'Weird,' as you say, is a relative term. I would say this puts you at a distinct advantage."

"An advantage for what?"

"Solving difficult murder mysteries, naturally. That is still your intent, is it not?"

"Yeah, well, I got fired from my first case before I even started. Not so sure I have a future in that."

I pinched the bridge of my nose, and my gaze strayed to my open closet. My purple cap and gown hung squashed to one side above a pile of discarded whims. I'd ended up with a business degree, but mostly because I'd wanted to take more courses from Liz than because I had an actual passion for it. Books on entrepreneurship, cartography, handwriting analysis, criminal justice, and French cooking teetered below, all artifacts from pursuits I'd abandoned because I hadn't been a natural at them. Because of that, I reasoned they couldn't have been "the one." Was this ghost detective gig—something I might actually be good at—destined for that stack too?

"Don't be silly," Auguste said. "Are you going to let one minor disappointment determine the course of your future?"

"Never stopped me before," I muttered.

With a *tsk tsk*, Auguste scurried up my chest until he touched my cheek and nudged my gaze back toward my bookshelves. To the evidence of the things that *had* been constants in my life. My mysteries and my friendships.

Then I sighed. The app did have a whole slew of ghosts

looking for a crime solver. I could even start with a cold case to get the hang of things. "Okay, you have a point."

"Of course I do." I'd swear his wrinkly little chest puffed up. "Ratiocination is my strong suit. Just like my namesake."

"You going to be my Watson on these cases? Come along and help me solve crimes?"

"My dear, I am clearly the Monsieur Holmes in our partnership."

I laughed, already feeling lighter. "And why, for the love of Sherlock, do you have a French accent? I'm pretty sure you were born in Metairie."

"Did you not name me after the magnificent detective Auguste Dupin?"

"Yes, but—"

He cleared his throat. "From Edgar Allan Poe's *The Murders in the Rue Morgue*, widely regarded as the first modern detective story?"

"Well, yes."

"Then there you have it." He held out his little paw in an *I don't make the rules* gesture. "Sometimes the correct answer is the simplest one."

Once I had my philosophizing hedgehog tucked into his snuggle sack, I headed down to the dining room to Ines and Bridget.

I sliced up some Gala apples for Auguste and grabbed three forks to share my birthday cupcake.

Before I even sat down, Bridget slapped two Red Vines into my hand like a surgeon passing a scalpel, and Ines slid me a fizzy orange drink.

"Have I told you guys lately that I love you?"

Auguste turned up his nose at my mimosa but munched happily on his apples.

"And we have another surprise." Ines flipped her ever-present laptop around, and Natalie Wong, the fourth in our tight circle of friends, waved back from her tiny rented flat in Notting Hill.

I squealed, troubles momentarily forgotten. It had been a few weeks since I'd talked to Nat. An eight-hour time difference can really put a damper on communications. "Nat! Oh my gosh, isn't it like four in the morning there?"

"We have a really early shoot today." Nat worked as a script supervisor on a TV show called *The Eternal Duke*, billed as a soapy Jane Austen with vampires. "I can't stay long, but I heard you could use some reinforcements." She raised a *Wicked* coffee mug.

My heart glowed again. After my off-kilter day, it felt so nice to be around my people, where I belonged.

After quizzing Nat about the goings on in the English moors and streets of London, I gave everyone a recap of my day, starting with the fortune telling machine's ominous prediction, then on to the Ghosted app and the dead body.

Auguste poked his head out of his snuggle sack. "Are you not going to tell them about conversing with me and about Austin's ghost?"

I stayed silent a heart-pounding moment, waiting for anyone else to acknowledge Auguste's new powers of elocution, but I still appeared to be the only one who could hear him.

If I could trust anyone to believe me about the more supernatural portions of the day, it would be these three, but I still stopped short.

I was still processing everything. I didn't know what to make of this myself, let alone how to explain it to others without sounding like they should commit me.

After saying our goodbyes to Nat, Bridget, Ines and I talked at length about the unfortunate demise of Austin Des Jardins over a few rounds of Scattergories. We'd made our own lists after playing the original lists so much that we knew them like the streets of the French Quarter.

I called for everyone's answers after the timer went off.

"Colors," I announced.

"Maroon."

"Magenta."

"Margarita," Auguste offered.

"Mermaid," Bridget said.

Ines laughed. "Mermaid is not a color."

"It's a shimmery aqua." She made fish lips and lifted her joined legs like they were her siren tail. "I guarantee you there's a Pantone or at least a nail polish color called mermaid."

Ines shrugged, her caramel curls bouncing off of her shoulders.

"Okay, we'll allow it," I said. "Murder weapons."

"Machete," Bridget said.

"Mail with anthrax," I said.

"Mardi Gras beads," Ines said.

"How do you kill someone with Mardi Gras beads?" Bridget made a face.

Ines mimed a strangling, and I froze mid sip of mimosa. The image of Austin's injuries and the weird circular pattern of the bruising on his neck came back to me. Had someone used plastic beads to strangle him? It was summer, well past Mardi Gras season, but beads were a ubiquitous New Orleans souvenir year-round, available at every gift shop and corner drugstore. Including the one where I worked. How terrible would it be if I'd sold the killer their weapon? But beads seemed more like an improvised weapon, not something a premeditated killer would choose. Especially one associated with a group as dangerous and powerful as Austin suggested.

"Paige, you okay?" Ines looked back at me, concern creased into the light brown skin of her forehead.

"Yeah, fine." I shuddered, trying to shake off the image, and plastered a smile back onto my face. "Who wants more mimosas?"

Ines narrowed her eyes. "What is it? Beyond, well, the obvious."

After a moment's hesitation, I told them about the purple pattern on Austin's neck and the theories that had followed.

Ines studied me with her trademark penetrating gaze. "You're not going all vigilante justice on this, are you?"

"Who, me?" I tipped more champagne and orange juice into Bridget's and my glasses.

Ines and Bridget shared a knowing look. "This is like the time with the llama," Bridget said.

"I think worse," Ines said.

"Okay fine, maybe I considered some amateur sleuthing."

"Do you think that's a good idea, what with an actual murderer on the loose and all?" Bridget said.

"If it gets too dangerous, I can back off."

They both made incredulous noises. Even Auguste snorted. *Rude.* No hedgehog treats for you.

"What?"

"You're not the best at backing off when you haven't found answers," Bridget said.

I scoffed.

"Do you remember the time with the food truck?" Ines said. "And the roofie guys. And the llama?"

"Okay, fine. Point taken. I know I can get a little—"

"Obsessed," Ines supplied with a grin.

"Single-minded," Bridget chimed in.

"Preoccupied," Auguste added.

I narrowed my eyes at them. "I was going to say *focused*, but fine. In any case, I'll be careful. I promise. *If* I even pursue this."

I sat down in a huff. Could I let it go, even if Austin fired me? Of course I could. Probably. Maybe.

There was at least a twenty-five percent chance.

After we finished several more rounds of Scattergories, I tapped the tarot book Bridget had brought down. "Okay, how about some mysteries that aren't so dangerous."

"Ooh, yes. The enigmatic machine. Remind me the card it

gave you again," Bridget said, flipping through the paperback in her manicured hands.

"The Tower," I said. "There's a dude falling out of a window on it."

"Let me see that app of yours," Ines said. "Maybe I can figure out where it came from."

I unlocked my screen and passed her my phone. Navigating technology was Ines's superpower. She made a living white-hat hacking through corporations' firewalls to help them find weak spots and shore up their security. The woman never met an electronic device or system she couldn't pick apart. She loved them almost as much as sports and got super competitive about both.

Her curly brown hair with streaks of gold fell over her face, and she frowned. "I don't see any Ghosted app listed in your downloads. Did you delete it? Because it looks like it's gone."

My chest tightened. Had Austin explained his misgivings about my newbie detective skills to the powers-that-be, who in turn decided I wasn't Ghosted material after all?

"Chaos. Personal upheaval. Violent and sudden changes," Bridget read in a doom and gloom voice from the Tower card's interpretation. "Ambitions and pursuits built on shaky premises."

"Personal upheaval—check." I grimaced. If I believed this card, so much for my notions of a calling in ghost investigations.

I took the phone back from Ines and scrolled through. The purple icon with the ghost in a deerstalker cap appeared on my home screen. Relief pummeled into me with a force that caught me off guard.

I clicked on it and showed the screen to Ines. *No new messages,* a pop-up read. It took me to the *cold or fresh* screen. Ines wrinkled her freckled nose. I didn't want to click the matches tab and confirm that Austin was no longer interested in working with me.

I passed it back to Ines, but the moment the phone left my hand, the app disappeared.

"Weird," we both said at the same time.

I grabbed the phone again, and the cold or fresh prompt reappeared. With another click, I brought up Austin's picture. His messages appeared below.

"Perhaps it only responds to you. It is a thing made of magic and not technology," Auguste posited.

Bridget peered over my shoulder at the messages. "These must have been a few days old since he's dead now, right?"

I made a noncommittal sound.

"So sad," Bridget said.

"I wonder if it has something to do with retinal recognition," Ines murmured.

"Or it's magic," I repeated Auguste's theory with a wry smile.

Ines raised a skeptical eyebrow. Ines Gomez did *not* believe in magic. She believed in empirical data and technology.

Then again, I didn't think *I* believed in magic until this afternoon.

But when you see spirits and your hedgehog starts talking, it kind of tips things in magic's favor.

I studied Austin's picture for a moment longer, and the sad smile on his face made me think of our last conversation about the dangerous and powerful group he worried about me getting involved with. "What do y'all know about secret societies here in New Orleans?"

Bridget frowned. "Like the Enclave?"

I nodded.

"Only what I saw on that old *Unsolved Mysteries* episode,"

Bridget said. "Money, fame, power, pact with the devil. Sacrifices."

"Do you think that's real, though? That they could still be around? Or is it just a legend?"

"Hmmm." Ines's face went pensive.

"What is it?" I asked.

"Nothing. Probably nothing."

"Which one is it—nothing or probably nothing?" I prompted.

She bit her thumbnail. "Hudson asked me about them once. Before he disappeared."

I stilled at the mention of my ex's name.

Ines and Bridget shared a concerned look.

Hudson Bennett had been the ex-who-must-not-be-named for a long time. We'd dated for almost a year in college. From the moment we met, he'd been my kindred spirit.

That first night, we'd both ducked out of my sorority's crush party to get some air. I was overwhelmed from my sensory processing difficulties. And even after spending his whole childhood on stage—equally adept at a back flip as he was at playing the fiddle or banjo—crowds still made Hudson jittery.

As fate would have it that night, we got locked out on the roof, both with dead cell phones. By the time rescue arrived, we'd talked all night, and I was smitten. His quietly confident ways, tender heart, and quick mind were a powerful trifecta. In the year that followed, he'd made me feel like I'd always have a place with him, even if I didn't know where I was going yet. If I'd been the betting kind, I'd have put money on Ines and Bridget throwing me a bachelorette party for our wedding right about now. Until our relationship ended abruptly when he ghosted me.

He left his apartment, his final semester of graduate studies, everything, with only a handwritten letter for me.

Paige,

I'm leaving town. I wish it didn't have to be this way, but maybe it'll hurt less if I do. I'm sorry. I'll always be sorry. I owe you so much more, but this is the best I can do. Please don't contact me. Let's make this a clean break, okay? You deserve every happiness.

-Hudson

I still had the letter, somewhere amid the altar of discarded dreams in my closet.

"It's fine. We can talk about... him," I insisted. "It's been what? Two years? Three? Three years, eleven months, and some change?" I grabbed Ines's discarded ultra lite beer bottle and picked at the label.

"We could still take a seam ripper to all his pants if we ever found him," Bridget offered brightly.

"Or break into his place and put Legos everywhere, so he couldn't walk without stepping on them," Ines suggested.

"It's okay. I've long since moved on. I hope he's somewhere safe and well," I said. And I meant it. At least I *wanted* to mean it. But his disappearing act had sent me into a tailspin. I'd been so sure that I knew him, *really* knew him, and that he was the person I'd wanted to spend the rest of my life with. His leaving made me question every instinct I'd ever had. Even after the worst of the fallout. I still felt the ripples today in the way I pulled back from potential career paths and relationships when things seemed too good to be true.

"Do you ever still wonder what happened to him?" Bridget said after a moment.

"I guess. Every once in a while. I wonder if there was a plausible explanation that we missed." I inhaled a cleansing breath and stroked Auguste's quills. He burrowed into me, as if sensing my need for comfort. "You never mentioned the Enclave stuff before. When did he start looking into that?"

"About a month before he took off. He wanted to know about searches on the dark web. For some paper he was writing, he said." Ines looked up at me.

I frowned. "He had all clinical psychology and art therapy classes that semester. What on earth would he have been writing a paper on the Enclave for?"

"I never thought anything of it. He asked in a real off hand way then told me never mind the next day. Do you think there was more to that question?" Ines asked.

In all of my imaginings about why Hudson had ghosted me, his being taken out by a secret society wasn't anywhere on the list. He wanted to be an art therapist, for goodness sake.

I shrugged. "I guess that's probably reaching."

Like Auguste's namesake had said, sometimes the simplest answer was the correct one. Hudson was probably just a guy sorting out who he was, dealing with some personal issues, and being a jerk about how he handled it. But that explanation had never sat right with me. Hudson had been all about honor and commitment. Then again, even people who have the best of intentions are human and screw up royally sometimes. And leave the people who love them wrecked and eating Cookie Butter from the jar.

But what if I'd missed something important?

Auguste piped up, his French accent still in full effect, "Perhaps this is the clue to solving more than one of your mysteries."

NINE

The next morning, despite my intentions to sleep in and give myself a chance to recover from yesterday's events, my eyes popped open, wide awake at an hour that would put even Ines to shame. Auguste snored, curled up with his favorite blanket, so I couldn't talk things out with him and confirm that I did indeed have a talking hedgehog and not a concussion. He looked so cute, all snuggled up like that. I had to take a picture.

Since I was up anyway, I decided to hit an early yoga class and clear my head. I did my best thinking with my body busy and my mind free to wander. And I had a *lot* to think through.

The bells jangled as I entered the studio. Several people I recognized were already doing warm-up stretches in one of the studios, but the reception area where we signed in to keep track of our number of classes stood vacant. And the clipboard wasn't on the counter as usual.

"Hello?" I called out.

Then I spotted a blonde woman sitting on an exercise ball facing the empty studio. Maybe a new receptionist. When I got closer, I realized it was Carlie, the part-time barista from Crumbles. Liz hadn't mentioned her quitting, but maybe she'd started a second job.

"Hey," I tried again.

Carlie nearly jumped out of her skin at the sound of my voice. She shot to her feet and swiped loose strands of hair from her face. "Hi. Hello. Sorry. Spaced out there for a second."

"No problem," I said. Upon closer inspection, Carlie didn't look her polished, fresh off the marina self. Dark circles pressed into the skin under her eyes. She'd twisted her normally immaculately styled hair into a messy bun. And not the cute on-purpose messy bun that she sometimes wore. This was a greasy knot with nary a spritz of dry shampoo.

"I didn't know you worked here," I said.

"Just started this week."

"How you holding up after last night?" I asked. Judging by her out-of-sorts appearance, I'd guess Austin's demise had taken its toll on her too.

"Fine. I'm fine." She shook her head, as though trying to clear away bad thoughts. "Great time to start a new job, huh?"

I signed the clipboard she passed me and hiked my mat bag over my shoulder.

She squinted like she was seeing me again for the first time. She must have really taken it hard. "You're Liz's friend. Cinnamon latte, right?"

"That's me. I'm Paige, by the way."

Her features tightened. Did I imagine it, or had she shrunk back at the mention of my name? Or could it have been my connection to Liz? Did she not know Carlie worked here too? I couldn't imagine she'd mind. Sweat beaded her forehead.

"You sure you're okay? You don't look so well," I said. "It's totally understandable with what happened last night."

"Fine." She mustered a too-bright smile, crouched behind

the counter, and rifled through drawers. My spidey senses tingled like crazy. Something was definitely up here.

Then an alternative idea struck me.

"You were a friend of Austin's, weren't you?" I said gently.

She froze and white-knuckled the brochures in her hands. "Something like that." Her voice teetered on the razor's edge of tears. "I mean, I didn't know him well or anything, but we'd been friendly."

"Same here," I said. "In any case, I'm sorry for your loss."

She sniffled. "Me too."

I extracted my mat and headed toward the studio, but stopped. "Hey, you don't know who he'd been hanging out with lately, do you?"

She frowned. "Why?"

"I don't know. Just something he said made it sound like... he'd gotten mixed up with the wrong people."

Hey, even if I wasn't officially on the case, that didn't turn off my curiosity.

Carlie's eyes widened a fraction. "No. No idea," she said in a rush. "Like I said, I didn't know him that well."

I studied her. As my buddy Shakespeare would say, the lady doth protest too much. Had the people who'd hurt Austin threatened her too? Or was I just reading too much into a perfectly normal expression of grief?

Her throat bobbed, and she inhaled a deep breath, seemingly trying to compose herself. "Okay, well, enjoy your class," she said.

"Thanks."

As I stashed my stuff in a locker, my phone buzzed with a notification. I went to unlock it, but my gut seized up and I fisted my hands. What if it held a message from Austin officially kicking me off his case?

Sure, I kicked myself off of my pursuits on the regular when

I caught a whiff of failure, but having someone else make the preemptive call that I wasn't cut out for something? That kind of confirmation of my self-doubts tied my stomach in knots.

I'd need every bit of Zen from my yoga practice I could gather to deal with the sting of rejection. I stuffed the phone in my locker. That would have to namastay tucked away until later.

All through my sun salutations, I mulled over yesterday's events. Austin's death. The bewildering fortune machine with the Tower card. The Ghosted app. My first actual spirit sighting after all my time in the ghost tour biz. Auguste's new loquaciousness and French accent.

It was all connected. It had to be. But why me? How was I chosen (and then rejected, *sigh*) for this? Was it something that ran in families? If so, it had skipped at least one generation, probably two. I couldn't imagine my workaholic scientist parents squeezing in a ghost PI side hustle. And I couldn't see my skeptical Grandma Alice or Grandpa Am getting involved with something like this either.

But then again, there was the whole estranged branch of my family on my mother's side I'd only met as a baby before I could form memories. This side also included my great grandmother, Magnolia, who I'd never met, but had written all the Matilda Mayhew girl detective mysteries. A lot of those contained ghosts who wanted Matilda's help to solve their murders. Was it weird that the person in my lineage I felt most connected to passed away before I entered this world? Was it possible to miss someone you never even knew?

I let out a deep breath and relaxed into downward dog. Grandma Magnolia was definitely the most likely person the skill had been passed down from if it were hereditary. If only I had some way to talk to her and get her guidance on how to make sense of all of this.

I made a plan to take a detour later today to the Nu Omega garden on my old college campus. Magnolia and the other women she'd founded the sorority with had gifted the garden and its fountain to the university through fundraising. It was the place I went to ground myself when I felt lost. A place I could feel closer to her.

I was her legacy in the sorority. Why not her legacy in the family ghost PI business too?

Just when I pretzeled myself into pigeon pose, another thought occurred to me. If there were multiple ghosts on the app, there must also be multiple ghost detectives like me. Were there more of us in New Orleans, or were they more spread out?

I leaned over my bent front leg, enjoying the deep stretch in my thigh muscles. On second thought, with all the ghosts hanging around the Crescent City, there *had* to be more here. I could track them down and get some help. After all, what better way to jump into any new endeavor than to find your community?

I toweled off after class, feeling renewed and invigorated with my new goal in mind. Even if Austin didn't think I was up to the job, I could accept that, move on, and still find my way forward if I wanted. I'd find my people, try out a cold case or two and learn the ropes.

With a deep breath, I pulled my phone out of my locker. I'd handle this rejection with grace and style.

See? Yoga clarity magic, y'all.

But instead of an *it's not you, it's me* text from Austin, two other notifications lit the screen. The first came from the Ghosted app with the subject: Mentor Match.

I clicked that right away. See, even better than I'd anticipated. My people were finding me.

Unlike with Austin's, no photo accompanied this message, only an avatar of the Emperor tarot card and the initial H.

I've been assigned as your mentor. Meet me at Miss Peacock's 3pm today?

My heart skipped a beat. A mentor!

Hello, so nice to "meet" you. I'm Paige. What's your name? Hunting down ghost murderers going well today, I trust?

A minute ticked by without a reply. Wow, this person really didn't go in for small talk. Then the three dancing dots appeared.

Sure. Does 3 work?

I suppose I can squeeze you in, I typed back. *How will I find you?*

Are you living or dead? I wondered, but didn't ask. That seemed a little overly familiar.

The mysterious H answered, *I'll find you.*

I rolled my eyes at the drama laced in that statement. This was going to be an interesting meeting.

After I closed the Ghosted app, I clicked over to a text from Liz. My stomach dropped when I read the words.

Can you come to Crumbles ASAP? Something bad's happened.

TEN

When I arrived at Crumbles, still sweaty in my pink yoga outfit, the place was in shambles.

Wind billowed the curtains out of both busted windows. And across the door and shutters, someone had spray painted MURDERER in angry red letters.

Despite the closed sign on the door, I ran in. "Liz?" Broken shards of glass crunched under my sneakers. Liz strode out from the back with a grim look.

I frantically looked her over for signs this had been more than breaking and entering, but all 5 foot 3 of her seemed unscathed. At least if you didn't count the hard line of her jaw and ever-deepening crease between her eyebrows. "Are you okay? When did this happen?"

"Thanks for coming. I didn't know who else to call. It was like this when I got here." She rubbed her wrist where a thin red line stood out against the light brown of her skin.

"You're bleeding," I said. "I'll get the first aid kit. Let's get you fixed up."

She waved me away, but I still led her to the sink, cleaned

and bandaged the wound. "I tripped over a glass shard and landed wrong. That's the least of my worries."

With Liz's arm patched up, I turned to take in the rest of the scene, my heart plummeting with every new detail. The tables, specially designed to match the ones in Liz's auntie's cafe in Santa Monica, lay overturned and broken in a sea of colorful chairs.

Liz's hand trembled on the way to her mouth. I followed her gaze to the worst slight of all. More graffiti marred the lovely French Quarter mural. The one Liz's sister painted just before her last round of chemo. One-of-a-kind, with Laini's signature whimsical touches. She'd been so proud of it.

"Oh, Liz...."

She swallowed. "What am I going to do? I was already scraping by since we stopped catering, when Laini got too sick. I don't know how I'm going to pay for these repairs. Plus, how long will I have to stay closed with all of this?"

I righted a fallen chair and guided Liz to it. After rummaging in the pastry case for a cranberry orange muffin for her, I put the electric kettle on and grabbed a bag of her favorite Earl Grey.

"How can I help?" I asked. "I've probably got sixty-five people on group texts who would be here in a heartbeat to get this all cleaned up. Bridget probably has some plywood panels lying around too. We could put them up until you can get the windows replaced."

She nodded and gave me a watery smile. I know how much she hated asking for help, so if I could carry any of her burden by jumping in, I was on the job.

"Have you already called the police?"

"On their way. I hope it's Officer Friendly and not the other one."

Declan, aka Officer Friendly, often stopped by Crumbles on

Liz's and my puzzle nights. He must have rounds during that time.

"Me too. What was up with that other guy? Do you know him?" I asked.

"Unfortunately. Friend of my ex-husband's."

I wandered over to a broken chair, one that Liz and I had sanded and repainted before the grand opening. "Remember when we worked on these?" I asked with a sad smile.

"There are a lot more pinks and purples since you offered to pick up the paint."

"There's more candy-colored paint where that came from," I said.

The corner of her mouth quirked up. "I had sawdust up my nose for weeks."

"Hey, Laini and I both told you to wear a mask while you used the sander. It's not our fault you didn't listen."

She laughed, but then a shadow clouded her features again. She cut a glance at the front door. "Hey, um, before the police get here, I wanted to show you something." She motioned to the office.

My neck prickled with alarm, but I followed. Liz waved a hand at a small canvas doll on her desk. Each stitch on it had been intricately detailed. Black yarn hair cut into an asymmetrical bob framed its face with a single streak of gray. The doll wore a red Crumbles Bakery apron. Two enormous pins stuck out of it, one impaling its wrist and the other its abdomen, just below the C in Crumbles. Chills snaked down my back.

I stepped closer and my face contorted at the brown button eyes staring up at me from the doll's face. Its mouth looked like someone had intentionally silenced it, stitched shut with a jagged X. The likeness resembled Liz way too much for my comfort.

I shuddered and looked back at Liz to gauge her reaction to

the obvious threat. She cradled her bandaged arm to her chest and donned the same blank mask she'd used to keep the emotion from her sister's passing from flooding out and consuming everything.

"Do you recognize this type of Voodoo doll? Are they something you sell at your gift shop?"

I leaned in to inspect it.

"Is it too much to hope they're mass produced?" Liz said, tugging at the grey streak in her hair.

"Looks custom to me." I grabbed a pen and prodded at the poppet. "The craftsmanship is high quality. We don't sell anything like this at Deveauxs'. We just have the tourist tchotchke kinds. I think I know the company that makes these, though." Sure enough, a navy blue tag with the word Talisman on it stuck out from its right heel. "We had a sales rep come out to try and get us to stock these. She said they were like the Build-a-bear of Voodoo dolls. Custom karmic torture for the enemies in your life. Said they'd be all the rage."

Liz made a disapproving face.

"Yeah, I told her thanks, but no thanks. I can see how it might be cathartic to process your negative feelings without actually stabbing someone. But it felt like bad energy, having people making little custom sacks of hatred in our store."

"Could you call your rep and see which stores sell them or if they do custom orders online? Maybe that could give us a lead on who did this."

"On it. Let me take some pictures in case they'll help identify the specific purchaser."

I noticed the doll's hands were pulled behind her back. "Hmmm." I cocked my head and flipped her over with the pen. Felted handcuffs encircled her wrists.

Liz's eyes rounded as she met my gaze.

Someone was trying to set her up for Austin's murder. Or at

the very least, rattle her enough she wouldn't go looking for the real culprit. The question was, why?

And if this was the work of Austin's secret society, how far would they go to protect their secrets?

✦▲✦▲✦▲✦

THE POLICE ARRIVED SHORTLY AFTER, roaming the cafe, making notes, taking pictures, and bagging evidence.

I stood by while Liz led Declan Durocher around, cataloging the damages while he scribbled notes. My shoulders had slumped in relief when he arrived with no sign of Officer Jerkface from yesterday.

Liz picked up the broken frame holding the $5 bill from their very first sale and clutched it to her. I'd never seen my indomitable professor look so deflated.

Liz rubbed her wrist and winced. My neck prickled, remembering the pins sticking out of the doll. *Coincidence*, I chided myself. It had to be. Magic used to harm others didn't exist. At least, I really hoped it didn't.

A few minutes later, Officer Crowder, the rude one from yesterday, blustered in, his upper lip and generous mustache curling with distaste.

"Miss Pickett, I'll need you to come with me," he growled at Liz, who had just dragged herself from the sight of her sister's ruined mural.

I edged closer to Liz.

"I understand you have lockers for your personal things here. I'm going to need you to open them all up. Starting with your own." Crowder didn't seem to register the damage or the emotional toll the break-in had taken on everyone present.

"Okay, but what's this about?" Liz met my gaze, and fear flickered in her eyes.

"Got a tip," Crowder said. "From a reliable source." He hitched up the belt with all of his police gear. "Just need to follow it up."

No way I'd let this officer bully Liz with no witnesses, so I followed them to the staff room. There, a row of cheery yellow lockers lined one wall next to bakers' racks brimming with flour, sugar, and sundry bakery supplies.

"Ms. Harrington, your presence is not required here," Officer Crowder said to me in an annoyed voice.

"Oh, that's okay. I volunteer as a concerned citizen," I said, deliberately mistaking his meaning. I flashed him a grin, pulled out my phone, zoomed in on his badge number, and snapped a picture.

Liz gave me a smirk and shook her head. Good, she needed some levity.

"Just want to make sure nothing untoward is happening here, officer," I said.

Crowder's nostrils flared, but he didn't kick me out. "Which locker is yours?"

Liz pointed and produced a small key to open the padlock threaded through the closure.

"Don't you need to have a warrant to search that?" I asked.

Officer Crowder looked uncomfortable.

"It's okay. I have nothing to hide. Might as well get this over with," Liz said. She pulled the door open and went to reach in, but her hand faltered. Her face went as white as her vanilla frosting, and her jaw worked. "I... I don't know where these came from. I didn't put them..." She trailed off, her hand shaking.

"I'm going to need you to step aside, Ms. Pickett." Crowder slipped on plastic gloves.

I stepped up to Liz's side to provide any comfort I could and see what had put her in a state of shock.

Officer Crowder pulled out a brass candlestick and several strands of Mardi Gras beads, all covered in what looked like dried blood.

My mind flashed back to the gouge on Austin's head and the strange pattern of bulbous bruise marks around his neck.

"I'm going to need some evidence bags in here, Durocher," Officer Crowder called.

"Those weren't there yesterday," Liz said.

"She's right. You guys checked the whole place," I said. "Are you saying y'all did substandard police work?"

"What I'm saying is that maybe someone hid them elsewhere yesterday, and then she stashed them here after we left. I understand I'll find the other candlestick in the matching set in your living room."

Liz's lips parted.

I stepped forward. "Did you miss the part where someone broke in here last night and probably planted all of this?"

Crowder shot me a glare. "Or she did this herself and made this look like a setup. Where's the laundry?"

The remaining color drained from Liz's face. She pointed to the corner.

After bagging the candlestick and beads, Crowder rummaged through the heap of red Crumbles aprons.

"Uh huh, just like I thought."

A black hoodie, the kind Austin's pusher reportedly wore, dangled from Crowder's gloved fingers.

"Ms. Pickett, I'd like you to come with me."

ELEVEN

No. No. No. No. No. This was *not* how things were supposed to happen. The police weren't supposed to arrest an innocent professor/cafe owner for a murder she didn't commit.

Watching Liz's face as Crowder escorted her to the police car crumpled me up inside. She'd agreed to go to the station for more questions even though she wasn't legally required to, sticking to what she'd said earlier: she had nothing to hide. But instead of her usual defiance and chin thrust in the air, she hung her head, hair shrouding her face as her fellow business owners on Chartres watched on.

That did it.

Whether or not Austin wanted me on the job, someone intended to frame Liz, and I wouldn't let her take the fall for their crime if I had anything to do with it. And I was about to have a whole lot to do with it.

I secretly hoped that Austin would reconsider because it would be a lot easier to smoke out the killer with his insider knowledge.

I just prayed I wouldn't find myself on the other side looking for a living detective of my own.

I called my lawyer friend Angelica and asked her to meet Liz at the station to be with her during questioning. Meanwhile, I rallied an impressive cleanup crew for after we got the all clear from the police.

"I'm sorry, squirt." Declan sauntered over after most everyone had left, his handsome-and-I-know-it-face looking sadder and younger than usual. He removed his hat and rumpled his hair. "You can count me in for clean-up crew duty after my shift. I already called Griffin to get the windows boarded."

His brother Griffin was married to my boss, Julie, and co-owned a construction company with their dad.

"Thanks," I said, managing a half smile.

"I'll check on Liz after I get back to the station. Wilson and Velasquez will patrol the area," he said.

He reclined against the pastry case next to me and nudged my arm with his. "We're going to find out who really did this."

I leaned into the cool glass.

"And by 'we' I mean 'we.'" He waved a finger between himself and the other two cops who would be patrolling.

So I wasn't in the circle of trust here. My lips pursed. "But I can ask around. See who Austin hung out with who might also be a homicidal maniac."

"I know you'd like to help, but whoever did this has already killed once. I don't want you getting anywhere near their cross-hairs."

I made a non-committal harrumph.

"Paige." Declan's thick eyebrows slanted in at me. He really did have arresting eyes.

"Okay, okay when you put it that way." I held my hands up in surrender. At least, I hoped it looked like real surrender. "I get it. You want me to leave it to the trained experts." That wasn't *technically* committing to backing off. Just showing his concern was noted.

Lord, help me.

⁺▲⁺▲⁺▲⁺

AFTER WRAPPING things up at Crumbles, I headed back home for a much needed shower. I'd also hopefully get some guidance from my mysteriously talking hedgehog and prepare to meet my mentor.

But much to my chagrin, I found a loathe-to-be-woken Auguste and got no response to my call or email from Valerie, the custom Voodoo doll rep. I had to help Liz, and until I could contact Austin's ghost again or train with my mentor, I wasn't entirely sure where to start.

About to burst with nervous energy, I visited a website and played with designs for my *Paige Magnolia Harrington, Ghost PI* business cards that I almost certainly did not need, but really wanted. I was especially partial to the pink metallic ones with smiley skulls. I may or may not have ordered a sample.

But as soon as I did, after feeling quite pleased with myself, I noticed that recognizable hitch in my momentum shuttling me into the second-guessing game.

In the past, I'd relied so heavily on my instincts, and this felt like a pursuit that aligned so perfectly with my skill set. This had the potential to be my thing, my way of making a positive impact on the world, using my talents for good. But then the memory of Hudson and his stupid, perfect dimple and how I'd been so epically wrong about him came barreling back. The familiar sensation of the mental brakes slamming on knocked the wind out of my confidence. I'd been wrong before, and how much pain had that caused me?

How could I believe this would be any different? How could solving ghost mysteries be the thing for me if I had no earthly idea what to do next?

I pulled on jeans, an Edgar Allan Poe tank top, and a cute pink cardigan, trying to push away my misgivings. I hated how they could sneak up on me and strike a blow at my confidence without warning.

But Liz was in trouble. She needed someone looking out for her. And maybe I wasn't an expert, but rookie or not, I'd be darned if I didn't do everything in my power to clear her name.

✦❧✦❧✦

I GLANCED at my phone again as I strode just outside the touristy part of the Quarter to Miss Peacock's to meet the mysterious H, my ghost justice mentor. The smell of red beans and rice and gumbo wafted out of nearby restaurants. My stomach grumbled. In my agitation this morning, I'd forgotten to eat after my granola bar at around ten. I'd have to order some of my favorite Parmesan truffle fries.

When I got to the door, I hesitated. My slick palm slipped on the handle. *Imposter*, the wicked part of my mind taunted. *You're going to fail at this just like you fail at everything else.* I shook it off. *No. You can do this.*

With a deep breath, I stepped inside and walked smack into a ghost from my past.

TWELVE

F rom his perch at a table made of *Sorry!* Boards and game pieces encased in resin, Hudson Bennett raised a hand in a tentative hello. The lines around his deep-set hazel eyes tightened as if he were bracing for impact.

My disappearing ex, returned to New Orleans after four years of radio silence, sat at our usual spot just like he'd never left.

So many emotions punched me in the gut while I goggled at him to make sure I'd seen right. That perfectly tousled brown hair that I'd delighted in mussing fell into his eyes. Under my scrutiny, the expression on his midwestern boy-next-door face oscillated between guilt, an impassive mask, and a hint of longing that scrambled my senses even after all this time. How did he look so darned earnest after what had happened in our past? A little more haunted and world-weary, yes, but yeah.

Sure enough. It was him.

As much as I hated to admit it, he still had that smile that could melt my butter from across the room.

He was alive and whole.

And he'd still abandoned me.

Holy mother of goat yoga, I was not prepared for this. On this, of all days.

I turned tail and zoomed back out.

Breathe, I coached myself. Just as I leaned against the cool windowpane outside, a car's brakes squealed, making me jump. A brass band's trumpets and horns bleated down the street. My breath had lodged itself somewhere between my head and heart at the sight of him. He was concrete evidence of two things I really didn't want to face right now. One: The biggest and most important mystery I'd failed to solve, and two: proof of how very bad things could go if I relied on my instincts.

A couple strolled inside and folk music blared from Miss Peacock's, creating a cacophony with the brass band's warm-up. My shoulders tensed and inched toward my ears. The whoops and hollers from a boisterous group of tourists pressed in all around me. I wrapped my arms across my middle. My head pounded with the relentless discordant rhythm. The events of the last few days came crashing back: Austin's body hurtling down, the mess of Crumbles, and Liz being hauled off. Seeing a freaking real life ghost. Spots of color danced in my vision, and I squeezed my eyes closed. By now, I recognized the signs of sensory overload. This by-product of my anxiety accosted me frequently and left me shaky and needing to hide away some-where dark and quiet to decompress.

Only I didn't have time to shut down today. There was a murderer on the loose, and I had to meet my mentor and help track them down before Liz paid the price.

I sucked in deep breaths and worked through the grounding exercise my therapist had taught me. Name five things I could see, four things I could hear, three things I could feel. I could do this. I shifted my gaze and counted them off. The blue grey spires of the St. Louis Cathedral in the distance. The hand-painted wooden Miss Peacock's sign with its brightly colored tail feathers. By the time I got to the cool breeze on my neck, the spots had dissipated and my heartbeat had returned to normal.

Once I stepped back inside, I strode straight to Hudson's table. Best to rip the Band-aid off and have this uncomfortable conversation. I'd acknowledge him and then move on because I was a woman on a mission, and that's what I needed to do.

He looked up at me with a tentative smile that knocked me off balance way more than I cared to admit. I folded my arms over my chest and glared at him. I called up all of my anger and indignation to combat the other emotions I couldn't afford to dredge up.

"Hi," he said after a beat of uncomfortable silence. "Guess you weren't expecting to see me today."

I made a scoffing sound, and my tongue tied itself in knots.

"That's the understatement of the year," I finally managed. "Or the last four years," I added under my breath.

"You okay?" Concern etched Hudson's features from the square line of his jaw to the wrinkle between his brow. "I wondered if you had one of your episodes."

"I'm fine. Fine." Gah, as if repeating it would make it true.

My hands fisted at my sides. He didn't get to look after me anymore. He didn't get to just show up and pick up right where we left off. "I've just got a lot on my mind."

More awkward silence. Apparently we excelled at that.

"It's good to see you," Hudson said at the same time I blurted, "So, I guess you're back in town."

We both let out nervous laughs.

"Yeah, for a while, anyway," he said.

Our eyes met, and my gaze roamed over him as if this would somehow unlock the mystery of how I went so wrong, putting my trust and hopes in him. He bit his full bottom lip, making the cleft in his chin more pronounced. His nervous tell. Good, at least I wasn't the only one feeling the full force of awkwardness of this situation.

His muscles looked more defined under the sleeves of his soft-looking grey t-shirt than I remembered. He shifted and stretched his legs out under the table. At five foot ten, while advantageous for his acrobatic training, he'd sometimes been self-conscious about his stature. I'd always countered that he was perfect kissing height. Argh. Exactly what I did *not* need to think about right now.

I blinked at him. This was my former boyfriend who always had a smile for everyone. He noticed when I got overwhelmed even before my diagnosis and steered me to a quiet place to get my bearings back. How did I reconcile that person with the dude who'd ditched me like old garbage?

I wanted to smack him.

I wanted to hug him.

He shifted in his chair.

Rage and hurt bubbled under my skin.

After all this time, maybe this could provide closure for that wound that never truly healed around the Hudson-shaped hole in my life. My ticket to answers to the questions that had kept me up countless nights. But would any of that matter? Could any answer make me feel better and make it make sense? Probably not. Perhaps it was just as well to put it behind me and move on.

Goodbye, Hudson. I tested out the words in my head. My heart wrenched, but in a way more like an echo of three years eleven months ago. Maybe *that's* what I really needed. The chance to walk away on my own terms. I cleared my throat and gathered my courage.

The ghost of his dimples hovered just beyond reach of his sad smile. My throat bobbed.

"Well...I'd love to catch up, but I'm meeting someone." I cast around for a free table as far away as possible to wait for my mentor. I turned to face him. "It was nice seeing you after all this time."

And as much as it had stirred up painful memories, I found I meant it.

Especially if it might pave the way for a fresh start with no more lingering what-ifs. My chest puffed up as if a weight had lifted. This closure on my own terms was good stuff. Maybe the years of yoga and meditation had paid off.

"Yeah, about that..." Hudson said in an apologetic tone. He held up his phone with the Ghosted app open to our message chain from earlier.

Realization dawned, and I did a mental face-palm. H was none other than Hudson Bennett. Some detective I'd turned out to be, not to have put that together. Though I blamed at least part of that on the shock of his presence.

"Oh, heck no." I rubbed my temples and sank into the chair opposite Hudson. So much for my nice, tidy closure.

"Trust me, this is not the way I wanted to roll back into your life," Hudson said. "I know this is not ideal. For you or for me."

"Oh well, sorry that it's inconvenient for *you*," I said. And so much for being the bigger person.

How was I supposed to solve a mystery with the distraction of my very attractive and confusing ex?

Hudson held his palms up in surrender. "That's not what I meant. None of the others from the bureau would touch this case with a ten-foot pole with the Enclave involved. Even if they would, everyone local got called away to help on a big sting down in Savannah."

"But not you?" I raised an eyebrow at him.

"When I heard the details of Austin's case and saw the call for a mentor, I volunteered to stay. I promise I didn't know you were on the case until after."

Just then, a bartender placed a sizzling basket of fries on the table. "I ordered those Parmesan truffle fries you used to like. I took a chance they were still your favorites."

My face scrunched up. "My tastes have changed a lot in the last few years."

Hudson picked up a fry, and it crackled as he dunked it into the culinary perfection of Miss Peacock's lemon aioli sauce. My mouth watered.

When the fry passed his lips, Hudson made a happy groaning sound that took me back to *before*. The man could not eat delicious food without this kind of verbal appreciation. "These still taste just as good as I remember."

I glanced at the door and stood up. He looked up at me with the most earnest pleading in his eyes, and I wavered. Argh, why did he have that effect on me? At least this way I'd learn something. But after that, we were parting ways.

My traitorous stomach rumbled.

"Sure you don't want one?" He waggled a fry at me and pushed the basket in my direction. "Consider it a peace offering."

I huffed back into the seat across from him. "Fine, I'll have a fry. Or two."

He smiled, and I dipped my chosen fry into the aioli. I groaned from the fried goodness stuffed in my mouth, and Hudson chuckled.

"I guess some things never change," he said. "Still think you can beat me at *Parcheesi*?" The dimples made an appearance and lord help me, a rosy colored nostalgia fluttered. No, no, no. Things couldn't just go back to the way they were, world's sexiest dimples be darned. He had too much to answer for, and I had my own life to lead. My nostrils flared. "You bet your butt I can. But you're wrong on the first count."

A crease of uncertainty dented his brow.

"Everything changes. You taught me that."

Something that looked a lot like regret flashed in his eyes, and he gave a solemn nod.

Good, I hoped he felt bad for the way he treated me.

"Is that where you've been all this time, doing ghost investigations? Is that why you took off?" Surely that wouldn't require his level of disappearance.

My chest tightened with my held breath. Finally, after ages of wondering—some answers.

He shook his head. "I've only been at this the last two years."

"And before that?" My voice cracked. "Where did you go?"

He rubbed the back of his neck. "That's a long story."

That he clearly didn't want to tell. The urge to dig deeper intensified, but I refrained. "Did you get an arcade fortune telling machine too?" I asked instead.

He nodded. "It showed up at the county fair I was playing at one day along with the Ghosted App on my phone. Then the next thing you know, I was out on an odd job for a friend, and I find the guy there strangled by his tie caught in the garbage disposal. His ghost shows up behind me telling me that someone did this to him."

"Was that your first case?" I asked.

"Yep."

"Did you get a prophetic card from the Madam Sophia machine like I did?"

He nodded. "The Hanged Man."

"Ooh." I wiggled my fingers, which got a laugh out of Hudson. "So who did it?"

"The next-door neighbor. She got tired of the guy's dog pooping all over her garden and him neglecting to clean up."

I grimaced. "Yikes. I guess you never know what will set people off."

"I vowed then and there if I ever got a pet, I'd always clean up after it."

"And did you ever?" I asked. "Get a pet?" Hudson had dogs growing up, big chocolate labs, that wore flannel sweaters in the winter. I knew he missed them and had wanted to get one of his own as soon as he got his own house.

His smile took on a sad tint. "Never stayed in one place long enough."

That too seemed out of character with the guy I knew. It made me sad. He'd spent so much time on the road performing as a kid, living out his mom's dream. After all that, he wanted to put down roots. At least, the person I thought I knew did.

"How long have you been back here?" I asked.

"Couple of weeks. I stayed away for a long time."

"Why?" I hated the plaintive note in my voice. The loaded question hung in the air between us.

He scratched the back of his neck. "I didn't want you to have to run into me."

I twisted the napkin on the table. My heart thumped out a frantic beat as the questions bubbled up. It would have been far better to keep it light and pretend the past never happened, but I could never leave well enough alone. "Why did you leave in the first place?"

"It was the only way," he said with no inflection. "At least it seemed like it at the time."

"So you said in your Dear Jane letter. But the only way for what? To hurt everyone who cared about you all in one go?"

Hudson's hazel eyes flashed with hurt, making him look even more haunted. "I guess I deserve that. If it makes you feel any better, I regret those things every day."

I blew out a breath. This was getting heavy, and I was getting tangled up inside. I needed to get back to business, to solving Austin's murder. But my stubborn mind wouldn't let go.

"So what changed? Why here? Why now? Of all the ghost detective apps in the world, why did you have to walk in to mine?"

Hudson leaned back in his chair and rubbed his lightly stubbled chin. "I saw a way to put things right. And I took it."

"That's going to take much more than cheese fries. Even these cheese fries," I quipped.

"I know. And I hope one day when you know the whole story, you'll understand." Hudson's jaw ticked. "But this is bigger than that. This case, the people behind it. They're related to why I left too."

"The case no other ghost detective will touch because it's too dangerous?"

"Yes."

My head swam, and I needed a minute to reckon with all this. Had he somehow gotten on the Enclave's bad side and had to run for his life? That certainly shifted things.

Hudson turned his steady gaze on me. Emotion flickered between us. Four years of words unsaid.

"And that's why I'm taking over the case."

THIRTEEN

"Wait, *what?*" My eyes bugged at Hudson, sitting across from me at Miss Peacock's.

"I'm taking over the case. It's better that way."

I leaned in and snatched the fry he'd just picked up. "Uh uh. You're doing no such thing."

"Please don't fight me on this, Paige." Hudson leaned forward on his elbows with conviction. We hovered inches from each other, eyes blazing with indignation. This close, the scent of his aftershave wafted over. Something that made me think of freshly cut wood and the sea, which stirred a visceral memory.

"You won't have to work with me," Hudson reasoned, dangling the prospect like an appealing carrot. "I can get you transferred over to Griselda for mentorship when she gets back from Savannah. You'll like her. She's this hippie from Atlanta. She has a whole indoor pod garden and sells catnip online. You can start with an older case to get you up to speed after she wraps up there. And you won't be in harm's way."

I blew out a breath. "Not working with you *is* tempting. But this one's personal." I filled him in on how the evidence had been planted, pointing fingers at Liz.

"Wait, *Liz*, Liz, your favorite economics professor?"

"Yup." I got worked up all over again, relaying the way Officer Jerkface had it out for her and how the anonymous tip had come in. I'd just recounted how I'd taken down his badge number when Hudson studied me for a long moment.

He tipped back in his chair and pinched the bridge of his nose. "You're not going to let this go, are you?"

I shook my head. "I can't."

"Not even for your own safety?"

"What about Liz's safety?"

Hudson let out a groan of frustration and muttered to himself. "After all this, you're just going to throw yourself in the mouth of danger, anyway. Perfect." He turned his heated gaze on me. "I can't let you do that."

"I don't need your permission. I'll do this on my own if you're just going to thwart me at every step."

"It'll be more dangerous if you don't have all the background on the Enclave that I do."

"So where does that leave us?" I asked.

He fell silent.

I twisted my lips in contemplation. As much as I dreaded the idea of being around him regularly and all the messy emotions that would stir up, I could stomach it to catch Austin's killer and keep Liz out of jail. I'd just have to keep him from steamrolling me in the name of do-gooding.

"You seem to know how they operate. Since time is of the essence, we work together—"

Hudson held up a hand and opened his mouth to protest, but I continued.

"*On this case only* and then part ways," I said. "Again."

Our eyes met and that old something that always sparked between us zinged, leaving me in a heap of conflicting feelings and misgivings.

Hudson's jaw ticked.

I sensed more protestations about my safety coming, but I held his gaze and my ground.

Luckily, Austin chose that moment to materialize in front of the colorful liquor bottles, keeping them at bay, at least temporarily. Today he'd decked himself out in board shorts and a white guayabera, his hair hanging in loose waves. He waved and floated over with a sunny smile, looking much more alive and adjusted than yesterday.

"Hey, Paige. Nice, looks like they set you up with a mentor like I asked. How's it going?"

"Great, just working out the details," I said as brightly as I could manage. "Learning all the ghost detecting secrets."

Hudson frowned, and at that moment, I remembered all of Austin's dubiousness from before. What if they both teamed up to push me out of the case? *Please be on my side here*, I prayed.

I can do this, I reminded myself. Somewhere deep inside, I knew that I could, knew that what I lacked in experience I could make up for in heart and determination to get justice for the souls I worked with. I'd never felt so right about anything in my life's direction before.

Except with Hudson. And look how disastrously wrong I'd been about that.

I bit my lip. My defense mechanism kicked in, and I could feel my confidence backpedaling. Maybe they were right, and I should just quit before I ran afoul of the wrong people in my determination to prove myself. Ugh. I was so tired of this mental back and forth.

Austin looked between Hudson and me, his happy-go-lucky expression fading. "Uh oh. Am I sensing some tension here?"

I held up my fingers in the symbol for a smidge.

"Austin, meet my mentor—and fun fact—also my ex, Hudson. Hudson, Austin."

Austin's mouth formed an O, and his gaze moved between Hudson and me. "That's... unexpectedly complicated."

Silence stretched out for a long moment.

"Are we sure this is a good idea?" Austin whispered to me. "We could ask for a new one."

I filled him in on the no-one-wants-this-case on account of the Enclave's homicidal tendencies thing.

"Oh. Well then," Austin trailed off awkwardly.

"It'll be fine," I assured him and tried to believe it for myself.

"If you're sure?" Austin said.

I looked at Hudson.

He shrugged. "We can work together." It looked like it pained him to say the words. Ugh. "But I'm taking the lead. If things get too risky, though, you have to promise to pull back. Those are the terms or no deal."

I sighed. Why did I go for the guys with a protector complex? He could think he was the leader, and I'd welcome his expertise, but I knew I'd do whatever I needed to get this job done.

"Mmm hmm, yeah. I'll do my best," I said.

Hudson's eyebrows dipped skeptically.

I held out my hand so we could shake on it. Hudson's strong fingers enveloped mine with a warmth that sent a wave of memory through me. We shook. I wanted too badly to hold on and just remember. But no. Bad. Bad idea.

I pulled back, retrieved my notebook and pen, and flipped to a fresh page. "Now that the gang's all here, how about we get started?"

Hudson's gaze lingered on mine for a beat too long. His eyes on me kicked up a krewe of glittery Mardi Gras butterflies inside me I did not want to be pleasant at all. I broke our gaze, with Hudson looking equally flustered.

He cleared his throat, pulled out his phone, and opened the

Ghosted app. "There's a section under each case file for your notes, research and suspect info," he said. He tapped the screen and showed me the different sections and other app functions. "But for the record, I still don't like this."

"Noted," I said.

"So, Austin, about the night you died..."

FOURTEEN

"Right, the night I died." Austin drew out the last word. He fidgeted in his seat at Miss Peacock's with the background noise of people playing board games and a dude strumming a guitar in the back corner. "I don't like this part so much."

I frowned and reached out to pat his hand, still on edge from the buzz of Hudson's touch a moment ago, but my fingers passed right through. "Take all the time you need."

Hudson leaned forward. "Paige and I could do a rundown of the basic tenants of ghost detecting if you need to work up to it. Protocols. How you should always keep one of these handy to cut down on the weird looks." He tapped his Bluetooth ear piece.

I looked over at Austin, who clenched and unclenched his fists. Poor guy, he looked like he was on the edge of fight or flight thinking about his untimely demise. I worried if we didn't get right to it, he'd spook out any second, leaving me alone with Hudson until he gathered up the nerve again.

"I think it may be easier for Austin to get this part over with." I motioned to Austin, hoping Hudson would use his powers of observation and get the hint.

Austin let out a shaky ghost breath. "Yeah, that might be best. Better than having it play on a loop in my mind." Austin shook out his arms like a boxer psyching himself up for a match. "Just jump right into it like cold ocean water, yeah?"

I gave him my best encouraging smile. I couldn't imagine having to relive something so awful.

"Where should I start?" He looked to me, his translucent eyes pleading for direction, reminding me of a forlorn shelter dog my friend fostered recently.

I hesitated, at that moment feeling every bit the rookie I was. I slid a glance at Hudson.

He jumped in. "How about we start with the beginning of the end?"

"Okay, I can do that." But Austin still frowned like his story was a whole ball of tangled up yarn, and he wasn't sure where to find the thread that would give him a way in.

"How did the night start?" I prompted. "Maybe tell us where you were and who you were with."

Austin nodded. "All right. So I was at Ben's place, making dinner plans. There was this new Vietnamese fusion place in the CBD we wanted to check out. But then we both got the text from Ravenscroft, that's the code name for our pledge leader, that we had an official task to complete, and it might be our last one if we were lucky."

"Who's Ben?"

"Ben Park. My..." He didn't finish the sentence, but his eyes took on a faraway sheen tinged with sadness. He rested his chin on his hand. Clearly whatever their relationship had been, powerful emotions simmered there.

"Was he involved?" I asked.

"*No.*"

I reared back at the ferocity in that single word.

"I mean, yes, he was *there* as an Enclave initiate. It's how we met. But he definitely didn't, uh..." He dragged a finger across his neck.

"And you know this because...?" Hudson tapped something on his phone.

Duh, because he was in love with him, I wanted to say. But that was only a hunch, and I wanted to let Austin unfold the story in his own way. Then another painful thought occurred to me. What if Austin had put his trust in Ben like I had in Hudson and then been betrayed as well? Only in a much worse and more permanent way. My heart clenched.

"I'll get to that part," Austin said.

"So you got the text from the Ravenscroft guy. Did you know his real name?" I asked.

"No. And we only saw him in a cloak with his face covered."

I frowned. "He dressed like that in public places?"

"No. We'd get a message to meet him somewhere secluded, controlled by the Enclave, and we'd get our instructions. They were really adamant about the initiates not knowing the identities of some members until we were 'chosen to ascend.'"

"Ascend? That sounds more like a cult than a secret society," Hudson said.

Austin held his hands out in a *what are you going to do?* gesture.

"Where'd you usually meet?" I asked.

"All different places. This time the tunnels under the old Ursuline convent. That's where they hold most of their ceremonial stuff too. We met him at the entrance."

"Those tunnels *are* real. I knew it." Despite the serious nature of the conversation, I couldn't help the tingle of excitement that zipped up my spine.

Hudson took in my wide-eyed *magic-is-real!* face, and his eyes twinkled in a way that twisted a painful nostalgia for better days between us.

I stuttered. "W-Where's the tunnel entrance?"

He described a place at the south end of the convent grounds and how this Ravenscroft guy led him, Ben, and the other four acolytes to an underground room.

"Anything off about this Ravenscroft or any of the others you remember from this part?" Hudson's brows furrowed into his deep thought look.

"Ravenscroft did seem more agitated than usual."

"How do you mean?" I asked.

Austin rubbed his chin and considered. "He was usually all solemn and loved making everything feel ceremonial and sacred. But that night, he kept glancing over his shoulder while he led us down there. Almost like he didn't want to be seen. He also sounded different than normal. Like maybe he had a cold."

"Do you think it's possible the Enclave leaders didn't sanction whatever this event was?" I asked.

"Now that you say that, it's definitely possible, but I didn't think that at the time." He sat back in his chair. Well, floated, so the back of the chair looked like it had gone through his upper torso. I grimaced.

Hudson followed my gaze and whispered, "You get used to that."

"Far into the tunnel, he unlocked a stone door that led into this big circular room. It looked ancient. Moss growing out of the cracks in the walls and stuff. I think there's a chance they used it for rituals. Stone steps led up to a raised dais in the middle. There was a table with packages on the dais."

"Were there torches on the walls?" I asked, rapt.

"Yes. Oh, and there wasn't a door handle inside of the room. Once he locked us inside, there was no way out."

A thrill of fear shivered up my back, and I scratched out some notes.

"Hold up. We're going to need more background," Hudson

said just as I was coming to terms with the confirmation of real underground tunnels under the French Quarter. Until this point, they'd existed only in whispers and legends.

"Yeah," I added, "When you say 'we,' who do you mean?"

"All six acolytes from my class. So, me and Ben, Carlie Lightfoot, Roman di Rossi, Nick Ortega, and Mina Lennox."

I scribbled down the names, leaving space for notes on possible motives and details that might be important.

"Ravenscroft did his thing and gave us instructions to read the notes and open the packages addressed to us on the table. He told us the room would not be unlocked again until we completed the task assigned."

"And nobody thought this was totally weird to get locked in a room and told to kill someone? If that was the task, which I'm guessing it was?" I asked.

"Bringing us places to do tasks of dubious legality was kind of their thing. It was part of the process to get selected to ascend through initiation."

"Kind of like sorority pledge period," I said. "Except instead of stuffing marshmallows in our mouth when we messed up reciting the Greek alphabet, there were felonies and misdemeanors."

"Exactly. They demanded complete obedience and loyalty. They were building up dirt to hold over us if we stepped out of line."

Hudson's fist curled so hard on the table his knuckles turned white.

"What kind of stuff did you have to do?" I asked.

"Just small things at first. Sneaking into someone's house to reprogram their security system. Planting embarrassing photos of someone's political opponent." Austin cleared his throat. "Then it got more intense. Stealing. Flooding the senator's mansion."

"That was you?" Hudson asked.

Austin nodded. "Releasing a swarm of cockroaches into someone's home. Vandalism. But I never thought—"

"Wait." I held up a hand, a realization dawning. "Is that why you stole from Crumbles?"

Austin hung his head. "I'm not proud of the things I did for them. That most of all. The owners were always so nice to me, even when one of them caught me at the cash register. I'd even saved up the money to pay her back. But I hadn't worked up the nerve to face her yet."

"Then why do it? What's the attraction? All that money and power too seductive to live without?" Vitriol laced Hudson's words, but it didn't seem entirely directed at Austin. I frowned. I'd have to keep digging on his personal connection to this.

"I mean sure, there's that," Austin said. "But that wasn't really it, you know? This probably sounds stupid, but for a kid who got cut off because I wasn't living up to my parents' expectations..." He shrugged again. "I guess being chosen was a pretty powerful drug. Feeling like destiny plucked me out of obscurity to be a part of something."

A tingle of sympathy and kinship stirred inside my chest. "It doesn't sound stupid to me," I said. "Everyone needs to feel wanted."

"Yeah, well, look where that got you," Hudson said.

I glared at Hudson. "Mr. Perfect, are you? Why don't we talk about some of your *excellent* life choices?"

Hudson returned my frosty look.

"No, he's right," Austin said. "I probably could've walked away if it was just that. But then my dad was at the vetting party, smiling and introducing me to people. Like he wanted me back in his life again. It messed with my head."

My mouth dropped open. "Your dad was a member? Did you know before you got the invite?"

"There were times he'd disappear. Important plans he'd cancel last minute. I knew he was hiding something, but I never imagined this.

"At the party, the initiated all had their faces covered, but I knew it was him. The guy taught me how to read and to spot a fine whiskey.

"For the first time in years, he looked at me like I was someone worth knowing. I thought maybe this was his olive branch, that he regretted cutting me off and was giving me one more chance to prove myself. And the way he acted, it was like he trusted I'd succeed."

I met Austin's watery gaze, my heart hurting for him. I knew the ache of never feeling like I measured up to my parents' expectations well.

"But instead of winning my dad's love and acceptance back, I got, well, ghosted."

Hudson just sat stone faced.

"Hudson here knows a thing or two about ghosting," I muttered. Not my finest moment, but I couldn't help the jab. It was petty, but anger kept the other confusing feelings at bay. Plus, I felt protective of Austin already.

Hudson flinched, guilt and maybe pain flashing across the green-gold landscape of his eyes. Maybe that had been too harsh. I curled my fingers into fists, stuffing down my yearning to soothe someone I cared about in pain. *Cared* about. Past tense, I reminded myself.

Hudson marshaled his anger. "So, back to the story. Ravenscroft locked you in this room."

"The understanding was that there were six acolytes, but only five of us would get to ascend. He reminded us if we succeeded, this would be our final task to find out which of us would go on and become full members and be set for life."

"No pressure," I said, imagining the feeling.

"Right," Austin said with a small smirk.

"We were given gloves and told to put them on. Ravenscroft said we'd each find a package addressed to us, that we should read the note attached, open the boxes, and we'd know what to do. Ben and I hung back. I think we both had a bad feeling."

"Did you believe him?" I asked.

"What do you mean?" Austin asked.

"Ravenscroft. You said he was acting suspicious. Do you really think he had no idea what was going down?"

"Hard to say. I don't know if they change the tasks up for different groups of acolytes or if they stay the same for generations. I get the feeling they like the mystery of it all."

"Did you ever ask your dad?" I asked.

"I tried, but he pretended not to know what I was talking about."

"Then what?" Hudson asked. His tone had gone considerably less hostile with Austin.

"Roman and Nick ran to the table like career tributes in *The Hunger Games* out for the best boxes." Austin rolled his eyes. "Even though each one was addressed specifically to one of us. Typical."

"What are their stories?" I asked, scenting a clue.

"They're both too handsome for their own good and used to getting what they want. Nick's family's some kind of oil royalty in Texas. He could charm the pants off anyone in a two-mile radius. Roman comes from money too. He's a serial entrepreneur and loves playing with daddy's money. Last I heard, he was after a marijuana dispensary license."

I jotted down some notes. Hudson asked for some vital stats, what they each looked like, where they lived, worked, etc.

I took a different tack. "What was your relationship like with them? Any reason they'd be out to get you?"

"I tried to be friendly at first, but it didn't really take. Everything was a competition with those two. They saw me as the obvious choice to get cut and not worthy of investing their time and attention into."

"Why would you be the obvious choice to be cut from the group?" I asked.

Austin shrugged. "Everyone else was a social climber, from money, aggressively ambitious, or all of the above. Carlie comes from a political family, and Mina was a first-year lawyer, one of the youngest Black women to score a place with the state Attorney General's office. Ben's making incredible strides in AI technology. I'm more laid back. A service industry dude cut off from my family money and connections. To be honest, I wondered why they picked me in the first place until I saw my dad. Nick and Roman loudly echoed my doubts."

After noting some impressions, I gestured for Austin to continue the story.

"Anyway, the rest of us followed Nick and Roman up the stairs to the dais. Each box there was identical. All black tied with white ribbons. I found the one with my name on it and stepped back to read it."

"What did it say?" I asked.

"'Be brave. Do not fight back.'"

I gulped and shook off the shiver of dread. Hudson kept his eyes on Austin, but leaned forward like he was going to touch my hand in a show of comfort and support. Muscle memory, maybe, because I looked down and saw that to my horror, I'd reached his way too. Again. I pulled back immediately and turned back to Austin.

"One by one, we slid the ribbons off and opened our boxes. Carlie pulled out strings of Mardi Gras beads. Roman had an old-fashioned candelabra. Nick had a wrench, Mina a gun, and Ben some sort of heavy statue looking thing."

The image of the blood-stained beads and candlestick planted in Liz's locker flashed in my mind. I shuddered.

"I asked everyone what their cards said. I had a very bad feeling, but I was still holding out hope that maybe this was a puzzle we had to solve. They held up identical cards with the message, *Kill the prey.*"

"What was in your box?" Hudson asked.

"At first, it looked like nothing. But then I rummaged around in the tissue paper and found it.

"Another card with a single word on it.

"Prey.""

FIFTEEN

"Ben saw the message from my box too. He stepped in front of me." Sadness etched Austin's features, and it struck me once more how young he looked. How much life the Enclave had stolen from him.

"We all exchanged uneasy glances," Austin continued. "Every muscle in the room was coiled tight. 'Let's just talk about this calmly, okay?' Ben said. Mina moved toward Ben and me too. The three of us had bonded through this experience, and we were all tight. I guess they were part of the reason I stayed too. Roman slapped the candelabra into his palm with this menacing gleam in his eye.

"'Sorry, preppy, no hard feelings. It's just business, right?' Nick said, stepping up beside Roman.

"Then Ben, always the voice of reason and decency, jumps in again. 'This can't be what they want us to do. They want loyalty, right? So this is a test. No one hurts Austin.'" Austin's eyes went a melancholy sort of wistful again.

I really wished I could hug him or at least feed him a French fry.

"Mina stepped forward too. That woman could scare a

hungry alligator back into the water with one of her glares, but I could tell even she was shaken.

"She said 'This is not what I signed up for. I'm not killing anyone or watching any of y'all kill anyone. Come on, Austin.' She grabbed my arm and pulled me down from the dais to the door. But then we noticed the lack of a handle on the inside. The two of us along with Ben pushed and pounded, but no one answered."

"Geez, sadistic much?" I said, beginning to see why they stirred up so much ire in Hudson.

Austin nodded. "Then it really went downhill."

I glanced up at Hudson, who watched the whole confession with a black look, and noted that he was trying to look at me rather than Austin. Which also seemed to make him uneasy, probably because he was considerate by nature and knew it would make *me* uneasy, given our history and tenuous partner-ship. I, on the other hand, had been turned toward what everyone else in the bar must have taken for empty space, giving Austin my full attention. One of the other patrons with a feather boa shot us a curious glance. I gave her a nervous smile before angling my body back towards Hudson—more awkward, yay—and looking at Austin through my peripheral vision.

Hudson noticed my change of posture and nodded in what I took for appreciation at picking up on that detail.

Austin continued, "Then on the far side of the room, a screen I hadn't noticed before lit up with a clock that started counting down. My whole body seized up. That's when I knew they were serious. That the Enclave really meant for one of the others to kill me. The ultimate test of loyalty and blackmail fodder. I wasn't chosen after all. I didn't pass my dad's test. And I was out."

"I'm so sorry, Austin," I murmured.

"Those dumb heads," Hudson said, only he didn't say dumb

heads. I softened toward him ever so slightly at his new protectiveness of Austin.

"I think Ben and Mina felt it too. And we all wondered what in the ever-loving heck we'd gotten ourselves into."

"What about the others?" I asked. "Nick and Roman dismissed you, but do you think they could be that easily provoked into hurting you?"

Austin frowned. "Hard to say. Roman talks a big game, but he's more the type to hire a hitperson rather than get his own hands dirty."

I considered, but the corner of my mouth hitched at Austin's use of the gender-neutral 'hitperson.' Once again, I wished I'd known him better when he was alive. I think we would've been friends.

"But maybe I was wrong about that," Austin said. "And Nick was always hard to read. Besides some details about his family's oil business, I didn't know much about him. He could turn on the charm around people he wanted to impress, but he was more a fan of monosyllabic answers any time I tried to be friendly."

"And what about Carlie? She seems like the wild card in all this. But she had the beads," I said.

"She just stood there in the middle of the room, with tears streaming down her face. She called out to Ravenscroft, 'Please tell me this is a joke. Let us out.'"

"But then a voice from the tablet's speaker said, 'Your escort has taken his leave. Your task is not yet complete. Nine minutes remain.'

"'So we wait out the clock,' Mina said, like that was that, God love her.

"Then Nick says, 'Great idea. Who wants to do some trust falls while we wait? Sing *Kumbaya.*' He was going for snide, but his face was as grim as the rest of ours.

"Roman kept his steely, impassive thing going, white knuckling that candelabra. Maybe he was psyching himself up to do what needed to be done. He was an entitled prick and thought I wasn't worthy of being chosen. In the end, I guess he was right."

"Don't say that," I said. "You are every bit as worthy as any of those people. They didn't deserve you."

A sad smile stretched across Austin's face. "Thanks. But every time I think about Roman, I don't know. Would he really murder me for his shot at power and a charmed life? Even for him, that seems like a stretch."

I rubbed my forehead and considered his assessment. Roman was in my top two likeliest candidates so far, but we needed a lot more information. "His weapon was the one that killed you. The candelabra was in Liz's locker with blood on it," I said.

"Along with the beads," Hudson added.

Austin's ghostly form flickered, and I could've sworn he looked greener when he reached for his throat.

"And the beads possibly point to Carlie," I said.

Austin cringed at her name, and I made a mental note to follow up on that later.

"Unless someone else grabbed them," Hudson continued. "But what happened after that?"

"Mina was good in a crisis. She, Ben, and I searched the room for another exit, a trapdoor, a hidden passage, anything, but no dice.

"My hands started shaking around the three-minute mark when our time was dwindling. Ben refused to give up, though. He reached out and squeezed my hand." Austin's throat bobbed. "It was the first time he'd ever touched me in public. He was really shy about that sort of stuff. 'We'll find a way out,' he said.

"But before I could answer, the voice from the speaker came on again.

"'You have two minutes to act, or you will *all* be sacrificed. Choose your course wisely.'

"Carlie cried out and dropped to the floor. She kept saying, 'It wasn't supposed to be like this. It wasn't supposed to be like this.'

I frowned and jotted that down. Did she know something the others didn't?

Austin went on. "The tension reached a fever pitch. Everyone drew closer together. Nick looked at Ben's and my hands laced together and smirked and said something I didn't catch to Roman. Ben tried to slide in front of me again, but I grabbed his shoulder and stopped him.

"If it was me or all of us, it was not worth losing him and Mina if that was how this played out. I squeezed his shoulder and shook my head. I took a good look at that shy, heart-stopping smile of his one last time.

"I opened my mouth to tell him all the things I wanted to say but held back because it felt too soon. But before I could get the words out, the lights went down.

"The room plunged into darkness except for the countdown screen. The torches snuffed out too. They must have been electric."

My heart raced. Even though I knew how this would end, I still found myself sending up a prayer for a different ending for Austin and his friends.

"Everything was still as death y'all, except for footsteps. Then some shuffling. Then something like an explosion lit up the room behind us before darkness again.

"I pushed Ben and Mina away from me so they wouldn't get hurt in the crossfire. Then something hit me, and I toppled over. Everything was chaos. Screams. Another gun shot went off.

Mina screamed. Hands groped at me. I wasn't sure if they were there to harm or protect. I remember the smell of wintergreen. Then something circled my neck and pulled until I couldn't breathe. Something struck my head.

"And then — well, you know the rest."

"Welp, I think we could all use a drink after that," I said. By the time Austin wrapped up his tale, my heart hurt for him. He was a lost soul, looking for a place to belong. And he'd put his faith in the wrong people.

Austin drifted with me to the bar where I ordered three bishop shots, the fact that Austin couldn't drink one be darned.

"Those were always my favorites here," he said mournfully. The bartender slid the three shot glasses filled with red liquid sideways to me and went back to the other end of the bar. "I tried to recreate them, but could never figure out the secret ingredient."

The bishop was one of the bar's signature drinks, which the bartenders could only deliver by sliding diagonally over the chess board counter top.

"Now you can just peek over someone's shoulder and find the recipe," I said. "Did you come here a lot? I'm surprised we never ran into each other." It seemed weird to talk about lighter topics after our sobering conversation, but I felt compelled to make small talk to take Austin's mind off of things.

"Yeah, mostly late nights after my bar shifts. By that time, it was the service industry crowd and tourists who'd had three too many Hand Grenades."

The bartender cocked her head at me and scurried back. "Did you need something else? I thought I heard you talking."

"Oh sorry," I flushed. "Phone." I pointed to the ear that was turned away from her, like there was an ear piece there. I was going to have to follow Hudson's advice and stick one in whenever Austin was around.

Hudson's face took on a bemused look at the sight of three shot glasses when I returned. "You know ghosts can't drink, right?"

I slid one in front of a mournful-looking Austin, took one for myself, and left Hudson to grab the remaining one.

I raised my glass. "To Austin. You left us way too soon. I wish I'd known you better in life. May we bring whoever did this to justice so you can rest peacefully and have as many pies as you want in that great pastry shop in the sky."

Austin's eyes shimmered.

Hudson lifted his glass too, and after a surreptitious look around the bar, looked straight at our ghostly client. "To Austin. And the long line of people the Enclave's hurt and covered up after. I'm sorry you got tangled up in this, man. Let's bring them all down." He threw back his shot, and in the following smile, I glimpsed a flash of the Hudson I'd known and depended on. The principled, always in-your-corner, funny Hudson.

I downed my shot.

After snagging an empty water cup from the next table over, I poured Austin's drink out into it ceremoniously. I couldn't help a little giggle. "I've always wanted to do that."

Hudson rolled his eyes, but couldn't suppress the smile threatening at the corners of his mouth.

"What? It's tradition. Going back to the days of the ancient Egyptians. Pouring a libation for the honored dead."

Austin pressed a hand to his heart.

"Let's just do this right so we don't have anyone pouring out liquor on our behalf anytime soon," Hudson said.

"I'm on board with that," I said. "So, Obi wan, where do we start?"

Hudson leaned forward and shifted into business mode. That twinkle he got in his eye whenever he was attacking a new project came out in full force. "First, we remember that we're dealing with a person or people who have already killed once and take the necessary precautions."

"And by 'we' he means me," I stage whispered to Austin. "Somber and serious, check."

Hudson sent me a withering look. "I'm not playing around, Paige."

"Me either. Did you miss that second item on my checklist?"

He shook his head and pinched the bridge of his nose, probably second guessing his decision to pair up with me. "Now we draw up a preliminary list of suspects. Suss out their motives, means, and opportunity. Then get started talking to them and narrow it down," he said.

"Well, the first part should be simple," I said. "We've got a locked room mystery."

Both Hudson and Austin lowered their eyebrows at me in question.

"Come on, don't you ever read mysteries? It's a classic trope. There's a murder that only someone inside the room could have committed. Or so it seems. Usually it's locked from the outside or something and only the dead body is inside. So obviously someone got inside, but how?" I twirled an imaginary mustache.

Hudson and Austin nodded. Austin's lips quirked with amusement, and Hudson went back to his pensive look.

"Only in my case," Austin said, "we were all locked inside together."

"Right, so it comes down to which of the five of your fellow acolytes did the deed," I said.

"But we also have to think about the big picture," Hudson said. "Who in this organization was pulling the strings? And why?"

"True. We also need to find out if this is a ritual they do with every class of acolytes or if this was a deviation, something more personal." My pen flew, jotting down questions in my notebook. "The cards instructed everyone to kill Austin. Was he randomly chosen, or was he a threat to someone? And was the mastermind a member of the group or someone higher in the organization?"

My last thought made my stomach sink like I'd just done a shot of lead instead of vodka and juice. I let the gravity of that prospect sink in, that there might be something much bigger and badder than a single newbie to the Enclave at fault. If they did this to their loyal acolytes as a matter of course, what would they do to a twenty-something ghost tour gift shop manager asking too many questions? Certainly they wouldn't give a second thought to ridding them-selves of me and sweeping it under the rug. I'd have to tread lightly.

I turned to Austin. "What does your gut say? Anyone inside or outside the group have it out for you? You told us a bit about Nick and Roman, but what about the others?"

Before I could answer, Hudson exhaled and shook his head. "Guts have no part in solving cases. We need facts, and we need evidence."

My insecurities reared their ugly heads. If I'd looked with my eyes and not my heart at my relationship with Hudson, could I have predicted how it would end? This was a question I could never answer. But it didn't change the fact that the relationships and facts were much more intertwined than he gave them credit for.

"Of course, but how do we even know where to look for facts and evidence before we know about the people and relationships involved? Which groups of people are close? Who's been acting shady? Where are the animosities and resentments? Who's spurned who? If we don't pull on those strings, how can we possibly know where to start looking? Austin's impressions and inside knowledge of these people and their relationships are exactly what we need to know about to find out who did this," I argued.

Hudson rubbed his temples but didn't object.

Point for Paige.

I turned back to Austin, who nodded at me appreciatively, but then his almost-translucent lips dipped into a frown.

"I'm not sure if my gut can be trusted if I didn't see this coming."

My gaze shifted to Hudson. "Believe me, I know the feeling. But don't beat yourself up. How could any reasonable human imagine something like that happening?"

"Have you seen the Saw movies?" Hudson deadpanned.

"Okay, unless you watch too many gruesome movies. How about we start with anything out of the ordinary? Was anyone besides Ravenscroft acting off?"

Austin thought for a moment. "Now that I think about it, Carlie didn't look so good that night. And not just after they locked us in the room."

"How do you mean?" I asked.

"She was paler than usual and kept wiping her hands on her pants. I figured it was just nerves about this last task. But I also caught her looking at Ravenscroft a few times like they were having an intense, silent argument. I got the feeling she knew who he was, unlike the rest of us. But Carlie and I weren't exactly on the best of terms over the last few months."

"What's the story there?" I asked.

He scrubbed a hand through his hair. "We hooked up near the beginning of our acolyte period. We'd both been drinking. She was superinsistent about it being a no-strings thing after, saying how she wasn't about to get into a serious relationship with a *bartender*."

"Rude," I said.

"Yeah. But I shrugged her off. Not too long after, I got involved with someone else." Austin's throat bobbed, and I hated seeing the look of sadness and regret on his face.

"Ben?" I ventured.

He nodded and cleared his throat when he caught me looking at him and ran a hand through his floppy hair. "Anyway, Carlie kept flirting with me and texting me, wanting to hook up. She was *not* happy when I broke the news I was seeing someone special."

"So we've got a woman scorned." I made some notes next to Carlie's name. "Did she seem like the vindictive type?"

"She had the beads and the opportunity," Hudson said.

"I mean, maybe? Slashing someone's tires while blaring Carrie Underwood or passive-aggressively skewering them on social media, sure, I could see that. But murder?" He made a face. "I don't see it."

Something about his description of Carlie's behavior in the chamber nagged at me, but I couldn't quite get a handle on the connection yet. I tapped my pen to my lips.

"You've got two people who were allies, from what you told us: Ben and Mina. Carlie's a wild card. Nick and Roman are on the hostile list," Hudson said. "Six acolytes, only five moving on, that had to bring out the competitive side for at least some of these people. Any past behaviors lead you to believe one or the other more capable of violence?"

"Or more desperate?" I added.

"Roman was a prick. He made no secret that he wasn't in this to make friends that wouldn't directly help his social climbing. And I seemed to be of no use to him," Austin said.

"There wasn't so much animosity between Nick and me, but he did have a Machiavellian view of the world. He was an 'ends justifies the means' kind of guy. I heard a rumor about Roman and anger management classes too. There was one time Nick showed up with a black eye, but nothing he shared with the class about."

"I'll do some digging and see what I can find. I say we shake out those guys first," Hudson said.

Austin float-squirmed in his seat, looking dubious.

"What is it?" I asked.

A heavy sigh whooshed out of him. "I guess part of me doesn't want to know the truth. What if it turns out people I thought I knew, I didn't know at all?"

My gaze lifted to Hudson's. His eyes were deep in thought. Regretful? My throat bobbed. I could relate.

Austin's gaze snagged on a newspaper abandoned on the next table and his eyes bulged at the headline: *Local bartender pushed from balcony of French Quarter bakery.* "Another problem: These guys, especially Roman and Nick, are not just going to offer up details about a secret society they've sworn never to speak of to outsiders and murder they committed. Especially one that was probably supposed to be covered up and is now front page news."

"I'm pretty good at getting people to open up," I said.

Hudson clenched his fists. "We'll have to track them. See who they talk to and about what. Wait for them to slip up," Hudson said.

"Ooh, stakeout!" I was already mentally preparing my dark sunglasses, Slushee, and pack of Red Vines. "Maybe we can borrow one of those fancy PI cameras. Ines might have one." I tapped my lip. But then I remembered Liz getting hauled off to the police station and sighed.

"We might not have time to wait for that to play out. Liz could take the fall for this. We're going to have to be more proactive, but still inconspicuous."

I let my gaze unfocus, trying to think of a natural way of cozying up to Roman or Nick. I couldn't exactly go knock on their front door, but between social media and asking around, it probably wouldn't be too hard to find out where they went to unwind after work and casually chat them up. But that could still take time. My gaze landed on a different article that had made front page news. An event announcement that contained a picture of none other than Roman di Rossi.

My lips curled into a triumphant smile.

"I think I found just the way."

This was the perfect opportunity. The event Roman would attend Sunday was the Crescent City Forty Under Forty Gala. The gala was a huge annual event for young business leaders. Held in one of the swankiest ballrooms in town, people got glammed up to sip champagne, munch on hors d'oeuvres, raise money for charity, and heap praise on the up-and-coming entrepreneurs and others making a community impact. It was the same event where my boss Wendy and her husband Alec were being honored this year for their game app that was sort of like *Pokemon Go* but for French Quarter history and ghost sightings.

And since Roman was another of the forty under forty himself, chances were he'd be in attendance, especially if he was as much of a social climber as Austin said.

It would've been on my weekend agenda anyway, except that my parents were supposed to be visiting, and I'd planned a dinner and show for the three of us. As a silver lining to their last-minute cancellation, I was free to seize the opportunity for some face time with suspect number one, Roman di Rossi. And possibly his acolyte friends.

And if there was one thing I excelled at, it was talking to people at events.

After telling Austin and Hudson about my plan, I jumped on the phone.

"Are you sure there are no more tickets? Not even for special last-minute donors?" I pleaded with the event organizer.

Hudson listened in with cautious hope.

"I'm sorry," the organizer said, sounding sincere. "I really wish there was something I could do, but we've got to follow fire code too."

"Okay, well, thanks, anyway." My shoulders slumped, but I shook it off. That was only my first call. Surely I could find someone who had a cancellation.

Hudson frowned. "Let's hit this from another angle."

That little voice of doubt whispered in my ear. *First move of your ghost investigation and you've already struck out.* I shook it off. I was *not* giving up that easily. And I was nothing if not resourceful.

"Patience." I laced my fingers together and stretched out my arms. I didn't need either Hudson or the devil on my shoulder messing with my head. At least the unexpected bonus of ticket scarcity meant Hudson couldn't easily muscle his way in and bulldoze everything I tried to do in my fledgling investigation.

A few more calls to my bosses and coworkers, and I was in. Wendy told me that Declan's date had canceled, and she thought Norman's girlfriend had gotten sick this week. I tried Norman first, all of my fingers and toes crossed that this would pan out. Attending with my eccentric work buddy would be much preferable to being the plus one of the police officer who'd told me in no uncertain terms to stay out of the investigation I'd be there to conduct.

"You had me at secret mission," Norman said when I

explained I was looking for a spare ticket for a little undercover sleuthing.

I offered to pick him up since he couldn't drive and was using a wheelchair to get around. The damage to his leg after the skateboard incident had been relatively minor, but he wouldn't be able to drive until the cast came off.

I hung up, feeling a little smug. I suppose I could've called Declan about the extra ticket for Hudson, but A) I did *not* want to answer all the inevitable questions from my friends and coworkers about my disappearing/reappearing ex and B) I wasn't sure I was up for spending more time with him than I had to. This was all still new and confusing, and I needed time to wrap my head around him being back.

Hudson said he'd see if he could find more intel on our suspects, where they lived, where they worked and hung out, and who they spent time with.

✦✦✦

AFTER AGREEING to meet up tomorrow and discuss what we'd learned, I parted ways with both Hudson and Austin and walked towards the campus of my old alma mater. I needed some time to clear my head and go over all the details to see if there were connections I hadn't seen before, more threads I could tug.

I could do this. Right?

Facts and evidence. Right.

I flipped open my notebook as I walked, but those pesky doubts still nagged. I needed to be in a place where I felt centered, where I felt like I belonged and was worthy. And I knew just the place.

A welcome sense of calm settled over me as I passed under a brick archway and stepped onto the path that wound through the towering halls of Ursuline University. It was a small private school, but it had been the place where I'd first followed in the footsteps of my great grandmother Magnolia. She'd attended in the 40s during World War II and had founded my sorority, Nu Omega, with her friends. During that time, she'd also penned her first Matilda Mayhew mysteries.

Ducks quacked from the pond, mallards with their jewel-toned heads swam close to the edge, looking for breadcrumbs from passers-by. Finally, I made it to the Nu Omega Memorial Garden. Vibrant summer flowers vined and dripped from the arched arbor that heralded the small space.

Sun dappled the grass through the sheltering branches of the live oaks, and I sat on the bench next to the fountain and the troughs of wildflowers.

I ran a finger over the plaque on the fountain with my Great Grandma Magnolia's name along with the names of the other 12 founders of Nu Omega who had planted and cultivated this garden as a gift to the college upon graduation.

I sunk down to the bench and pulled out my notes from this afternoon again. Obvious animosity between Austin and both Nick and Roman. Roman and his anger management and Nick and his black eye. The jilted lover thing with Carlie. Romantic relationship with Ben and friendship with Mina. I felt like there was something else missing, though. I needed to see the dynamics of these people in person to understand more about what was there without being said. Was there any way to observe that?

The closest thing, in my mind, would be to talk to Austin's friends first, get their impressions and insider knowledge. Maybe they'd seen something Austin hadn't that night. Or would be forthcoming about the aftermath of the cover-up. Or knew of an outsider with influence over this whole thing.

My gut said talk to the friends first and go from there. But

Hudson was adamant about working from the most obvious to the least likely suspects. He'd been at this a lot longer than me.

Were my instincts actually leading me to take the easiest way out? To veer away from the danger?

I didn't want to think so, but I was new at this. I really wished I had someone experienced to help me navigate this that I didn't have such a complicated and adversarial relationship with.

I thought of all the cases my great grandma had written with so many twists and turns in her books. Did she have someone helping lead the way through the beginning of her career, or did she just stumble along until she found her way?

"Great Grandma Magnolia, I wish you were here. I could really use your help." Saying this out loud felt a little silly. But ever since I'd seen my first ghost yesterday—had that really only been yesterday?—a part of me had harbored the secret hope that maybe Grandma Magnolia wouldn't only be a distant relative that I'd never get to meet.

But that was silly, right?

"I wondered when you'd come, my darling."

I sucked in a breath of surprise at the voice so close by. You would've thought I'd be beyond surprise with the events of the last few days, but all the hairs on the back of my neck stood up at the sound of the female voice. Smoky and low. Foreign, yet familiar at the same time.

"I rather always thought it would be you to carry on the family gift. Didn't I, Moisha? Didn't I call it from the start? Ever since you were six years old and followed that ice cream truck you figured out was overcharging and skimming your friends' pocket money."

A second female voice chimed in unison with the last sentence, as if this were an oft-told story. "Yes, yes, so clever, this one. A regular clairvoyant, you are," the second voice ribbed in a playfully annoyed tone that suggested a close-knit friendship rife with inside jokes. "Likes to be right too, this one," Moisha said.

"Well, I usually am, aren't I?"

"Fair point," Moisha conceded. Then she whispered an aside to me, "And she'll never let you hear the end of it."

I finally spun around and came face to face with my great grandmother.

EIGHTEEN

Two young female apparitions dressed like they'd stepped out of the 1940s whacked one another with their gloves and giggled.

The taller blonde ghost swept closer and put her hand to my cheek. It tingled, cool and fleeting where she touched. "Paige, my darling, we meet at last."

My throat constricted.

Looking at her was almost like looking in a mirror. She had the high rosy cheeks and heart-shaped face common to the women on my mom's side of the family. But unlike me, she'd swept her golden locks into perfect victory rolls with the back of her hair hanging loose. She wore a dress with a high-waisted A-line skirt and beautiful detailing on the bodice. The entire outfit was the same faint powder blue as her eyes, which now glinted with mischief.

"Magnolia?" I sputtered. "I mean Great Grandma Magnolia?"

"Magnolia will do. That 'great' business makes me sound old."

"Well, you are getting on in years, Mags," Moisha teased. She floated to Magnolia's side.

Magnolia smirked. "No more than you."

Despite neither of their feet touching the ground, Moisha stood about half a foot shorter than Magnolia, with brown hair set in pin curls and a generous dusting of freckles across the fair skin on the bridge of her nose. She sported long, flowing trousers, a cute pussy-bow blouse and an over-sized mustard cardigan that dwarfed her petite frame.

"Speaking of old, Paige, meet my oldest and dearest friend Moisha."

"Moisha Mosher-Harter," I murmured. I'd seen that name next to Magnolia's on the plaque hundreds of times.

Moisha grinned. She touched one hand to her nose and pointed at me with the other. "I see my reputation precedes me." She fluffed her hair and preened.

"And you say I'm the one that loves attention," Magnolia quipped. The low smoky quality of her voice made me think of a golden age movie starlet.

"You were a founder of Nu Omega," I said. Before initiation, we'd had to memorize the names of all thirteen founders along with our Purpose and the Greek alphabet.

"And one of the first female doctors to serve in the US Army."

"We learned about that during my pledge period. You're my friend Indira's career idol."

"Moisha was also the brains behind the name Nu Omega."

I raised an eyebrow, eager to soak up any stories they cared to tell me.

"I liked that it looked like the letters N and O, a little nod to our fair city of New Orleans," Magnolia said.

"And I liked the idea that we could walk around with the word NO on our chests," Moisha said. "In a society that wanted women to follow the rules of the patriarchy and say yes to their every whim, it was a subtle way to give them the old middle finger."

I burst into laughter. "I have a feeling we're going to get along very well."

"Speaking of," Magnolia said, "before our time runs out, how are you holding up with the news that the supernatural is a lot more natural than you might've thought?"

"Okay, I guess." I told them about the fortune telling machine, the Tower card, the app, and getting matched up with Austin.

"It was carrier pigeon messages from the people upstairs in our day." Magnolia pointed to the sky.

"Just as cryptic, though," Magnolia said.

"But a lot messier." Moisha wrinkled her nose.

"They do have a flair for the dramatic," Magnolia said. "So, how can we help on the case?"

I looked back and forth between Magnolia and Moisha, so lively, so *real* in front of me. So much like I'd imagined, but even more. My hopes from my loneliest days had come true. And not only that, with Magnolia, I had help. The non-judgmental kind that didn't come from someone who just wanted to take over and do it his own way. I blinked back the tears that stung the back of my eyes.

"What is it, love?" Moisha asked in a soft voice.

I sniffed. "Nothing. I just never thought this could really happen." I studied Magnolia in her ghostly form. Impossible, but here nonetheless. Maybe this was the most magic thing of all. "You, your stories—once my mom finally told me about them—changed my life, set me on this course. I never really felt like I fit with anyone in my family until I read them. Until I found you."

Magnolia's eyes softened and glistened.

"True stories, those books of hers," Moisha said.

"Wait, what?" My brows furrowed. "Seriously? Even the one with the devil?"

"Well, I did take quite a bit of dramatic license here and there. But yes. I wrote down my ghost detecting adventures and gave them to Matilda."

"No. Way."

"Cross my heart." Magnolia glanced at her watch.

"Do you have somewhere else to be?" I asked, hating the pang I felt.

"I wish we didn't. But I'm afraid our arrangement has some limitations. This isn't usually done within the agency, the dead who have already crossed over coming back to earth, but I can be persuasive when I want to be."

"Isn't that the truth," Moisha said.

Magnolia continued. "We're allowed to visit you for an hour each day. You can call us as needed to consult on your cases. And we can only go where you go. You'll be our tether to the world of the living. I understand you also have a living mentor to help you anytime we're not available."

I frowned, thinking of the way Hudson had swept in and wanted to take over, dredging up the pain I'd almost put behind me. "That's a little complicated." I filled them in on our history and how this afternoon had gone. "Plus, I think he'd rather run the show than teach me how to do it myself."

Moisha gave an exasperated sigh. "Eighty years later and they're still pulling those shenanigans."

"He did give me a little to go on." I told them about his strategy and my idea to chat up Roman at the gala tonight.

Both Magnolia and Moisha listened intently.

"So what do I do? Where would you start? I feel like talking to Austin's friends is the quickest way to get more background, but Hudson's insistent on knocking out the most likely suspects first."

"As much as I hate to say it, he has a point. Especially if your professor Liz is in trouble with the police. Time is of the essence. I think I'd have started there too. It sounds like you already have that in motion, in any case," Magnolia said.

"True." I mulled this over. Speed was a factor even if I was working with the training wheels still on, with Liz's freedom hanging in the balance.

Still, I was in this estranged relationship with my instincts. I'd relied on them so heavily for most of the decisions in my life. I was constantly taking in information, processing it quickly, and feeling my way through. How could I ever be good at this if taking the correct steps didn't come naturally?

"I know that look." Magnolia regarded me with a rueful smile. "Don't be so hard on yourself. You don't go from rookie to expert your first day on the job."

"Technically, it's day two," I said.

Moisha laughed. "Like grandmother, like granddaughter."

"I don't mind putting in the work," I said. "I *want* to put in the work." The next part was tougher to say out loud. *What if I put in the work, and I'm still a failure?*

"Then do it," Magnolia said. "You have all the raw materials you need. You have a knack for reading people and connecting to them. The rest you'll pick up as you go. The most important quality successful people have in common is the courage to risk being appallingly bad at something before they have the experience to get better."

I wanted to believe her. I wanted to take her words and wrap them around me like a warm blanket.

"There's just so much at stake here. Liz's freedom, my friends and family potentially getting in the cross-hairs of the Enclave if I upset the wrong people. One of those inevitable mistakes and someone could get hurt. Or worse. Hudson's solution is looking smarter and smarter," I said.

"Nonsense," Magnolia said. "It's wise to weigh the costs. It shows me you're mature enough not to enter this lightly. You can start with something easier, and I wouldn't think badly of you for it, but if you wish to do this, you have help. I have no doubt you can make all the difference for many people doing this work."

"Were you scared on your first case?" I asked.

"Petrified."

"But you probably aced it on the first go."

"Let's just say there was a very disgruntled alligator wrangler. And some misplaced prized pralines. But it turned out all right in the end." Magnolia winked at me.

"Needless to say, that one didn't wind up in the books," she said.

I exhaled and took in a breath of the vining jasmine and trees of the garden, trying to psych myself up. I could do this. I wasn't alone. Veteran ghost detective grandma and Moisha on my side. Hudson to fill in the gaps.

"Okay, so any pointers on how to get answers out of a suspect without being too obvious?" I said.

Magnolia and Moisha exchanged delighted grins, and we launched into preparations before the hour drew to a close and both of their apparitions started to fade away.

"I think our time is almost up," Magnolia said with an apologetic smile.

Discussing a game plan with them had bolstered my spirits. I hated to see them go already.

"So, does Cinderella have a gown for this ball tonight?" Moisha said as her hair flickered in and out of view.

"I'll dig up something," I said. That was next up on my agenda.

"Too bad we can't wave our wands and be her fairy godmothers. Hedgehog footman, squash blossom coach, a pretty, frilly confection to wear," Moisha said.

"For someone who loves trousers so much, you sure have a thing for ballgowns," Magnolia said. Her forearm faded in and out.

Moisha shrugged. "Eh, I like both. So sue me."

"I wish you could come to the gala with me tonight," I said.

"Me too, darling, but you'll be great." Magnolia squared her shoulders and lifted her chin like her word was final. I tried to soak in her confidence.

She fixed me with a knowing gaze. "See you tomorrow for your first stakeout."

✦▲✦▲✦

A FEW HOURS LATER, Ines and I raided our collective closets for gala formal wear options.

"Too *Addams Family* on you," she proclaimed when I wriggled into a black sheath cocktail dress of hers.

"I think it's pretty. Understated. I'm trying to blend in," I said, turning this way and that in the mirror. But I did see her point. With my pale complexion and sunny disposition, head-to-toe black tended to look out of place on me.

"Face it. Most people have a little black dress. You have a little pink one."

I laughed. That was true. I held up a floor-length dress in shimmery pale pink with ruching in the bodice that was much more me.

Ines gave a thumbs up.

"So, you never told me. How did it go with the person who might help with your investigation this afternoon?"

I froze, then faced away from the mirror under the guise of unzipping myself. "Um..."

A poker face was something I did *not* possess. Well, maybe with strangers, but Ines, Bridget, and I had been friends long enough that they knew all my tells. Any direct eye contact, and boom, my eyelid started twitching. Then all the stuff I never intended to say came tumbling out.

Rather than coming clean about the specific details of the whole ghost thing with my skeptical friend earlier, I'd focused on the practical bits and told her about the potential helper I was going to meet. I hated keeping even that much from her, but add to it the bombshell of Hudson showing up in the middle of things, and it all felt like too much to digest. As much as I was dying to spill everything, getting all up in my feelings right now was a distraction I couldn't afford with so much at stake tonight.

"I don't know if that guy will work out. But I got a lead on some other retired investigators who can spare a bit of time here and there."

"That sounds promising," she said.

I tried to wriggle out of the Wednesday Addams special, but the zipper stuck. My jaw twitched, and beads of sweat popped up on my forehead.

"Here, let me help." Ines laughed and worked the zipper back on track.

"Thanks." When I turned around, I came face-to-face with Ines. I felt the weird-o smile pasting itself onto my face and stretching. Okay, add to the unfortunate side effects of this new gig: life and death danger and keeping stuff from my friends.

Ines raised an eyebrow and considered me. "What's with the face?"

"What face?"

"The 'I'm keeping a secret, possibly against my will, and I will burst if I don't let it out' face."

"What?!" I stepped behind my dressing screen and clapped a hand to my cheek. If this kept up, I'd make a terrible investigator. I blew out a breath and switched dresses. "Just nervous," I said, which was also true. "The thought of interrogating a possible murderer does that to a girl."

Ines was quiet for a moment. "Sure you don't want me to cancel my plans and come with you?"

"No! I mean no, I do not want you to cancel your bread baking class with Sam. You've been wanting to do that forever. But thank you for offering. Norman will be there with me."

She laughed. "Right. Norman is the very picture of inconspicuous. Didn't he catch his eyebrows on fire at your last work event?"

I laughed. "Ah yes, the famous baked Alaska incident." I smoothed the pink dress over my shapewear and stepped out to face the mirror in my sparkly pink glory.

"Yep, that's the one."

Ines nodded her approval and grabbed the perfect necklace from my dresser to go with it.

"They're almost all grown back now. He does still look surprised most of the time. But the whole Deveaux family will be there too if I need backup. Unfortunately Officer Stay Out of It will also be in attendance with them."

"You can handle Declan."

I could. We had the overprotective cop/cheeky meddling sleuth thing going. He'd probably step in if he knew I was digging, but I knew how to placate him.

A potential surprise appearance by Hudson, however, was another thing entirely.

I wondered again where he'd been all this time, what had been so wrong or so important that he'd run out like he did. My emotions warred inside me, and I cycled through sad and mad all over again.

I grabbed my purse, trying to put aside my issues with Hudson and steady myself for the task ahead.

"Hey, do you think you can run some names for me? Find out where they live, where they work?"

"Some leads already? Nice. Write them down for me, and I'm on it." She grinned at me. "Paige Harrington is on the case."

NINETEEN

"All right, what's our secret mission here?" Norman whispered as we entered the ballroom for the gala. I looked down at my friend who propelled his wheelchair forward with flair. He'd somehow managed to find tuxedo shorts, of all things, to go with his last-minute leg cast and sported a wine-colored velvet smoking jacket over his lace collared button up. His whole aesthetic was sort of casual Haunted Mansion chic. He doffed his requisite top hat to the person who took our names for entry.

After we passed the hallway to the ballroom, Norman swayed a little and wiped a bead of sweat from his brow with his pocket square. His face looked even pastier than usual.

"Are you sure you're okay to be here? You barely got out of the hospital 24 hours ago."

"Pain pills are glorious things," he said. "And besides, it's Wendy and Alec's night. How could I miss this?"

I gave him an indulgent smile. The Deveaux family had taken him in and made him part of their motley family, just as they'd done with me. "I'm sure they'd understand. Especially since you were injured in the line of duty. Well, sort of."

He waved the thought away. "But on that note, I understand pain medication does not play nice with spirits." He wiggled his index finger at me in a no-no gesture.

"You are correct," I said. "Bridget cracked open some wine after she had her wisdom teeth pulled, and it was not pretty."

"So," Norman raised his pointer finger in declaration. "I'm helping you with your secret investigation mission. You're on keeping-me-away-from-the-free-champagne duty."

I laughed and gave him a salute. "On it."

"Who are we looking for again?" he asked.

"His name's Roman di Rossi. He's on the 40 under 40 list." I pulled out my phone and showed him a picture. "And maybe a few others who were also with Austin the night he died. I'll know them when I see them." At least I hoped I would. Austin had been MIA since our meeting with Hudson this afternoon. It would be nice to have some additional insight from my ghostly client.

"And under no circumstances are we to mention to Declan Durocher what we're up to. Got it?"

"Griffin's brother? The police officer?" Griffin was our boss, Julie's husband.

"That's the one."

"No cops. We're out for rogue justice." Norman nodded his head sagely, the pain meds clearly in full effect.

I snorted.

At the end of the hallway, the ballroom stretched out before us. Glittering strands of fairy lights and crystal chandeliers cast a soft glow on the navy silk linens draped over the high tables dotting the room.

People in formal attire filled the space, which was arranged in two levels. The lower tier provided a showcase for silent auction items, a stage, and bar, while the upper level housed more tables with a magnificent view of everything happening below. Above the musicians on stage, an enormous video screen cycled through photos of the honorees and the contributions that earned them a spot in tonight's celebration.

"Come on, let's find Wendy and Alec and the fam before those pills put you to sleep," I said.

A band playing pop/country crossover music that Hudson probably would've loved crooned from the stage. I spotted Wendy's auburn hair in the crowd near the upstairs railing, and a few minutes later we were up there hugging her in congratulations.

Norman attempted to compose a sonnet about their win but lost his way when he tried to find a word to rhyme with ectoplasm.

Norman's antics seemed to defuse some of the discomfort for Wendy, who'd flushed three shades of crimson at all the attention. Now *there* was a woman who could rock an all black wardrobe. She twisted her combat boot into the ground and adjusted the tulle layer of her dress that was embroidered with skulls. Her husband Alec, who was always a quiet, steady presence, pulled her into a hug.

"Dude, what are you doing here, anyway?" Wendy gave Norman's shoulder a playful punch. "You were only discharged from the hospital yesterday."

"'Tis but a flesh wound," Norman answered. Because of course he did.

We mingled and said our hellos to the whole Deveaux and Durocher ghost tour clan, though Declan was nowhere in sight yet. Phew. But then, neither was Austin. When an appropriate amount of time had passed, I caught Norman's eye and motioned toward a spot at the railing, a little out of the way.

He nabbed a glass of champagne from a server's tray, which I swooped in and swapped him for a bacon wrapped shrimp.

"Thanks, spymaster," he said. "I almost forgot."

The cold rail of the balcony pressed into my midsection, and I bit my lip. A fizz of nerves bubbled up, along with my sip of champagne as I surveyed the crowd. This was it. I was actually doing it. And I had no idea if I would sink or swim here.

"What do we do first?" Norman whispered.

Heck if I know, I thought.

I froze, all of my instincts on vacation rendezvousing with their pal second-guessing.

No, hold up. To heck with that line of thinking. I thrust my chin up and thought back to my conversation with Magnolia and Moisha. I was not alone.

"First, we read the room," I said, parroting Magnolia's advice. "Find Roman. Look out for the others too. Pay attention to how he's acting. See if there's any sign of guilt or hiding something. Watch who he talks to. Follow the connections."

The last bit was my own. And it seemed to track with the sound advice of my veteran sleuth great grandmother.

"Ten-four," Norman said. "Over and out."

"I'm pretty sure you only have to say that if you're on walkie-talkies."

"Roger that."

I surveyed the crowd, recognizing many of the faces who cycled through on the big screen. Some were calm and more subdued, seeming to stick to a small circle of their friends and family, like Wendy and Alec were doing. Others, though, were aggressively social climbing. With their sharp suits and stylish dresses, they practically hummed with energy and ambition. Many flitted between prominent business leaders and folks bidding on the high-ticket silent auction items, while others moved through the crowd, gravitating to their fellow young, hungry, and beautiful people.

If the Enclave were looking for the next class of rich and

powerful to join their ranks, this would be just the kind of event to prospect for new recruits.

I also spotted several sorority sisters, like our newly elected Louisiana Governor, Gretchen Ginsberg. We were friendly even though she'd graduated and gone alum before I even started college. Unfortunately, though, no sign of Roman.

"I've got eyes on our perp," Norman said.

"Where? And he's not a perp. He's a suspect until proven guilty."

"Twelve o'clock," Norman said. "And can you get me another shrimp thingy?"

"On it." I flagged down the next server passing hors d'oeuvres and settled in to get a read on suspect number one, Roman di Rossi.

"Hey, isn't he the guy from those Calvin Klein ads?" Norman asked.

"That seems like something that would've come up in my social media search." But even if he wasn't, he still would've been right at home in one of them. Roman cut a dashing figure in his suit, which was probably bespoke. With his Mediterranean complexion—his family had roots in Italy, as I'd learned from my preliminary combing through his social media—and his cheeks that could have been chiseled from marble by one of the Renaissance masters, the man was striking. Besides winning the gene pool lottery, the two or three-day beard he sported also lent him a roguish air.

Roguish, but nothing about him struck me as sinister or capable of murder. Nor did he appear overcome with guilt.

Roman bent to shake hands with a distinguished-looking couple in their eighties. He turned just as much dazzle on them as he did to the female admirers he'd spoken with moments before.

Dang it.

"What is it?" Norman asked.

"Nothing." I sighed. "I just realized I was secretly hoping he'd be some mustache twirling tie-'em-to-the-train-tracks, dyed in the wool villain." The truth was far more murky.

"He doesn't look very villainous to me," Norman said, scratching his chin. "Unless he's into white collar crime. Embezzling from the rich and investing in state-of-the-art teeth whitening."

I grinned and watched Roman move effortlessly through the room. One thing became evident. This guy would be difficult to get on his own. He moved from group to group, with people sliding in for his attention at every turn.

After taking selfies with several people I took to be strangers to him, he waved at someone across the room and excused himself. His features tightened on his traverse over to none other than Nick Ortega. Score. Maybe I could get in conversations with both of them tonight.

Nick donned a sleek steel blue suit that complemented his medium brown skin. Trouble brewed on his youthful face, though I suspected when not in this state, he had charm for days. He'd been talking to someone very hairy.

"That's Nick," I elbowed Norman. "The other suspect."

"Why is he talking to Cousin It?"

Roman edged out the hairy guy, who took the hint and moved on. The two Enclave acolytes greeted each other with a half hug/slap on the back thing. But when Roman leaned closer to whisper something to him, Nick's countenance went even more stony. Nick cut a glance at the stage and shook his head at Roman. Curious, I followed his gaze to where a musician with long black hair obscuring his face rocked the guitar riff on an old Taylor Swift song.

Did they know each other?

Not now. Not here, Roman's face seemed to communicate.

Something was definitely up with them. Were they talking about the murder? Had I been wrong, and they'd both been in on it, or was one helping the other cover it up?

I needed some face time to get a better read on them. A chance for them to react to mention of Austin. "I don't know how I'm going to get Roman away from these people, but I'm going in."

Austin chose that moment to materialize next to me. I jumped. He'd outfitted his apparition form in a tux and bow tie for the occasion. "Don't worry. He'll want to talk to you. You're just his type."

"And what's that?" I asked.

"Beautiful, trusting, and you always look like you're keeping a secret. He'll want to find out what it is."

I gave him a wan smile. "Is that so?"

Norman frowned. "Who are you talking to?"

"Ghost friend," I said. Of anyone I knew, Norman was probably the only one who wouldn't blink at the mention of ghosts.

Norman shrugged with his typical nonchalance around the supernatural. "Cool. Tell them I said hi."

"My friend Norman says hi."

"Tell him I say hi back."

I did.

Norman gave a thumbs up and waved at the place Austin floated.

"You might want to get down there," Austin said. "I have a feeling he's going to slip out soon. There are other Enclave people here too. Nick's acting wiggy. I want to keep an eye on him, so I'm going to tail him. Get down there and see what you can get from Roman."

My palms began to sweat. Watching from afar was one thing. Actually running an investigation was another altogether.

I called up the image of Grandma Magnolia and her words. *I believe in you.*

With a cleansing breath and a mental crack of my knuckles, I steeled myself and looked down to find Roman again. He'd moved on from Nick and was now chatting with a generically handsome blond man and a woman with long dark hair. When she turned, I did a double take. Eliza?

Yep, there she was, in a form-fitting gold dress, a pair of pearl earrings, and a tasteful necklace that were way too under-stated for her usual style: my cousin Eliza. She lived in Metairie, a city close by, where she worked as a journalist. I'd spent summers with her and her brother Roscoe as a kid, and we'd gotten into all sorts of trouble. But what was she doing here? And more importantly, what was she doing talking to my murder suspect?

Another mystery to solve tonight.

An idea struck. "Norman, text me in a few minutes when I get to Roman and give you the signal, okay? Something about funeral arrangements."

He gave me a salute. "What's the signal?"

I pressed my lips together. "I hadn't thought that far. We need something that won't be easily mistakable. Any ideas?"

"Ooh, how about a casual chicken dance?" He flapped his arms like wings in slow motion.

I laughed. "I think this calls for a little more subtlety."

"Jazz hands?" Norman suggested.

"I can work with a less razzle dazzle version of that." I straightened my shoulders. "Okay, I'm really going in now," I said to Norman and Austin. "Wish me luck."

Just then, Declan Durocher, aka Officer Stay Out of It, aka the last person I needed thwarting my efforts right now, sidled up next to me on the railing.

"Going in where?" he asked.

TWENTY

I smiled sweetly up at Declan, hoping I didn't look like I'd just been busted. I scrambled for a plausible explanation as he looked back at me expectantly.

"Declan, hi," I said. "You startled me." I pressed a hand to my racing heart.

"You clean up nice, squirt," he said. "What'cha doing up here away from all the action?" He leaned against the guardrail next to me and cocked a perfectly arched brow.

"Keeping Norman here company. People watching," I said, going for nonchalance. Roman moved away from Eliza and her date and disappeared into the crowd, much to my chagrin. I turned back to face Declan in his tux, which accentuated his broad shoulders. "You're looking quite dapper yourself."

A nice smell wafted off of him, some kind of cologne or aftershave that made me think of the ocean. Driftwood? Did that have a scent? Why was I even thinking about the smell of Declan Durocher, anyway? Focus, gumshoe Harrington.

"We're on a top secret mission," Norman stage whispered to him.

I elbowed Norman and gave him a meaningful look. "To find those bacon wrapped shrimp again," I added quickly. "Because they are delicious. Have you tried one?"

"You wouldn't be casing the place for murder suspects, would you?"

"Who, me?"

Declan's eyebrow inched toward his hairline.

"Paige would make an excellent investigator," Norman said. "On account of she's so good at finding things."

"Like the shrimp," I said. "And bacon."

"Mmm hmm." Declan gave us both a skeptical look.

I put on my most innocent face. "Besides, I thought that was your job, officer."

"It is. I'm just making sure we keep it that way."

"Far be it from me to interfere," I said. I pressed a hand to my heart and batted my eyelashes.

"Mmm hmm," he said again with an amused grin.

Austin cleared his throat and pointed to the recently conjured watch on his wrist. I flicked a gaze back at the crowd and frowned. I'd have to wrap this up.

"Speaking of the investigation," I said, "How's it going? Since I'm most definitely not sticking my nose in it."

Declan chuckled, then his carefree features clouded. "It's not looking great for Liz, I'm sorry to say. Someone ordered a rush on the fingerprint analysis on the murder weapons. They sent her home until they get the results back. I have a feeling the person or persons who did this covered their tracks very thoroughly. My guess is her prints are all over them."

My chest tightened. "But she doesn't have any motive. Can't the other investigators see that this has to be planted?"

"The lead investigator on the case isn't so sure about that."

"Who is it? It's that Crowder dingus, isn't it?"

Declan nodded. "Unfortunately."

"Then we have to find out who did this and clear her name," I said.

"Don't you think that's what I'm working on?" His grip tightened on the rail.

"Of course. Sorry."

We both fell silent for a beat.

"Got any leads?" I asked.

He frowned, but didn't elaborate. I wondered if that meant he didn't or he just wanted me to butt out.

Another server came by with a tray of champagne flutes. Declan and I took one, and I asked if she could come back around with water for Norman.

"Sure you're old enough to drink that, squirt?" Declan asked with a teasing grin. I took that as his attempt to lighten the mood.

I shot him a dark look. "Har. Har. I just turned twenty-five, so you know. Just because I don't look forward to getting mail from the AARP and spend a lot of time thinking about dentures like you do doesn't mean I'm a kid. What are you, thirty?"

"Hey now, don't hate because I plan for my retirement." He sipped his champagne. "And I'm thirty two for your information."

"Good to know." I took a sip and looked out into the crowd again. No sign of Nick or Eliza. Dang it.

But I did see Roman, thankfully, heading in the bar's direction. Near the stage, alone for the first time tonight.

I wanted to rush after him, but I bit my lip, considering an idea first. As much as I'd like to solve the case myself, it would be nice to have another ally, especially one on the inside I could trust with more resources to track down important information.

When I looked up, trouble was brewing again in Declan's brown eyes.

"What if I had some info that might help you? People Austin was with the night of the murder."

"And how did you come by this info?"

I shrugged. I didn't think he'd take as readily to talking ghosts as Norman did. "Talking to people."

"And do you have any proof these people were with him the night he died?"

"I know where they might have been." I shifted my gaze around, lowered my voice, and told him they might've been seen outside the old Ursuline convent. Austin fed me the specifics about the location of the tunnel entrance. "Can't you check CCTV or something like they do in *Killing Eve*? Or is that just a British thing?"

Declan shook his head and the corner of his mouth twitched into a smile before his features went pensive again. "I'd like to speak with this source of yours. They might provide me more details that would help us find the right person."

"I don't know," I hedged. "He was very clear that he couldn't talk to the police."

"Is he safe, at least?" Declan asked.

"Oh, I don't think he's in any more earthly trouble."

"Well, give him my card in any case. I'll keep things as quiet as possible if he needs help." Declan handed over a business card, then placed a second one in my hand. "One for you too. Should you find yourself in trouble. Which is completely unlike you."

I smirked. "Thanks."

Austin stewed once I'd passed on the names of the acolytes, and Declan made his way back to his brother and the rest of the family. "Are you sure it's a good idea to involve him?" Austin asked.

I wondered the same thing. But it'd felt like the right thing to do in service of getting Liz cleared. I couldn't answer without looking like I was talking to myself, so I just shrugged, hoping my instinct wasn't wrong on this, and I hadn't made my first colossal mistake.

✤❧✤❧✤

AS ANXIOUS AS I was to get to Roman and find answers to my myriad questions, fate delivered me to my cousin first. At the bottom of the staircase, she was deep in conversation with the same guy I'd seen her with before: Mr. tall, blond, and disdainful.

I'd have to make it quick and promise to catch up so I could stay on task. The music pounded in my ears, and I knew sensory overload was not far away if I didn't find an anchor to focus on. After I finished with Roman, she'd actually be the perfect person to parse my impressions with, with her background in investigative journalism.

"Eliza," I said, my smile stretching wide at my favorite cousin. "You didn't tell me you were in town."

Her sparkling green eyes bugged out at the sight of me.

I threw my arms around her. "I could've made up the guest room if I'd known. It's so good to see you."

Eliza stiffened in my embrace. Weird. She was normally just as much of a hugger as I was.

"Uh," she said, wriggling away. "I'm afraid you've got the wrong person. Could you stop with the... squeezing?"

My cheeks flared. I swept my arms back in a flash and stepped away. "Oh my goodness, I'm so sorry. My mistake. I saw you here, and you look so much like my cousin." My gaze swept over this doppelganger again: the same tall, slightly curvy build. Same enviable sable hair, long and stick straight, even in the southern humidity. Her makeup and jewelry were all wrong: much more understated than Eliza's vibrant swaths of color and penchant for metallic eyeliner. Even so, I would've sworn under oath that this was her.

I was about to bumble on about how I didn't usually go around hugging strangers and how she even *sounded* like my cousin when I caught sight of the scar from her clavicle to her shoulder. The one from when the two of us and her brother Roscoe snuck into the Anderson's backyard to spy on a kid who swore his dad had a secret candy factory in their basement.

No candy factory, alas, but there were two ginormous Dobermans that chased us away. One of them nabbed my brand new shoe in its slobbery mouth while we climbed the fence to make our getaway. Eliza cut herself on the fence after she wrestled the dog and got my shoe back for me.

Eliza tracked my gaze. Her hand shot up to cover the area.

This was most definitely my lovable older cousin, instigator of many a questionable plan. So why would she pretend otherwise?

I eyed her quizzically.

Eliza cleared her throat and shot me a pleading look in answer before smiling back at her companion. "I guess I have one of those faces."

I wondered if she'd finally landed the undercover assignment she'd been hoping for.

Her date's face pinched as he regarded me. He didn't stand out too much from the other up-and-coming politicians I'd encountered. His type abounded at my boarding school. Every dark blond hair in place, every word measured and deployed for maximum personal gain. And yet something about his features and particular brand of disdain struck a chord of familiarity.

"Well, sorry to have bothered you," I said, still stewing on his connection to someone I knew. "Have a good night."

"Come on, Eleanor. There's someone you should meet," her date said with a last cursory glance at me. With a hand on the small of her back, he guided her toward the silent auction tables.

Eliza didn't look back.

TWENTY-ONE

In my haste to get away, I feigned intense interest in a glass of bubbly from a nearby server. I snagged one, spun around, and careened right into Roman di Rossi.

The whiskey in his glass sloshed down my dress. Meanwhile, my champagne arced onto my hair and Roman's tux sleeve. Roman caught my arm to steady me and pulled me into his personal space.

Well, I guess that was one way to make a splash. And an introduction, I supposed. Win?

"I'm so sorry!" I exclaimed.

His brown eyes twinkled, and for a moment, I couldn't help but be a bit dazzled.

"Your big night and here I am getting your suit all soggy."

"Not to worry. It was probably my fault, anyway. If it takes fighting a spill for us to meet, it will have been worth it."

I choked on a surprised laugh. Did my murder suspect just quote *Hamilton* to me?

That didn't seem right.

A wave of luxurious dark hair fell onto his forehead. "Come, let me get you another and something to clean up with." He nodded to my empty glass.

"I should get *you* another drink," I said.

He waved the thought away as we approached the bar, and he procured some cloth napkins and sparkling water.

"Champagne?" he asked.

"If you're outside that region of France, I think it's just sparkling embarrassment."

He grinned, the big bad wolf raking his gaze over me.

I flushed against my will.

"To serendipitous meetings." He handed me a fresh glass fizzing with bubbles and clinked it with his own.

I smiled, suddenly unsure how to proceed, and sipped my drink instead. He led us to a high table close to the entertainment. An angsty country ballad charged the air. It was a song I'd played repeatedly after Hudson left. I pushed the thought of him out of my head, so I could concentrate on my task at hand. The plan had gone out the window, so I had to do my best to wing it here.

"So, where were you headed in such a hurry earlier?" Roman asked. This close to the stage, we had to talk louder to hear one another. He leaned near enough that his breath tickled my ear.

"Oh, just trying to escape an awkward situation," I said.

"Fleeing the unwanted advances of the masses?"

I gave him my best enigmatic smile. "Something like that. I'm Paige, by the way."

"Roman, but you knew that already, didn't you?" He enfolded my hand in his and stroked the back of my hand with his thumb.

"I did. Well, at least I recognized your face from the pictures when I stopped being mortified." I flung a hand in the direction of the screen over the stage, still rotating through the photos. "I have friends being honored here tonight too. That's why I'm here."

"Oh yeah, who? Maybe we know each other."

Crud. I was definitely not supposed to connect myself to my friends and employers when talking to a suspect. Wasn't that Undercover 101? How could I divert the conversation in another direction? Spilling another drink was out.

"I must decline to tell you. For secret reasons," I demurred with one of my favorite EB White quotes before I could think it through. Austin said he liked women with secrets, right?

Roman's lips tugged into a tantalizing smile.

"They just prefer to stay out of the limelight," I added.

"So..." Roman said.

"So..."

He lifted a strand of my hair, still wet with champagne, and coiled it around his finger.

"How come we've never met before, Paige? You stay out of the limelight like your friends?"

I shrugged.

This would be a perfect time to change the subject.

"You shouldn't hide yourself away like that," Roman said.

Praying Norman was paying attention, I did the best surreptitious rendition of jazz hands I could manage. All while holding Roman's gaze.

My phone buzzed.

I sagged in relief and pulled it out of my purse. "Sorry, I need to check this real quick."

My curl uncoiled from his finger.

Blah blah blah funeral arrangements blah, Norman's text read.

I suppressed a grin and put on a grave face instead.

"Something wrong?" he asked.

I sighed and let my face fall. "Just some info on funeral arrangements. A friend of mine died earlier this week."

"I'm sorry to hear that." His facial muscles tensed—was that guilt? —but the concern in his eyes as he studied me struck me as genuine.

"Maybe you know him—*knew* him," I corrected. "Since you seem to know all the people worth knowing." I managed a rueful smile. "Austin Des Jardins."

The muscles in Roman's throat worked.

"The guy who fell from the balcony." His tone flattened, his eyes distant.

I nodded. "I remember him mentioning someone named Roman, now that I think about it. Must be why your name sounded familiar. Were you a friend of his too?"

Now came the moment of truth. My breath caught in my throat. I looked up.

Roman stayed silent a moment before speaking. "A friend? Not exactly." Roman rubbed his angular chin. "If I was a friend, I should've been a better one." He looked unsettled. Remorseful. But did that mean he'd murdered Austin, or just regretted he hadn't stopped whoever had?

Either way, it surprised me he copped to knowing Austin at all if he wanted to cover his tracks. Would a guilty person do that? Maybe one who thinks he's untouchable.

"How'd you know him?" I asked.

"We had some mutual interests."

"Business?"

"No. We had some acquaintances in common."

"Same," I said.

Roman raised an eyebrow and seemed to consider me in a new light.

"Sad what happened to him," I said.

"He deserved better than that," Roman agreed.

I nodded. This remorseful guy didn't seem like a stone-cold killer.

"Did he seem off to you lately?" I asked.

"How do you mean?"

My heart stuttered. Did I really want to go there? I was certain Hudson wouldn't approve of this line of questioning. Would Grandma Magnolia and Moisha?

"I don't know. He'd been cagey lately. Canceling plans at the last minute."

Roman seemed to consider.

"Some things he said made me think he'd gotten mixed up in something," I pressed on before I could stop myself.

"Like what?"

I demurred. "Promise you won't laugh? This is going to sound nuts because it probably doesn't even exist."

He drew an imaginary X over his heart. "Promise. What exactly do you mean?"

I pursed my lips. "I'm probably way off here."

"Try me."

"The Enclave?" I said with a blush.

"The secret society," Roman repeated.

"Mmm hmm. Told you it was out there." I sipped my champagne and gauged his reaction. "You wouldn't know where a girl could get an invitation to something like that?"

My lungs squeezed, but my breath stopped in my chest as I waited for his answer. As a follow-up, I winked and played it off as a joke that maybe wasn't entirely a joke.

The tension in his frame seemed to relax a fraction. "And why would I know about that?"

"I mean, look at you." I swept a hand from head to toe of his handsome frame. "You're successful, promising, well-connected. If I were in charge of secret society recruitment, you're the exact type of person I'd be dying to have."

"I do seem the type, don't I?" He relaxed a bit more at the flattery, his charming facade slipping back into place. "Even if I were, I could neither confirm nor deny my involvement. What good is a secret society without the secret part?"

I gave him a coy look. "In that case, forget I asked."

The sad ballad ended and the opening chords of *The Devil Went Down to Georgia* rang out from the stage, jolting another memory loose. Great, yet another song to remind me of Hudson. This was his favorite to play for a crowd. He told me getting swept into its rhythm whisked away his anxieties, even if only for a few minutes. His love of playing had stuck with him, even after years of performing had him frayed around the edges. I wondered if he still loved to play and what he was doing tonight, if he'd sneaked in somehow and requested this song.

"But, speaking of recruitment, I'm doing a little of my own tonight," Roman said. "And you might just be the perfect candidate."

"For what?" I said, returning my focus back to the conversation at hand.

"A little venture I have going. I have an unexpected vacancy, and I've been tasked with finding a successor."

When my brain caught up with his words, my whole body hummed like I'd touched a live wire. Did that mean what I thought it meant? Was he hinting at me taking Austin's place as an acolyte?

"What exactly are the qualifications for this position?" I asked. The bass notes from the stage hammered along with my heartbeat, commanding my attention.

"Someone who has a way with people." Roman leaned in closer. A little too close for comfort. Was it my imagination or did the music just get louder? More frenetic. I felt the shift of the crowd and the pull of the music. Whoever was on the fiddle was good, like Hudson-level good. "Someone who can be persuasive. Discreet."

"And you think I fit that profile?"

"Mmm hmm." Roman took a sip of his whiskey, and my attention strayed to the musicians. The fiddle player commanded center stage now, electrifying a rapt audience. His bow raced along the strings at a punishing pace, coaxing out the melody and making it look as natural as breathing, which I knew it very much was not. From under the curly black wig, the fiddler looked up and caught my gaze without missing a beat with his bow.

Hazel eyes in the thrall of performance fervor winked back at me. My heart stopped. If the devil ever went down to New Orleans, he would meet his match in Hudson Bennett.

I should've known.

Finally, my sense surfaced, and I pulled my attention back to Roman. "And what exactly does this position entail?"

"That is a story for somewhere more private." Roman angled his body in front of the performers. "Can you keep a secret, Paige?"

"Yes, mmm hmm. Discretion is my middle name," I babbled, still off kilter.

"Good. I thought so. Why don't you give me your phone number, and I'll text you the details? You can meet with my associates and me on Tuesday night."

TWENTY-TWO

The emcee took the stage and announced that the awards ceremony was about to begin.

The band dispersed to make way for the ceremony, and Hudson hopped down and swaggered into the space Roman had newly vacated.

I tucked Roman's card into my purse for later.

Hudson swiped a forearm across his face.

"Nice mullet," I said, nodding to his ridiculous wig. "Looks like you found a way in after all."

"I'm not the only one with a talent for using all the resources at my disposal." Hudson winked at me.

Lawd. He was sexy, with his skin glistening, riding high on the energy of his performance. Ugh, it was hard not to get swept up in it right along with him.

"Nice playing up there." I grabbed a program discarded on a nearby table and fanned myself.

Hudson bowed his head and mimed touching the brim of his imaginary cowboy hat. "Thank you, kindly."

He drained a cold bottle of water. "I thought we agreed on reconnaissance only until we reconvened?"

"Did we, though?" I teased.

His nostrils flared.

"I saw an opportunity, and I took it. Sometimes it's better to ask forgiveness than permission."

Hudson groaned and ran a hand through his hair, but it knocked his wig askew. I tugged it back into place.

"Careful," I whispered. "Don't want to blow your cover, oh wise one." On the way down, my finger grazed his cheek. He inhaled sharply. Our eyes locked for a second, and old feelings stirred in that long, heated moment.

I snatched my hand away, and we both laughed nervously, defusing the tension.

"Back to you going rogue," Hudson said. "You promised—"

"That I would be careful. And I was. And guess what else? Guess who has two thumbs and spent the afternoon training with her ghost hunting, mystery solving great grandma?"

Hudson's eyes went wide. "Really? Your Grandma Magnolia?"

I nodded, feeling my entire face light up with the memory of Magnolia and Moisha's visit this afternoon and their unshakable belief in me.

"But how? I didn't think that kind of thing was allowed."

"Apparently, my great grandma can be very persuasive."

"Must run in the family."

I beamed. "Anyway, they get to help me for an hour a day as long as I need them." I couldn't imagine ever *not* needing them. But would they have to fade away eventually, anyway? I pushed off the thought.

"Did you know most of her stories were inspired by her real life doing what we do?"

Hudson looked at me with one of those smiles that made me feel seen. "That's amazing, Paige. I know how much her books meant to you."

"Yeah." It was so hard to meet his warm hazel eyes without forgetting all the baggage that stood between us.

"Did you learn anything useful in your conversation with Roman?"

"He admitted to knowing Austin. Seemed genuinely upset at the mention of his death. He didn't exactly scream killer to me. But I guess all of Charles Manson's victims probably thought the same thing. I suppose he could just as easily be a talented actor and sociopath."

"We play that game a lot in our line of work—innocent person or thespian sociopath?" Hudson balanced his hands back and forth like a scale.

"He invited me to his place on Tuesday. Said he had an unexpected opening and an opportunity he thinks I'd be perfect for." I puffed up like a little pink peacock for making some actual progress.

"Wait, you made a date with the murderer?" Hudson's already square jaw hardened.

"Relax, it's not a date. And he's only a potential murderer until proven otherwise. I think he wants to recruit me to the next pledge class of the Enclave." I whispered the last part.

Hudson closed his eyes, and I could practically hear him counting to ten to calm down. "You're supposed to be flying under the radar, not kicking the hornets' nest."

"I'm supposed to be shaking people down, getting the info we need to solve the case."

"Inconspicuously," Hudson said. "And no shaking down. Please. At least not yet anyway."

"You can follow me to Roman's house Tuesday. We can even get you set up in one of those unmarked computer surveillance vans, and you can rush in if anything untoward happens."

Hudson shook his head in what looked like half amusement, half exasperation.

"You missed me. Admit it," I chided.

He shook with laughter, then smoldered down at me. "You have no idea."

⁕▲⁕▲⁕▲⁕

"THIS NIGHT just keeps getting weirder and weirder," I said to Norman once I'd made my way back upstairs. I thought about tracking down Nick again, but then I spotted Norman nodding off against the railing, talking to Wendy and Alec.

At least I'd made one big stride forward with Roman, even if it was a little risky. Nick would have to wait for tomorrow's stake out.

Norman perked up and tried to follow my debrief on Roman, Hudson, and Eliza, who may or may not be undercover, but his eyelids kept drooping.

"You know what, why don't we take this conversation to the car and get you home to rest," I said.

"But you have more spying to do," Norman protested. His head listed to the side.

"That can wait," I said. "Let me just run to the ladies' room real quick and we'll head out."

I said my goodbyes to the Deveauxs and Durochers, enlisting Declan to keep an eye on Norman until I got back. After I'd finished washing my hands and sampling the complimentary lotions, a familiar face appeared in the mirror beside me.

I glanced around to see if there was anyone else here. One set of feet below the bathroom doors.

"Eliza?" I whispered. Maybe now that she was away from her companion, she'd let me in on what was up.

She touched up her deep pink lipstick. "I told you, I'm Eleanor. Eleanor *Doolittle*."

Excitement fizzed, and I nodded in understanding. That was her code name when we'd do stealth missions with walkie-talkies as kids. Mine was Agatha Raisin Bran.

"My mistake," I said.

I turned to leave, and Eliza bumped into me from behind.

"Sorry!" She stooped to pick up a folded piece of paper from the floor. "Here, you dropped this." She held it out.

"I don't think—"

"You *did*." She gave me a knowing look and pressed the note into my hand.

TWENTY-THREE

Call this number at midnight. Not from your own phone. 504-998-6848

I reread Eliza's hastily scrawled message for the millionth time as the clock slunk toward midnight.

I hated to wake Ines since she was a 5 a.m. riser, but she was also the only one I trusted to steer me right on setting up a temporary, anonymous phone number. I started with a basic web search, but as Auguste reminded me, that didn't come with Ines's expertise in the pitfalls and loopholes I didn't even know to ask about.

With minimal grumbling, she rolled out of bed, her caramel curls sticking out at all angles.

"I owe you big time."

"Mrrmph." She pulled out a heavy duty, ancient looking laptop from her closet and let her fingers fly.

"How was baking class?" I asked.

Ines smiled sleepily. "Excellent. We made this weird orange marmalade thing with croissant dough. And lots of bread. Extras in the fridge."

"Nice. And Sam?"

Pink spots colored her cheeks. "Sam is good."

"Mmm hmm." I gave her a conspiratorial smile. Ines had been interested in him since they first met at work, and she still wasn't sure if this baking class he'd proposed was a date thing or a friend thing, though I know she was hoping for the latter.

I gave Auguste's head a scratch inside his snuggle sack and watched Ines in the zone.

"She is quite skilled in the magic of electronic devices," Auguste observed.

"I know," I said.

"Huh?" Ines asked.

I tensed. "Nothing. Just talking to myself." Note to self: do not respond aloud to hedgehogs or ghosts in mixed company. "Did it work?"

She moved her head as if to shake off the sleep, but her eyelids drooped. "Yep. Here," she said, handing the computer over to me. "Just plug the number in at the time you need it, and follow the instructions there to burn the number when you finish."

"You're the best." I beamed at her, feeling like a woman of espionage and stealth.

Ines smiled. "I'd ask about your night, but I can't keep my eyes open. I want to hear everything in the morning, though."

I left her to get back to sleep, and at last, the clock on my phone clicked over to 11:59. Auguste twitched his little brown nose. "Do you believe the business your cousin is involved with is connected to your investigation?"

I scrunched my brow. "No, I don't think so. What makes you ask?"

"She spoke to your suspects, did she not?" he asked.

"I guess that's true."

"There are no such things as coincidences," he replied cryptically. "It is all connected. Even when it's not."

I raised a skeptical eyebrow. "I'll keep that in mind."

"So, this Hudson, he is a thorn in your side, no?"

"He's—I don't know what he is, honestly."

"I do not care for him."

"Why?"

"He is the reason you wept so much when you first brought me home, is he not?"

"That was a long time ago," I murmured.

"And what about—" Auguste began, but I interrupted him.

"Oh, look it's time." I punched the number Eliza gave me into the computer, and she picked up on the second ring.

If a hedgehog can give withering looks, Auguste gave me one. "This conversation is not over," he whispered in his annoyed French accent.

"Hey. Who's this?" Eliza's voice answered cautiously.

"E?" I said, keeping it cryptic in case someone else was listening on her end.

"Oh Paige, thank goodness. I thought you were going to blow my cover earlier."

I let out a breath. "Oh good, so you are on assignment. I thought I was cracking up there for a minute."

"That's affirmative. Did you like my outfit? I looked all civilized and stuff, huh?"

I chuckled. "Very."

"How'd you like your birthday glitter bomb?"

I groaned. "I may still have Mardi Gras glitter implanted in my contacts."

"Aww, I thought you liked shiny things," she teased.

"Not exploding into my eyeballs. So what are you up to, anyway? If you can talk where you are now."

Shuffling noises sounded across the phone line. "Yeah, I'm good for now."

"Who was that guy you were with?"

"The one with the stick up his di—?"

My laughter covered the end of her words.

"That's Hartley. He's a little intense, isn't he? But turning out to be a useful source."

"For what? What's your assignment?" I asked. "I've been doing a little investigating myself lately."

"Ooh, do tell," Eliza said.

"You first," I said.

"Well, I'm not really supposed to say, but swear you won't tell anyone?"

"Pinky promise."

Eliza lowered her voice. "I'm infiltrating a secret organization and looking into some old missing persons cases."

"Whoa, that sounds important. And also maybe dangerous."

"Right? Which is why it's important to keep my cover."

"And what secret organization is this?" I ventured, my skin tingling with the possibility that it *was* all related.

Auguste scrambled up my arm and gave me a knowing look.

"Don't laugh, okay? I didn't think it was real either, but turns out it's alive and well."

"The Enclave?" I whispered.

"Yeah, how did you—?"

The tingles spider walked up my back.

"You know what, nevermind. You always did have a scary good intuition," Eliza said.

Auguste nudged me. "Ask how the man is involved. The brooding one. There is a connection here."

"And this guy you were with tonight, he's part of it?" I asked.

"Yup."

"Wow."

"I know, right? Hartley's an initiate. He's sort of a rising star in the ranks of the organization."

"How are you getting him to talk about all of this secretive stuff?"

"I have my ways." I could practically see her eyes twinkling. "I've been surveilling several suspected members for a long time. They set everything up so membership is fragmented and secretive. No one knows all the members except for the very upper echelons. I faked my way into an underground meeting with all the robes and candles and everything. Then I pulled my hood down after and talked to some members. They just assumed I was one of them."

"Impressive," I said. "What have you found out so far? About the disappearances?"

"Word on the street is there's some kind of ritual sacrifice every 3- 4 years that grants members their power and influence. It doesn't follow an exact pattern, but it's been pretty close."

My eyes bugged out. "Did you actually see this ritual in action?"

"No, but it was supposed to happen soon. Something to do with a failed acolyte getting sacrificed, but there was some kind of snafu."

"What do you mean?" Auguste nudged my arm repeatedly, as if to point me further in this direction. All the hairs on my arms stood at attention.

"There's a whole protocol to choosing the sacrifice, but someone went rogue. Or maybe an entire group of someones," Eliza continued. "There's an uproar because of what just happened."

"Like an acolyte's death?" I asked.

"Yeah, how did you know?" Eliza mused.

"This might all be related to the investigating I'm doing."

"Interesting..."

"Yeah. What's your theory on the breach of protocol?" I asked.

"Apparently, there are two factions within the Enclave. One is for bringing in a more diverse array of acolytes. The other is rooted in the old ways and invested in replacing old white men of the Enclave with young white men of the Enclave."

"Surprise, surprise," I said. "And which side is your buddy Hartley on?"

"He's team patriarchy all the way."

Auguste wrinkled his nose in disdain.

"Sounds delightful," I said.

She cackled. "Yeah. Although, he *has* been lobbying to get his sister in. So I guess he makes exceptions for nepotism. She might even be in this acolyte class, but he was cagey about it, so I can't say for sure."

I nodded. "And which side went rogue, do you think?"

"My money's on the traditionalists tampering with things. This is supposedly one of the most diverse acolyte classes they've had."

"So they wanted to tip the scales in their favor and pick the sacrifice?" I said.

"Somebody wanted to make a statement, that's for sure. But some parts still don't make sense. I do know that the body went missing, though and screwed up everyone's plans."

I let out a breath and prepared to launch into my knowledge of the events. "About that. I think the body may have fallen on my head."

TWENTY-FOUR

After getting Auguste settled into his habitat under his favorite rock, sleep didn't come easily, trying to make sense of all the night's events. I turned the recent information from Eliza over in my head again.

What did this ideological battle within the Enclave have to do with Austin's death? Maybe nothing. Maybe everything. Or was it all far more personal?

Unable to stand more tossing and turning, I dragged myself out of bed. I reached for the comfort of the cloth-bound covers of my great grandma's Matilda Mayhew books. Some people had their tarot cards, but I preferred bibliomancy.

For as long as I could remember, whenever I couldn't sleep and needed some direction, I headed to the bookshelf for guidance. Especially before I moved back to New Orleans and found my people.

Even now that I could talk to Magnolia in person, I craved the familiar comfort of this ritual.

I drew in a deep breath and closed my eyes, running my fingertips along the worn spines, concentrating on my questions until something in my chest glowed with warmth. *This one,* the warmth seemed to whisper.

Before I even opened my eyes, I knew which book it was by the heft.

I brought *Matilda Mayhew and Case of the Devil You Know,* one of the more obscure books in my great grandma Magnolia's series, back to bed and crawled under the covers again.

This is the one where a Valentine's Day dinner goes awry for Matilda's friend Betty when she accidentally summons a demon while trying to make pot roast. When the devil shows up to retrieve said demon, the reformed prince of darkness (who is way more attentive and appreciative than Betty's cad of a boyfriend) falls in love with her. They run away together, and she vows never to make pot roast again.

"What have you got for me tonight, Magnolia and Matilda?" I imagined my great grandmother, now with a vivid mental picture of her high cheekboned-smile and victory rolls in her hair to accompany it, guiding my hands to the right page and dropping my finger to just the right line to answer my questions.

Tonight's page was 51. My chest warmed as my finger dropped, and I read:

"You've gotten yourself into quite a pickle here, Betty. What are you going to do?" Matilda asked.

"Why, call on my friends, of course. And maybe the handsome devil who visited this evening."

I leaned into my pillow and mulled over the words. The handsome devil in question was the actual devil, who, in the book, was reformed and quite charming. Calling on my friends and grandma Magnolia, check. Was there a handsome devil in my future too who could help me dispatch my demons?

I had less faith in that coming to fruition.

Finally, after a bit more reading, I drifted off to sleep.

Strange dreams of Roman and the demons chasing me

ensued.

What exactly had I gotten myself into?

⁘▲⁘▲⁘

THE NEXT DAY, still examining the clues I'd picked up so far and more than a little worried for Eliza's safety, I headed to my shift at Deveauxs' Historical Haunts. I stopped by Liz's on the way to see how she was faring.

"Knock knock." I pushed open the front door and found Liz sprawled on the couch in pajamas. She licked peanut butter off a spoon and put it back into the jar.

"How are you feeling?" I asked.

She made a non-committal sound and lolled back onto the cushion. Her shiny black hair stuck up at odd angles.

My heart clenched at the sight.

"Why don't I find you something to go with that peanut butter," I said.

She waved the idea away, but I went to her fridge, anyway. It was still semi-stocked from pre-break-in days, but I made a mental note to do a grocery run later this week and make some soup and other dishes she could heat with minimal effort.

She filled me in on her questioning at the precinct while I whipped up a quick omelet and pulled together a fruit bowl.

"They let you go. They can't charge you with anything. Can they?" I said.

Liz shook her head and accepted the plate I passed her. "Not yet, but Crowder advised me to 'lawyer up.'"

I rolled my eyes, but Liz looked at me with a grave expression.

"He also said to 'get ready for the swift scales of justice to come crashing down on me' once the fingerprint and DNA analysis comes back on the murder weapons."

What lengths had the Enclave gone to with their aim of avoiding blame and sealing Liz's fate? And why frame *her*?

•▲•▲•▲•

AFTER PROMISING to check in again soon, I left Liz's and settled into work at the gift shop. I was restocking the snack items, still stewing over her state of mind, when Austin's mop of golden hair phased in next to the Cheetos. I yelped and dropped the candy bars in my hands.

Austin grinned. "Still not used to ghosts showing up yet?"

"Guess not." I retrieved the M&Ms and 3 Musketeers from the floor and looked over my shoulder.

Thankfully, Norman had just taken off with a small tour in his wheelchair, leaving me alone in the shop. I stepped in front of the fan, letting the breeze cool the ever-present beads of moisture that came with the sweltering summers in New Orleans. My aubergine dress clung to my decolletage, despite the air conditioning. Good thing Austin's ghostly presence came with a cool spot all around him.

"It's okay. It's still weird for me too," Austin said.

"I imagine," I said, giving him a sympathetic look.

"So this is where you work. I don't think I've ever actually been in here." He floated around to the area where we housed books on haunted history and gift items.

"You've never been on one of the Quarter's most prestigious and historically accurate ghost tours?"

"Would you believe I haven't?" he said. "I lived here almost my entire life and became a ghost before I had the chance to meet the others."

"You'll have to come along next time I lead a tour. Maybe you can get the lowdown on this ghost thing. And you can be my own personal air conditioner."

"So," Austin asked, "Any developments since last night? And how's it going with the ex?"

Hudson and the way it had felt to talk to him after watching him in his element on the stage last night wasn't something I was ready to make sense of. The case, on the other hand, I was keen to discuss since Austin could probably shed some light on the details.

I filled him in on what had happened with Roman and my cousin Eliza's unexpected involvement.

"You're saying my death wasn't supposed to happen?" Austin hovered back and absorbed the information.

"Not as part of this ritual they had going. It least it doesn't look like it."

"I guess that doesn't change anything, because it happened anyway. But still, it was supposed to be one of us." Austin paled at the thought. "And it was all because of some warring factions I had nothing to do with?"

"I still need to do a lot more digging," I said.

"Maybe my dad didn't have me bumped off after all," Austin said with false brightness.

I planted my hands on the counter and studied my ghostly friend. The tension around his eyes and mouth told me that theory wasn't as much of a joke as he pretended. "Is that really what you thought happened?"

He shrugged, and his jaw muscles ticked. "It's crossed my mind."

Once again, I wanted to hug him. "I can't imagine that's true."

"You don't know my dad."

Yikes. Sometimes, I felt like my parents didn't understand me, but this was something else entirely.

"Families, am I right?" Austin said with more false cheer.

"Have you gone to see your parents since you came back?" I asked.

He shook his head, his sun-bleached locks flopping in front of his eyes.

"Want me to go see them?"

"Please don't."

"Are you sure? I could—"

Austin shook his head. "I'm not exactly in a hurry to have my worst fears confirmed. They're probably irritated my funeral arrangements postponed their Mediterranean getaway."

"I bet you'd be surprised. They're probably up to their eyeballs in regret right now, wishing they'd treated you better when they had the chance."

Austin's silence stretched. "But what if they aren't?"

Those plaintive words that matched the lost look in Austin's eyes stopped me in my tracks. I'd always looked for the best in people. But what if some people were just rotten to the core? I hated to imagine that for Austin.

"I'm just not ready to have my worst fears confirmed. If they're not mourning me, I'd rather not know, okay?"

I nodded, determined to respect his wishes, even though I itched to find them and prove they cared.

"That name you mentioned, Hartley, that sounds familiar," Austin said. He floated behind the counter with me while I pulled out some paperwork.

"Could he be a friend of your fellow acolytes?"

"Not sure. Do you have a last name?"

My face fell.

"Shoot. No. Rookie mistake. I should've asked Eliza. Hopefully, I can get ahold of her again." Again with the insecurities. Maybe I should just call Declan, tell him what I knew without mentioning Eliza's name, of course, and let the pros handle this.

I tried to push my snafu aside and keep digging.

"How much did you know about the inner workings of the Enclave? You said one of you wouldn't make it to ascend. Did you have any inkling about this ritual sacrifice thing or what they had planned for the one who didn't make it?"

"I mean, there were rumors. There have always been rumors. Ben and Mina and I talked about it when they told us only five of us would ascend. I couldn't believe that they'd really do something like that in modern times."

"What was the ceremony like for you to become an acolyte?" I wasn't entirely sure where I was going with this line of questioning, but I hoped the more background I had on the organization, the more something might pop out at me.

"After the vetting party, they sent us all invites with instructions to be ready."

"Ready for what?"

"It didn't say, but on that day, after I'd gotten home from work, someone rang the doorbell. Only before I saw their face, they put a hood over my head and smuggled me into a van. Ben and Mina and the other acolytes were there too."

"Was it always only the six of you?"

"There were more that night, but we were, um, narrowed down."

My eyebrows lifted. "That sounds ominous."

"It was."

"Where did they take you?"

"Same tunnel entrance on the grounds of the convent, I think, but they hooded me until we got to the underground room, so..."

"Did they take you to the same room as for your final task?"

"No, someplace else. It was a circular room, and they led ten of us prospective acolytes to the raised platform in the center.

"When they finally took my hood off, this gargoyle statue was staring me down. It was as tall as me and the mouth was open. There were five more of them on the outer edges of the circle. All these black hooded figures—the already initiated—packed in around the platform on medieval stadium-like rows and did a chant in Latin."

I shook off a chill. "What did they make you do? How did they choose the six of you?"

"One of the hooded dudes came up and introduced himself as the High Hierophant. He said we were the chosen, the elite. But to proceed and pledge our lives to the Enclave, to learn its secrets and claim its privileges, we first had to pass a test. And only six of us would go forward."

I leaned in, thankful for the shop's lack of traffic.

"Then flames leaped out of the gargoyles' mouths. I flinched back. It was wild, like something out of a movie, not real life, you know?

"One of the other hooded dudes gave us all a parchment scroll and one of those old-timey feather quills."

"Can't use ball point for a secret society ceremony, I guess," I said.

Austin smiled. "He told us this was our test. To write down our heart's deepest desire—no matter how audacious or depraved—and our greatest fear, then feed those secrets into the gargoyle's mouth."

"He said our benefactor enchanted the gargoyles. If the fire turned blue, we were worthy and would be offered the opportunity to pledge. If it didn't, an enchanted powder would poof into our faces, knock us out, and we'd be returned to our regular lives with no memory of the Enclave or its existence."

"What did you write?" I asked, but quickly backpedaled when Austin's cheeks pinked. "Sorry, you don't have to answer. Especially if it's too personal."

"It's okay," Austin said.

His features tensed and he air-surfed the perimeter of the

shop for a bit. Just when I thought he'd closed the subject, he drifted back, but looked down at his shoes. "For someone whose family gave up on him so completely—" He shook his head and sighed. "Still wanting their love and approval, even with its strings and conditions makes me the world's biggest idiot, doesn't it?"

"Oh, Aus," I whispered. I wished again I could wrap him in a hug. Wasn't that what we all wanted? Someone to love us and approve of who we were regardless of our mistakes? My parents might get intense about their work, to the detriment of all else. I might've questioned whether they approved of my career whims, but I'd never had to question their love for me. "It just makes you human."

His jaw twitched, and he finally met my gaze with a rueful smile.

"Families are complicated," I said.

"Tell me about it."

"Have you gone to see them? In your ghost form?"

Austin shook his head, but didn't elaborate.

I understood what he left unsaid. If they weren't mourning, he wasn't ready to see that. Time for a subject change.

"Speaking of family, want to hear the rest of what my cousin Eliza had to say?"

"Yes. Tell me everything. Also, have some of those M&Ms and tell me what they taste like."

I grinned and obliged him.

"Eliza's looking into the disappearances that have cropped up every three to four years. She thinks they might be connected."

"But if they marked me for sacrifice, why move my body to a balcony and toss me off? That seems clumsy for an organization that's made people disappear and kept its secrets for centuries."

"I agree. That doesn't track."

TWENTY-FIVE

"Did my, um, body have any strange markings on it? What are the hallmarks of a ritual sacrifice, anyway?" Austin said. He lounged on the counter of the Deveauxs' Historical Haunts gift shop.

"Nothing that I remember. No gargoyle tattoos or anything. But then again, I was in shock. I could talk to my cop friend and see if there was anything like that. Though he might not be so forthcoming on investigation details. Who do I know at the morgue?" I pondered whether I knew anyone who worked in the morgue or coroner's office. There had to be someone.

I sent off a quick text to Ines and Bridget: *Who do we know with connections in the morgue?*

Bridget answered back right away: *I've waited my whole life for this text.*

I snorted a laugh.

"Eliza thinks someone on the inside went rogue. Either they knew who the chosen sacrifice was and staged your death to prevent it, or this was part of a coup by one of the warring factions within the organization. What I don't know is if there's been a replacement sacrifice or not."

A group of tourists came in then, halting our conversation and leaving each of us to our own thoughts for the next few hours while people streamed in and out and lined up for the early afternoon tour. I took reservations, gave suggestions on souvenirs, and rang up people's orders at the register. Talking to people energized me, and all the everyday work activity had a soothing effect. For the first time since Austin fell off of the balcony, my brain had some mental white space, and it felt nice.

When Austin showed up again during a lull, he looked more introspective and broody even with his Hawaiian shirt and board shorts. His eyebrows hunched over troubled features.

"You're good at this," he commented. "How'd you get into this gig, anyway? Ghost tour gift shop management. Was this always something you wanted to do?"

"Nah," I said. "A friend of mine knows the owner's mom. They were looking for some help, and I applied. Why?"

"I don't know. I've just been thinking—what if there's one thing we were put on earth to do, but I never got to do mine?" He laid back against the counter and tugged his arms across his chest. "Do you ever feel that way?"

Hoo boy, did I. "Yeah."

"I made a big thing about how I was into this laid-back life-style, how I wasn't going to fall prey to the corporate grind and succeed at all costs mentality. And it's not that it wasn't true. It was. But maybe there was more to it."

"What do you mean?" I asked.

"I think I was in a holding pattern. Maybe I was just scared to try something else because I might fail at it."

I let out a long breath. "Did you know I changed my major nine times in college? I almost changed again my senior year, but I stuck with the more practical business degree."

"See, you weren't afraid of change. I should've been more like you, kept trying until I got it right."

I shook my head. "No, I don't think that's what I was doing at all. I think it was more like what you were saying—fear. Except mine was of staying in the wrong place, committing to something and that being the wrong thing."

Austin gave me a sad smile.

"Everyone around me always seemed so *sure* of what they were doing. My parents are working on a cure for cancer and practically came out of the womb as budding scientists. My friend Bridget is an engineer, and she's into fandoms and cosplay and does these amazing maker videos for her gazillion YouTube subscribers.

"I guess I just expected to feel this wave of certainty when something was right for me."

"Like a choir of angels singing and parade floats in your mind?" Austin grinned.

"Something like that," I said with a sheepish smile. "And when I didn't feel it right away, I hurried up and moved on."

And when it did feel right, and I stuck it out, I got burned. See Exhibit 1: Hudson Bennett.

"What if it doesn't happen like that?" Austin mused. "Maybe it starts small and grows from there."

"But what if sticking with it and being bad at it hurts?"

"Maybe it's supposed to. Maybe that's the test."

"Want to know a secret?" I asked.

"Who better to confide in than your best ghost pal?" Austin said.

"Sometimes, I'm scared it'll never happen. That I'll never find that one thing. That I'm not special." I'd never said those words aloud before, but they felt freeing.

"At least you're not the ghost of a yard margarita guy who got murdered for a ritual sacrifice," Austin said in that light-hearted way of his.

"You know what I think? That you have great things to do in the afterlife, my friend. I have no doubt."

Just then, the bell on the front door jangled, and Valerie, the custom Voodoo doll rep, breezed in, holding some folders under her arm.

She was a little older than me, with medium brown skin and hair dyed an ombre red. She looked down her nose at some smudge sticks and other tchotchkes on her way to the counter.

"Hey, you're the one who emailed me about the custom dolls this weekend, right?" Her tone stayed light, but her gaze was cool and assessing. Something about it made me think of barbed wire.

"Yep, that was me," I said. "I wasn't expecting a personal visit in response. It was nice of you to come by."

She waved a hand like it was nothing and looked around the shop with her nose wrinkled, making me wonder why she got into this business with such disdain for the places that carried her products. And if she disliked this place so much, why make a house call?

I exchanged a puzzled look with Austin.

"I was in the neighborhood, so I thought I'd stop by," Valerie said. "Our company's all about the personal touch, you know." Her lips curled into a wicked smile.

"Was that a Voodoo joke?" Austin raised his eyebrows. He mimed poking a doll with a sharp stick. The motion and Valerie's weirdness made me shake off a shudder.

"Yeah, I remember," I said. "So, can you tell me anything about the doll I sent you pictures of? It was one of yours, right? It definitely looked like the same style."

Valerie shifted. She telescoped her gaze in on me and studied my face. A chill zinged up my arms from the intensity of her scrutiny.

"Yes, they were ours," she answered finally.

"Customs or some of your Build-Your-Own line?" I asked.

"What's your interest in these dolls? Change your mind about making an order?"

"Reconsidering, yes," I lied. "I was wondering if you could give me the name of the business or person who ordered them as a reference. See if they were happy with your products before making a big investment."

Valerie's smile thinned. "Where'd you get those pictures you sent me?" Valerie asked. Again with the intense look. What did she stand to lose or gain here? Was she protecting someone?

What could I tell her that wouldn't completely shut her down?

"My friend found them at her bakery."

"I'm sorry," Valerie said. "We don't give out our customers' personal information like that. You can talk to the Spinellis down the street at Crescent Gifts if you need a reference."

Her gaze bored into me for another minute.

"Okay then," I said when I couldn't stand it anymore. "Thanks for stopping by."

"Let me know when you're ready to place an order."

Austin turned to me when after she'd walked out the door. "That wasn't weird at all."

TWENTY-SIX

S ix o'clock could not come fast enough.

When it was finally stakeout time, I was still turning over Valerie's visit and possible Voodoo doll connection. Armed with cherry Slurpees, Red Vines, cheesy puffs for me, and watermelon and hedgehog treats for Auguste, I pulled my Prius to the curb a few houses down from Nick Ortega's house for my first stakeout.

I'd summoned my Grandma Magnolia and Moisha as soon as I pulled up, so they could get in on the action, but so far they hadn't made an appearance. I guess it wasn't like I could expect them to be at my beck and call at all hours of the day. Who knew what important ghost duties and plans of their own they had in the afterlife?

I pulled on my aviator glasses and set up a plate with watermelon slices for Auguste on the dashboard. He took a tour of the front windshield, sniffing along before tucking into his dinner. Ines gave me a listening device, a small silver disk about the size of a key fob battery with tiny wire transmitters. I had no idea if I could get it close enough to Nick's house without being seen, but it was good to have, just in case.

Nick's house was shotgun style, typical of the houses in Uptown, with a narrow front and long back portion. A porch and stoop wrapped in cream-colored slats fronted the grey building. An ancient live oak shrouded the place in secrets, and its roots pushed up parts of the sidewalk.

Hudson, who'd refused to let me pick him up for whatever reason, probably because he didn't want me to know where he lived, sauntered up from behind, also in dark glasses, and climbed in the passenger seat.

"Hey," he said. His hair glistened, probably still wet from a shower, and the freshly cut wood scent of his cologne infused the air.

I tensed. "Hey."

"What on earth is that?" Hudson nearly jumped out of his seat at the sight of Auguste nibbling at his watermelon on the dash.

"Who is zis uncouth creature?" Auguste said.

I laughed. This was going to be fun.

"Hudson, this is my talking hedgehog, Auguste. Auguste, this is Hudson, my official ghost detective mentor, for this case only."

"And don't forget, your cad of an ex-boyfriend," Auguste added. He sniffed, and I could swear he frowned in Hudson's general direction.

"And that, yes," I said.

Hudson's eyes widened, and he looked like he wasn't sure whether to be amused or offended. "Um, nice to meet you?"

"I'd say it was a pleasure to meet you, but that fact remains to be seen." Auguste went back to munching noisily on his fruit.

"So, when did you pick up this delightful talking hedgehog?" Hudson asked. He snagged a licorice vine from the center console.

"A little under four years ago." *After you left*, I added silently. "But the talking part only started this week."

Auguste made a tsking sound. "What did I tell you? The *listening* part only started this week."

"What, you didn't get a talking animal companion out of this deal?" I asked Hudson.

"Can't say that I did."

We sat in awkward silence for a moment. I took a drink of my Slurpee, and it made a screechy slurping sound. "Sorry."

"That's okay." He motioned to the second icy drink. "That for me?"

I nodded. I probably should've only gotten stakeout snacks for myself and Auguste, seeing as Hudson was hardly deserving of my kindness, but what could I say? Old habits.

"Thanks," he said.

"So..."

"So..."

Grandma Magnolia and Moisha, feel free to show up anytime now, I thought.

How had it gone from easy silences and comfort to the Olympics of Awkward between Hudson and me?

"Great conversationalist he is," Auguste said with a mouth full of watermelon.

The corner of my mouth hitched up.

"Any movement from Nick's place?" Hudson asked.

"Someone went in right as I pulled up," I said. "I didn't get a good look, but it was a dude, about the same height as Nick. Jeans and a white button up."

Hudson picked up my pink mini binoculars from the dash and peered into them. "Do you really have binoculars to see two houses down?"

"You never know when they might come in handy. I come

prepared." I turned my focus back to Nick's house. A light switched off in one room and turned on in another.

"So, what do we do now? Just wait? Stakeouts are much more boring than I expected."

"It's not the most exciting work. But if he comes outside and talks to people, we might get something. Or if he leaves, we can follow him."

"Great."

More silence. Broken only by the sound of hedgehog chewing.

Argh, this was painful.

"I'm going to check out social media for Carlie, Ben, and Mina. Maybe we can figure out how to best contact them."

"Good idea," Hudson said. "I'll watch the house while you do that."

I double checked their last names in my notebook and scrolled through their accounts. Mina was a stunning Black woman with dark skin and long coils of hair. Her feed was full of colorful monochromatic looks, thrillers she'd been reading, and references to the law. She hadn't posted a thing since the night of the murder. Ben wasn't much of a sharer, it looked like. There were a few pictures with friends, only one of him and Austin looking very sweet together, and posts promoting his family's hotel brand. There were a few shots of books he was reading, mostly fantasy and sci-fi mixed in.

Carlie, on the other hand, was all about curated food posts. Beignets under the green and white awnings at Cafe Du Monde, leaf and heart latte art, and heaping plates of muffins I recognized as Crumbles' specials. Not a single photo of herself. Just as I was about to scroll on past to see if I could find a picture of her elsewhere, a story popped up on her timeline. I clicked on to see her staring sad-faced at the camera with her long blonde hair.

The hairs on my neck tingled with recognition.

You never know how much impact a person makes on you until they're gone. RIP, friend. XOXO, read the caption.

I nudged Hudson. "I know her. Carlie Lightfoot. Look." I shoved the phone in his face.

"She works as a barista at Crumbles. Or at least she did until Friday. The bakery where someone tossed Austin's body off the balcony."

Hudson pushed his sunglasses onto his head and raised an eyebrow.

"This has to be connected to the cover up somehow. She had a key, or at least she probably did. I can check with Liz to be sure. Is she the one who wanted to frame Liz? Was it just to throw suspicion off of herself, so any scapegoat would do, or was there something bigger at play?"

"Maybe a group effort," Hudson mused.

"Could be. I saw her Saturday morning too. She just started working at my yoga studio, and she seemed weirded out to see me. She's usually Miss Immaculate, but she was in a sorry state that morning. Maybe she quit Crumbles because she couldn't stand the guilt?"

"That's good. I can go to the yoga place in the morning and act like I'm looking into classes and talk to her some more," Hudson said.

"I'll message Ben and see if he'll meet me for coffee tomorrow. I feel like a more direct approach might be best with him."

After this brief period of conversation, we fell into a lull again, both Hudson and I stealing glances at each other between watching Nick's house.

It was so weird having him back here. Like coming home and being ripped out of the new one I'd constructed for myself all at once.

There was an equal pull for me to know everything about

why he'd left and what he'd been up to all this time, and to keep that Pandora's box closed and go on with my life.

"Are you still doing the Halloween fundraiser?" he asked at the same time I said:

"Are you still making those mosaics you used to make?"

We shared an awkward laugh.

"You first," he said.

"Mosaics?" I repeated. Arts and crafts had always been his thing, working with his hands while his thoughts did their worst. It's why he wanted to go into psychology and specialize in art therapy.

"Not too much. The supplies were too heavy to cart around. I got into whittling for a while, though." He fished two little wooden talismans from his pocket and passed them to me.

"Aww, cute! Auguste, look," I said. One was a little hedgehog and the other a peregrine falcon with its wings outstretched. My favorite animal and his. Did that mean he'd still thought of me this whole time? Of us?

"Humph," Auguste sniffed. "Passable."

I ran my finger over my hedgie's quills, a spot of warmth blooming in my chest. But then confusion set in again. Is that even what I wanted—him pining away from afar? It didn't change the abrupt circumstances of his departure. And all the hurt that followed. I passed them back.

"I'm still doing that, but my favorite thing lately is subversive cross-stitch," he said.

"That I need to see."

He thumbed through the pictures in his phone until he came to a photo of a couple of projects: one with colorful euphemisms for swear words and another that said, *Spark joy or GTFO.*

I laughed. That's what I needed—to stay light-hearted, and

solve this case—not wander down the what-if path with Hudson.

Then I grabbed the binoculars because someone had pulled open a curtain from the lighted room. Three people were visible inside: Nick, the man I'd seen enter, and a woman. It was hard to see more detail from here.

After a time, my traitorous heart couldn't stand it anymore. I had to ask. Had to know. I'd always wonder if I didn't. Maybe I could broach the subject obliquely.

"Did you end up taking that entertainer job on the cruise line when you left?"

When you left. It hung between us like a heavy stone around both of our necks. So we were really going to do this? I guess we were. My palms slicked and my heart beat loudly enough that I could hear it in my ears.

"My mom would've loved that." Hudson shook his head. "I thought about it, but I needed to get farther away."

"Farther than the Caribbean?"

Hudson rubbed the back of his head. "Guess so. Plus, I thought you might look for me there. And I wasn't ready to be found."

I had looked for him there. I'd also called all the other cruise lines, just in case. My gut twisted. Were things so bad, he had to make the break so complete?

"So where did you go?"

A dimple punctuated his sad smile. "I ran away with the circus."

TWENTY-SEVEN

I snorted and rolled my eyes, tucking back into myself.

"Fine. Don't tell me, then. I thought we were being honest here."

"I am."

I shot Hudson a skeptical look.

"I got down to Florida and holed up in a little town called Gibsonton where circus performers go in the off season. It's legal to keep elephants on your front lawn there. Then I saw an ad looking for acrobats for a Cirque show doing a European tour. I auditioned, gave them a fictitious name, and set off."

I absorbed the additional blow.

Hudson had an unusual upbringing, to say the least, that included an uneasy relationship with performing on stage. His mom believed it was her destiny to shepherd a tiny pageant queen daughter into the spotlight she herself had missed out on, and was devastated when God had only seen fit to give her a boy child. Since there was no Little Miss Stone County in Hudson's future, his mom enrolled him in gymnastics, singing, fiddle, and banjo lessons and got him in front of every talent scout in the county.

By the time he hit twelve, he'd been performing six shows a day in the country music equivalent of a boy band at an 1880s-themed amusement part in Branson, Missouri. Grasshopper Hollow, breaking tweenage hearts since 1887.

"I thought you were over performing. But you left to do acrobatics on stage in a traveling show?"

"And some trapeze." That midwestern drawl and grin on his face were maddening.

I huffed. "Of course. Can't' resist the siren call of aerial stunts."

"It's my weakness," Hudson said with a sly smile. Then he looked into the distance and sobered.

"Paige, I didn't leave to join the circus. I panicked, and I ran. I had to find something to do with myself after I imploded my entire life. And this came along at the right time. So, I leaped."

"Literally and figuratively," I said.

"It was the only thing I could think to do."

"Oh."

Time stretched out. Where were my Grandma Magnolia and Moisha?

"So, how about you? What have you been up to since I—?"

"Since you left me with nothing but a vague breakup letter in your wake?"

Hudson winced.

The words were petty, but I couldn't bite them back. I crossed my arms over my chest. So much for keeping it light.

"Paige, I'm sorry. I'll never stop being sorry for how that went down. You deserved so much more, and I'm sorry I didn't give it to you."

The words walked the tightrope between us with an anguish neither one of us wanted to touch. At long last, the apology I'd waited four years for. The glacier around my heart cracked and whined.

Auguste farted.

I couldn't help but laugh, and neither could Hudson.

"Way to cut the tension, little guy," Hudson said.

Auguste glowered, and I rolled down the windows.

"Think he'll like me better if I give him one of these treats?" Hudson shook the bag of creepy crawlies.

"You may address me directly, you know," Auguste said. "And yes, I will permit you to provide me with snacks now that I have eaten my watermelon. You cannot bribe your way to my affections, however. So please disabuse yourself of that notion tout suite."

"Got it," Hudson said. "One dried bug feast coming up. With no strings attached."

"I've been doing pretty great, actually." I pasted on a smile and answered Hudson's earlier question. "Ines, Bridget, and I bought a house together and remodeled it."

"That's great. Did you switch your major to criminal justice like you were talking about? You seemed so excited about that." Hudson sneaked a look at me.

I bit my thumbnail, my nervous habit, but pulled my hand back into my lap when I noticed. "No. I decided it wasn't practical so close to graduation." I omitted the part where his leaving had made me shut down and second guess all my instincts in the realm of career prospects as well as love. If he'd been too-good-to-be-true, then the idea that I'd make an ace detective was too.

"I manage a gift shop in the Quarter. Deveauxs' Historical Haunts. We do ghost tours. And vampire and cemetery tours too. Sometimes I fill in as a tour guide. That's what I was doing when Austin's body fell from the balcony."

I thought back to my conversation with Austin this afternoon. Maybe the reason I'd stayed at Deveauxs' for so long was that it never represented some shiny, magical passion. It was okay, just as it was, and I didn't pin all of my future hopes onto it.

Just as I mused about that, Magnolia and Moisha materialized into the back seat. Magnolia patted the perfect victory rolls in her hair and straightened the trench coat she wore over a pencil skirt and blouse.

"Paige, dear, I'm sorry we're late. We got pulled into this dreadfully boring meeting about teaching hygiene in the afterlife."

"That's okay."

Moisha leaned between the two front seats and looked between Hudson and I with a conspiratorial grin. "Thought you might've brought him along." Moisha's mustard colored cardigan draped her arms.

"What's the scoop? And why don't you introduce us," Magnolia said.

I relaxed into my seat, glad for the diversion. I introduced Magnolia and Moisha to Hudson.

"That's the ex," Moisha stage-whispered to Magnolia.

My cheeks heated, and I rolled my eyes.

"Guilty as charged," Hudson said. He looked back at them with a sheepish grin.

"Pfft. Guilty is right," Auguste interjected. I also introduced Auguste to my ghost grandma squad, who cooed over him. He climbed back to my lap and then crawled up to my shoulder to talk with them.

"Well, it's an honor to meet you both," Hudson said to Magnolia and Moisha, every bit of the midwestern charm turned to the max. "Paige tells me you based some stories you wrote on true events. I wondered about that after I got into this line of work."

Magnolia preened.

"The one about the sea turtles?" Hudson asked. "Real or fiction?"

"That I mostly fabricated. My sweetheart at the time was rather fond of sea turtles. But I did go into the bayou after the suspect that time."

"What about the one where Matilda stops the blind serial killer?"

"I altered some events, to protect the innocent, you know, but that was by and large a true story." Magnolia's chest puffed at the memory.

"Really? That's some impressive work, Ms. Castile."

"Call me Magnolia." Her eyes glittered at him.

Great, just what I needed. My grandma was supposed to be team Paige all the way.

The front door of Nick's house opened and the three people who had been inside came out, beers in hand, and gathered around the Adirondack chairs on the porch.

"You guys, look!" I said.

We all followed their movements. The shadows mostly hid the woman, but we had a full view of Nick, who looked as intense and broody as he had the night before. He lit a cigarette, and the cherry glowed through the night.

Dusk dusted the sky, and the street lamps clicked on.

"What about the one with the lonely vampire?" Hudson asked, still not taking his eyes off Nick and the other two.

"Mervyn? Quite true, that one," Magnolia said.

I perked up here. "Wait, you're telling me that vampires are real?"

"Of course, darling."

I could not wait to tell Norman. He would weep with joy.

"I knew it," Hudson said.

"Oy, the constant lamenting with that one, though," Moisha

said with an eye roll. "My lost love this, 1773 that. It was all very touching at first. But you want to know the trouble with vampires? They don't sleep, so it just keeps going and going. I had to stay at a friend's place while he camped out at our apartment to get a break."

"They're quite fond of hedgehogs, though, and not keeping them as pets, if you get my drift, so I'd keep your quilly friend close if you ever meet one," Magnolia said.

"Mon Dieu." Auguste shuddered, and I hugged him to my chest. "Suppose it is because we are both nocturnal?"

"Don't worry, I won't let any vampires have you for a snack," I said.

I turned back to Nick's house, where the group still lounged on the porch. The woman stepped into the light, and I could finally get a good look at her. Long blonde hair, slight build.

"Wait, is that Carlie?"

She reclined against Nick's chest, and he wrapped an arm around her.

Hudson grabbed the binoculars for a closer look and then passed them to me. "Looks like it."

"That's new," I said.

Hudson and I exchanged an excited look, and both of us strained forward.

"Can you hear anything with the windows down?" I whispered.

We all went silent, but the only thing any of us could make out were muffled voices. Serious tone. And music wafting out of a speaker at Nick's place.

My phone buzzed with an incoming call. I rolled up the windows before answering.

"Hey," Ines said in her cheerful voice. "How goes the stakeout? Did you catch your killer? I thought I could be your computer genius backup since you went out there by yourself. At least if something happens, I can call 911."

"She's not alone, dear," Magnolia said. "You didn't tell her we were coming too?"

I waited a beat to see if Ines could hear the voice of my ghost grandmother. Maybe with actual auditory proof, she'd be more receptive to the idea of otherworldly entities.

"Hello, Paige, you there?" Ines said.

Dang it.

"Sorry, bad connection there for a sec. We've got eyes on the suspects, and they seem to be having an intense conversation, but we're too far back to hear, and they're out on the porch now, so I can't really sneak your listening device close enough to them without being seen."

I muted the call and whispered to Magnolia, "I don't think she can hear you."

"Ah yes, I always forget that part," Magnolia said.

"Wait, did you say we? I thought you were flying solo tonight," Ines said.

"Um,... Auguste and me."

"Oh, good call."

Hudson shot me a quizzical look, and his expression fell for a moment before he could school his features.

I muted the phone again. "This is complicated, okay?" I said to Hudson.

Then an idea struck. "Hey," I said to Magnolia and Moisha. "Do you think you could float over there and listen in on their conversation?"

Moisha's eyes twinkled at the prospect. She shot out of the car, went about ten feet, and then winked out of existence.

I gasped. A second later, with a very perturbed look on her face, she appeared next to Magnolia in the back seat again.

"What happened? Are you okay?" I looked her up and down for any sign of damage to her ghostly form.

"I was afraid of that," Magnolia said. "Since Paige is our earthly tether, we can't exist very far away from her."

I eyed the side of the property. "I guess if it were a last resort, I could go hide in the bougainvillea in the side yard," I said doubtfully.

"This Nick fellow saw your face at the gala, correct?" Magnolia asked.

I nodded.

"And mine," Hudson said, "I was in disguise, but still."

Magnolia pursed her lips. "One slip up here could jeopardize all your progress so far and attract undue attention."

Ines said something I missed in the commotion.

"Sorry, what was that?" I asked her.

"I said, why do you keep putting yourself on mute?"

Because I'm busy talking to two ghosts, my ex, and a hedgehog.

"I'm eating my stakeout snacks," I said. "I know how you hate mouth noises."

Ines gave the verbal equivalent of a shudder. "Too true. But I still don't like feeling like I'm talking to myself."

"Sorry. Ooh, someone just pulled up on the curb next to his place."

Auguste climbed onto the dashboard and sniffed around in the direction of Nick's house. "What do you see, Auguste?" I asked him.

"Nothing. Hedgehogs have terrible eyesight." He raised his cute little nose. "And I cannot smell a thing up here over all of those powdered cheese snacks."

A woman got out of the car. She wasn't yet in the pool of light put out by the street lamps, but her shape struck me as familiar. She waved at Nick, and her car beeped as she locked it.

"Who is it?" Ines asked.

When she hit the first stair up to Nick's porch, the light bathed the waves of her red ombre hair.

"It's the Voodoo doll rep! What if Nick had them made?" I practically squealed. "We have to find a way to listen to their conversation. Too bad we can't clip the listening device to Auguste's quills and send him in," I said, fiddling with the device. "Wait, that's actually not a bad idea."

"You really think you can slip your hedgehog out of the car and tell him to go spy for you, and he'll just listen to directions?" Ines said with a dubious tone.

"Stranger things have happened. What do you say, buddy? You up for a little undercover op?" I looked to Auguste for confirmation. He gave the hedgehog equivalent of a shrug.

He peered over the dashboard again. "Did you bring my booties? There is much mud after the storm, and I do not wish to sully my paws if it can be avoided."

"They're in the little pouch on your snuggle sack."

"Then I will go play my part in this game that is afoot. Souhaite-moi bon chance."

"What's that?" Ines asked.

"Nothing. Auguste is going in."

TWENTY-EIGHT

"Auguste, can you hear me?" I whispered into the receiver that came with the transmitter.

Auguste, outfitted in his pink booties, scampered along the sidewalk from our stakeout car toward Nick's place.

Silence. And what could've been a tiny hedgehog grunt.

Hudson shrugged. "Maybe it's one-way?"

I'd hung up with Ines, promising to keep her posted, so I'd have to check on that later if he didn't respond.

"The poor thing. He's a walking target for stray dogs," Magnolia said.

"And vampires," Moisha added.

My stomach clenched. I tried again. "Try to walk on people's yards outside of the street lamps."

This time Auguste came through loud and clear. "Like I said, there is much mud." I could practically hear him wrinkle his nose and ignore the suggestion.

"Would you prefer mud or attracting the attention of hungry neighborhood dogs?" I reasoned. Dogs have petrified Auguste since the time Bridget fostered a Mastiff. The dog tried to use Auguste as a ball, and I had to pry him out of the dog's slobbery jaws.

Auguste trotted off the path, not without an excess of moaning and groaning about the indignity of it all.

"That's one spoiled hedgehog you've got there," Hudson said.

"Hush, he's an indoor pet. At least he doesn't freak out about clowns."

"That was one time! And that is a perfectly common phobia. Look how much money those *It* movies and books have made."

Auguste sniffed. "I smell them. I think I am getting close."

"Auguste, darling, stay at the bottom of the porch steps if you can. It'll make for a quicker getaway," Magnolia said.

Auguste disappeared into the darkness. I said a little prayer he'd be all right.

"I am in position next to the steps. Can you hear them?" Auguste whispered. I wondered if he even needed to whisper, since the only people who could hear him were here in my car.

We all leaned in and listened intently.

I made out the sound of voices, all muffled and indistinct.

"Bud, you're going to have to get a little closer. All we can hear is chatter," I said.

"I will endeavor to climb the stairs unnoticed. The cigarette smoke is everywhere, but I can also smell flowers. Perhaps there are pots I can hide behind."

The sound of shuffling came next, and then, little by little, the voices grew louder until I could hear Valerie clearly. "I followed up on what you asked me about earlier." Her voice stayed low and unsure, like she wasn't confident what to say in front of Nick's other guests.

"And?" the voice I assumed belonged to Nick said. "It's

okay. They know. At least, the broad strokes. Did she know anything?"

"She seemed very intent on finding out who placed the order," Valerie said.

The hairs on the back of my neck stood on end, and my stomach turned to icy sludge. "I think she's talking about me."

"Oh, dear." Magnolia leaned her cheek into her palm.

"But why, though? Do you think she's digging into things she shouldn't?" Nick said.

The other female voice, that must've been Carlie's, let out a doleful sound.

"I don't know," Valerie said. "She knows the bakery people. I think she's just worried about them."

"What if it's more than that?" Carlie asked, distress clear in her tone.

"She's just a gift shop manager, not some private detective." This delightful retort came from the second man in attendance.

Carlie scoffed. "Yeah, well, I'm 'just' a barista, well ex-barista, now yoga studio receptionist—"

"Only until next week," the other guy cut in. "Then you'll have all the power and opportunities you can handle."

"Whatever, and look what I got mixed up in. I'm just saying don't underestimate people," Carlie said. The floorboards creaked, and it sounded like she was pacing.

"Carlie, baby, things are going to work out fine. We just keep doing what they say, and all this unpleasant stuff goes away," Nick said.

The other man added, "We should monitor this gift shop person, though. Just in case. I ran her name earlier, and something popped from a few years back. The higher ups will want to know if she persists in asking questions."

That was... not good.

Beside me, Hudson gripped the center console until his knuckles turned white.

"Who is this dude? Do you recognize the voice?" I asked him.

He shook his head. "This was a terrible idea, getting you involved."

"Sounds like I already was if he ran my name and something popped. What could that mean?"

Hudson's nostrils flared.

"He must be associated with the Enclave, right?" I said. "Probably someone further up in the ranks and already ascended. Is this guy the mastermind? Were Nick and Carlie his henchpeople?"

"They could simply be on damage control," Magnolia mused.

"We just need them to say something incriminating. Then we can have the police check it out," I said, trying to appease Hudson.

"Shhh!" Auguste hissed. "You will miss it if you keep blathering over their conversation."

He was right.

We'd definitely missed something talking amongst ourselves. I hoped it wasn't key information.

"I just want to know who pulled this stunt right before ascension and ruined all our lives," Nick said.

"Me too," Carlie added. "This was supposed to be the most important week of my life. An auspicious occasion. Then someone has to botch the whole sacrifice. You still don't have any ideas who was behind it? None?"

"I have some suspicions. I'm keeping my ears open," the mystery man said.

"What do you think the Hierophants will do if they find out who did it?" Carlie asked.

But we didn't get to find out the mystery man's theories. A dog's growl, low and menacing, reverberated through the speakers.

"Sacré bleu," Auguste whispered.

"What is it?" I asked.

"Canine," he choked out. "Hideously large canine. He has spotted me."

"Abort, Auguste," I said. "Get out of there."

"I don't know if I—"

The growling intensified.

"Paige, help!" Auguste squeaked.

Before I could think, I'd slammed the car into drive.

"What are you doing?" Hudson said. "You can't go up there. They're already suspicious of you!"

"There's a hat in the backseat. Put it on my head." I screeched to a halt at the curb in front of Nick's place.

Hudson secured the hat in place just before I dashed out and thundered up the porch steps.

Four pairs of quizzical eyes gaped at me in my purple camo fishing hat and aviator glasses at night.

But all that barely registered. I threw my hands up, eyes darting frantically along the porch.

"Has anyone seen my hedgehog?"

TWENTY-NINE

"Auguste?!"

"Here," came his tiny voice, a stubborn bravery shining through the quiver in it.

All four human porch occupants frowned at me like I was about five cards short of a tarot deck.

My eyes darted around the crowded space. Magnolia and Moisha had followed me out of the car and swept right through Nick and Carlie.

"Here he is, the poor thing," Magnolia made cooing sounds at him.

The dog growled, and I shoved past my lovebird murder suspects. A brown dog that looked more like a bear growled and bared his teeth.

"Down, Hoover," Carlie said in a firm voice.

I scooped up Auguste, who quivered head to quills, and pulled him to me. His booted feet left muddy tracks on my shirt, but I didn't care.

"Is he okay?" Moisha swept to one side and peered down at Auguste.

"I don't think the dog got any bites in, did he?" Magnolia said, checking him over.

"No, I am unharmed. But I shudder to think what would've happened had you not arrived in time." Auguste burrowed further into my chest.

"I'm so sorry, little guy," I said.

"I wondered what that growling was all about," Carlie said. "Down boy." She scratched Hoover's head and held him by the collar.

"Thanks," I said. I backed up, angling myself away from Valerie as best I could, lest she identify me.

Auguste let out a shuddering breath, but his heartbeat began to slow. Carlie'd cleaned herself up since I'd seen her last, and now sported freshly pressed khakis and a coral-collared blouse. Her blonde hair shined again, like she was trying to pull herself into some semblance of normalcy after the whole witnessing or possibly committing murder thing. Despite those efforts, the bags under her red-rimmed eyes were still present and accounted for.

"Is this one Nick or this one?" Magnolia asked, sizing up the two men. I nodded my head to my left, where Nick ran a hand through his thick mane of black hair.

"Try asking a few questions, so we can get a read on him," Magnolia said. "And perhaps if you get him talking, we can get a name for the other guy."

Nick beat me to it. "How did your hedgehog end up on my porch?" He gave me an amused smile, but I didn't miss the touch of wariness in his gaze.

I went for a lighthearted laugh. "Long story." Shoot, talking would probably allow Valerie to recognize my voice too. But what could I do, just shout, "Squirrel!" then point and run?

"The short version is I was visiting my friend down the

street—she has a rabbit. They like to play in her garden, but he got loose and went exploring the neighborhood."

"Is he wearing shoes?" Carlie leaned closer and rubbed Auguste's belly. "Aww, how sweet."

"Wait, Paige, is that you?" Valerie stepped into my line of sight. I very much wanted to leave my head down and disappear into a nearby hedge.

"Valerie?" I tried to sound surprised, but I'm not 100% sure I pulled it off with the way my palms slicked, and my heartbeat pounded in my ears. "Two visits in one day. What are the odds?"

She made a non-committal sound and frowned. "What's with the sunglasses?" she asked, her eyebrows scrunching together.

"Um... headache?"

"You don't sound too sure about that," Nick said.

"I'm sure. They scramble my brain a bit."

"Wait, I know you too," Carlie said, once I'd slipped off my glasses.

"Hey," I said with a little wave.

"I'm feeling left out." Nick extended his hand. "Nick Ortega."

"Paige." We shook.

"This is the client I followed up with today," Valerie said. "The one asking about the dolls."

Nick's hand gripped mine, and his charming smile tightened.

Uh oh.

Okay, play it cool. A bead of sweat trickled down my temple. "Are you interested in custom Voodoo dolls too?" I asked Nick brightly. "We're thinking of carrying some in my gift shop. Valerie's seem like excellent quality."

"The best," Nick said coolly.

An ominous silence descended for a beat. Magnolia and Moisha signaled for me to engage the stranger in the group.

"I didn't catch your name," I said, turning to the mystery man. He lounged against the wall, just outside the sconce light, shadows obscuring his features. Even in the shadows I made out his dark pants, and his arms crossed over a crisp oxford shirt rolled up to the elbows, revealing what looked like a very expensive watch. He appeared bored, but in a cultivated way, like he thought himself above everything else.

When he stepped into the light, I recognized him too.

The light played on his overly-styled, dark blonde hair.

Eliza's Team Patriarchy Enclave companion from the gala.

"Hartley," he said. "I believe you assaulted my date the other night."

Three living and two ghost faces snapped my way with expressions ranging from curiosity to horror.

I covered my face with my hand. "I thought she was my cousin," I said, mostly to Magnolia and Moisha. "And last time I checked, hugging is nowhere in the vicinity of assault. It was an honest mistake."

"What a coincidence you were just in the neighborhood," Hartley said. The note of accusation floated on the humid night air. He, Carlie, and Nick exchanged dark looks.

"Who'd you say you were visiting?" Nick stepped closer to me. "I know most everyone on this street."

"And that's our exit cue, darling," Magnolia said.

"They're actually a few streets over. I've been driving around looking for him all evening. Good thing I heard the dog growling and checked up here. I never would've thought he'd get so far away. You're practically a world traveler, aren't you Auguste?"

Another skeptical look passed between the others.

"I do not think they are buying it," Auguste said.

"Well, now that he's safe, I'd better be off. Nice running into you all again so soon. Y'all have a pleasant night."

I crept off the porch with the Enclave crew watching me like I held a lit stick of dynamite. With the evening I'd had, I prayed the next custom Voodoo doll they made wouldn't be of me.

The next day on my lunch break, which fell at 3pm since I had the late shift, I headed to meet Ben Park in the place he'd agreed to meet me. Students and business people grabbing their late afternoon caffeine congregated at wrought-iron tables in a common area shared by several small restaurants and coffee shops. Flowers trailed from extra large pots, which divided the space into various nooks and crannies. I'd chosen it for that very reason.

Finally, on to the part of the investigation I'd been looking forward to since the start: meeting Austin's friends and getting their take on everything that went down after Austin's story ended.

After last night, I felt like we were on the brink of uncovering something big. It was like getting all the edge pieces of a puzzle connected. I could see the overall shape of things. Now I had to fill in the details to get the full picture. I really hoped Ben could help with that.

Since I'd arrived early, I ordered a bubble tea and scoped out the place. Hudson looked up from a table near the tea shop where he pulled purple floss through his latest cross-stitch project.

He raised a hand in greeting. I hadn't argued about him coming along for backup after the incident last night had put me squarely on the Enclave's radar.

"Anyone tailing me?" I whispered as I pitched a piece of stray garbage into a trash can next to his table.

"Not that I can tell," he whispered back, keeping his eyes on his stitches. He pulled a threaded needle through the Aida cloth that read: *This took forever.* "I'll keep watching, though. Ben's already here. Other side of this flower pot. Someone's with him: a Black woman in her late twenties, early thirties. Hat and big sunglasses. Could be Mina, but I didn't get close enough to tell for sure."

Filled with a surge of excitement, I jumped into action. If it was indeed Mina, it would save us from tracking her down separately.

"Wish me luck."

"Luck," Hudson said, with a spreading grin.

I APPROACHED the table beyond the flower pot where a striking man of Asian heritage sipped a bubble tea. "Hi, are you Ben?"

He looked up at me with possibly the kindest brown eyes I'd ever seen, even if they were tinged with melancholy. Some people you meet, you can just tell they'd make a good friend. Ben was like that. He smoothed his already flawless black hair and pulled at his skinny tie, his movements measured, even the fidgety ones. Goodness seemed a baked-in part of him, like the sugar in the cinnamon roll he and Mina were sharing. I could tell why Austin had been so smitten.

"Paige?" Ben asked.

I nodded. "Thanks for meeting me."

I smiled at the woman with high cheekbones who I recognized immediately as Mina Lennox. "Hello."

Mina licked icing off of her fingers and eyed me warily through her sunglasses. She wore a taupe pants suit and her hair pulled into a ponytail under her floppy sun hat. She looked from Ben to me and sat up straight, one leg crossed over the other. Her gaze didn't waver as she assessed me. Everything about her posture exuded protective energy. I bet her clients valued this quality in the courtroom. I know Austin did.

"Hello," she said, almost daring me to flinch first.

I just smiled back at her, trying to look as nonthreatening as possible. "I like your hat," I said.

The stiffness of her carriage relaxed the slightest bit, and she allowed me a tight smile. "Thanks. What's this about?" She waved a finger between Ben and me.

Okay. The direct route. I could respect that. I probably shouldn't have expected any less, from what Austin had shared.

Ben gave her a *let's not go full gladiator mode* look and answered before I could. Was he as conflict-averse as I was?

"You caught me by surprise when you messaged yesterday," he said. "Austin never mentioned you, but I'm glad to meet another of his friends."

"Same here," I said.

I turned back to Mina, determined to break through her protective exterior, so she could see we were on the same side.

"Are you Mina, by chance?" I asked. "Austin told me a lot about you both. I was actually going to call you after I met with Ben. I'd like it if you stayed too, if so. If you can, that is."

"Funny he's been talking so much about us and never said a thing about you." Mina stayed put, muscles still coiled taut in lioness mode. "How did you know him, again?"

"He worked down the street from the ghost tour place

where I work. Deveauxs' Historical Haunts. Do you know it? We saw each other in passing a lot."

They exchanged a look. Wondering if I could be trusted? I'd be cautious too, after what they'd just been through. Who could you afford to take into confidence when the people in custody of your secrets ask you to kill one of your own?

"I can send you on a complimentary ghost tour any time you want," I said, determined not to give up here. Then my voice sobered. "I'm sorry for your loss. Both of you."

I wondered where Austin was now and how he knew when to pop in and out of existence in the living world.

It would be great if he could show up right about now and help me with my approach to earn their trust.

As if thinking that had conjured him up, Austin drifted into view behind Ben and Mina, his surfer hair rippling in the breeze. At the sight of his friends, relief swamped his features. He wrapped his arms around their shoulders as if he were still solid. Unfortunately, he wasn't, and his limbs passed right through them.

"You're alright." Austin's breath whooshed out. "You're both alright."

Mina shivered at his ghostly contact. She frowned and looked over each of her shoulders, momentarily shaken.

After she composed herself again, she said, "I suppose you want to know how we know Austin too."

"I kind of already do."

Both Mina and Ben seemed to shrink into themselves, and the air between the three of us charged with their worry and fear.

"What exactly did he tell you?" Ben shredded the piece of cinnamon roll in his fingers. Mina covered his hand with hers and he dropped the pastry.

As I sipped my tea, I contemplated how much to tell them. I

had a feeling Mina could sniff out a lie a mile away, so I'd stay as close to the truth as possible, lest they shut down. I turned to Austin for direction.

He shrugged.

Then a wild idea struck me. The words were out of my mouth before I could stop them.

"He told me everything."

THIRTY-ONE

"Define 'everything.'" Mina's voice wavered the tiniest amount, but I still caught it. She cast a furtive glance around the outdoor cafe space where she, Ben, and I had gathered.

Leaning closer, I lowered my voice. "I know what you three and also Roman, Nick, and Carlie were up to together."

Mina's plastic cup crumpled in her grip. She set it aside.

Ben held stock still, like a kid who still believes no one can see them if they don't move a muscle. The skin between his eyebrows creased.

"And what exactly was that?" Mina pressed her lips together.

"The break-ins, the stuff with Ravenscroft, the *organization* you're pledging."

Ben's knuckles went white where he gripped the table. Mina kept her poise but for a tremor in her hand. She fisted it and pulled it under the table.

"No way. He wouldn't," Mina said. "He knows — *knew* — what the penalty for that would be." She turned to Ben. "You know I'm right."

Dang it. Wrong move. I was losing her. I looked helplessly at Austin. He held his hands up, as much at a loss as I was.

He put his hands on Ben's shoulders as if he were kneading the tension of the past week from his muscles.

Ben loosened his grip on the table and looked over both shoulders. "Maybe he needed to confide in someone." Horror dawned on his face. "Maybe that's why..." He locked eyes with Mina.

Mina pushed away from the table and grabbed for her purse. "No. I'm not here for this nonsense." She turned her intimidating gaze on me. "Who are you really? Is this some kind of blackmail stunt? Because if it is, I'm leaving."

My chair screeched across the concrete as I stood. "No, wait! Please. Nothing like that. Don't go. Austin's my friend, and someone is framing my other friend for his murder. I'm just trying to find out the truth about what happened and help clear her name."

Ben put a hand on Mina's arm, and I sent up a silent prayer of thanks.

Mina pinched the bridge of her nose and drew in a deep breath. "Who's your friend?"

"Her name's Liz Pickett. She runs Crumbles Bakery in the Quarter. She was my favorite professor in college, and we've stayed in touch. You can call the cops and check it out."

"Let's hear what she has to say," Ben said. "Or ask."

Mina frowned but settled back into her seat. "You know we can't talk about any of that."

And now here it came, the other part of my completely mad idea. I sucked in a deep breath, looked around the courtyard to make sure we weren't attracting any onlookers, and blurted it out.

"I know what happened the night of Austin's murder. In the underground place. With the weapons and the messages. I know how that sounds. How could I possibly know, right? But Austin told me."

Austin's jaw dropped. "Not where I thought you were going with this. But okay."

"Not sure where I was going with that myself," I muttered. "But let's roll with it."

Too late to go back now.

Austin floated next to me to read Ben's and Mina's expressions.

Deep creases lined both of their foreheads. I could tell they were trying to make sense of what I'd just told them.

"Are you trying to tell us you're a psychic medium or something?" Ben asked.

I bit my lip and looked at Austin.

"I think you'll lose them both with the psychic scenario," he said.

Mina shook her head. I could tell by the look on her face that she was about as likely as Ines to believe in ghosts or psychics. "No. The only way you could know that is if Nick, Roman, or Carlie is a snitch or if you're an ascendant trying to test us," Mina said.

"I'm not working with any of the other acolytes. I don't even know them. Well, except for Carlie working for my friend Liz for a while."

Austin looked from his friends to me with a stricken expression. "That cinnamon roll is looking really good right now," he said.

I gave him a commiserating smile.

Mina followed my gaze to where Austin's ghost hung in the air, her voice tinged with annoyance. "What do you keep looking at?"

Ben studied my face and the place where Austin floated.

Mina turned back to Ben and lowered her voice. "There's

no way she could know this stuff unless she's got someone on the inside."

"Or unless Austin's here with us," Ben whispered. His kind brown eyes searched the space Austin occupied. He breathed in deeply, and a sad smile stretched across his face.

Austin's eyes widened. "Do you think he can see me?"

Ben's gaze followed his specter as he moved to his side.

"I don't think so, but maybe he can sense something."

A tiny ball of hope formed inside of me.

I felt so awkward talking to him out loud in the presence of others, but might as well go all in.

Mina narrowed her eyes at me.

I held my hands up in a peace offering. "Ask me something only Austin would know."

Mina rubbed her temples and sighed. "First that hellscape of an Enclave trial, and now we're talking to the ghost of our dead friend?"

I looked at Ben. His eyes studied the air next to him. I could practically see his rational mind vying with what he clearly wanted to believe. "What's my middle name?"

I relayed Austin's answer. "Sung-ho."

Mina countered, "Anyone with google could find that out."

"Okay, what was the first task the three of us bonded over?" Ben asked.

"Flooding the senator's mansion," Austin answered.

Ben and Mina shared a silent conversation.

"What did we find in the drawer of his night table?" Mina asked.

"She's trying to throw you off," Austin said. "We didn't go into the bedroom. But we found those weird Garbage Pail Kids collectible cards in his office drawer next to pictures of his mistress."

I repeated his message.

"This is too weird," Mina said. "I don't understand how you could know all this. Surveillance?"

I shook my head.

"Austin," Ben whispered. "I know this sounds totally out of the realm of possibility, but he's really here, isn't he?"

I nodded.

Mina shook her head in disbelief again. "I know what he meant to you, Ben, but I just..."

Austin held up a finger and asked me to relay his words. I did. "Okay, Mina, Austin says you're the most driven person he knows. You protect your friends and clients, and you'd probably work 24 hours a day if you didn't need to sleep. But on Sundays you curl up like a cat in the sun in your fancy schmancy cashmere lounge pants and don't move until you've watched at least an hour of bad reality TV. You always wanted a sibling, so you watch over him and Ben like the brothers you never had."

A small wrinkle formed between Mina's brows, and her lips parted. I could see the tentative sparks of belief break through the haze of doubt.

Finally, it was working.

"And Ben." Austin floated down, eye-level with him. His eyes glistened and his throat bobbed. I watched him struggle with emotion, my own heart squeezing at the sight. "People underestimate you because you're so gentle, and you think before you speak. But you're the best person I've ever met. You're brave, way more so than you give yourself credit for, and you would do anything for the people you care about.

"You also have a terrible singing voice, but you love to sing Beatles and Kanye songs in the car. It's the reason you drive even if you could take the streetcar.

"Also, when you eat Lucky Charms, you pick out all the marshmallows and eat them first. And for someone so straight-laced, you're incredibly proficient with a set of lock picks. You told me you mastered the skill when you were bored as a child, hanging out in the offices of your dad's hotel."

My voice caught when I repeated this. Their relationship may have been brief, but it was clear these two cared deeply for each other.

Emotion washed over Ben's face, grief, hope, but most importantly for our continued conversation, belief. I loosed a pent up breath.

"Okay, okay, let's not get out a pottery wheel, here," Mina said with a laugh and feigned exasperation. "Now what?"

I looked back at Mina now. Her keen brown eyes were still wary, but dialed way down from before.

"Now," I said, "if you help me, we can solve Austin's murder."

THIRTY-TWO

Once I had Mina and Ben on board and conscious of Austin's ghostly presence, I scribbled furious notes on their versions of events from the night Austin died, overjoyed to finally get somewhere. Who would've guessed the allies would be the hardest nuts to crack?

The scent of flowers from the over-sized pots filled my lungs, and the air shimmered in the sweltering heat. Moisture beaded on my arms, and I sucked down more tea.

Mina's and Ben's accounts of the night Austin died dovetailed with everything Austin had told me. And now finally, time for the part I needed most: what happened after Austin died and how did he come to be tossed off a balcony and land at my feet?

"And after the lights went out, what then?" I shook out my hand. It had cramped from so much writing, but I was still eager for more.

Mina had taken off her sunglasses by this time and relaxed a touch more with me.

"Everyone was pretty freaked out by that last ultimatum,

kill or be killed." Mina shuddered and rubbed her arms despite the heat. "One of them must have snapped."

We all leaned together and spoke in low tones.

"Who do you think it was?" My neck prickled, and I glanced over my shoulder again, imagining that Nick or Hartley or anyone else had followed through on the threat to keep tabs on me. The dread that someone was watching us intensified the closer I got to answers.

"We disagree on that point," Mina said. "I say Carlie talked Nick into it, but Ben thinks Roman did it. My alternate theory is all three of them worked together."

Austin rubbed his chin like the last hypothesis interested him most.

"Why?" I asked.

Ben considered. "Ever since Roman found out Austin's dad is an ascendant way up in the ranks, Roman's had a chip on his shoulder. He was so sure that Austin had an automatic in he didn't earn."

"Like that guy earned anything he's got," Austin said with an eye roll.

Ben continued, "We did some digging recently too. Turns out he had several assault charges scrubbed from his record. He got out of it with hush money and anger management classes."

"And Carlie is vindictive as all get out," Mina added. "I wouldn't put it past her to have a daily grudge journal the way some people keep one for gratitude. Nick's always spoiling for dark thrills. He enjoyed all of our tasks in proportion with how much harm they'd cause."

"And you guys still want to be in a secret society with these people?" I said incredulously.

Mina huffed a mirthless laugh. "Not like we have much of a choice now. They don't take kindly to defectors. Especially ones that know any of their secrets."

"What'll they do if you want to quit? Whammy you with that powder they gave the 'unworthy' at the acolyte ceremony?" I asked.

Ben's eyes took on a dull, hopeless sheen. "I'm pretty sure there's only one way out at this point, and that's not it." His gaze moved to where Austin hovered at his shoulder.

"Wow, I'm sorry," I said.

Two sad smiles reflected back at me.

"We're not giving up quite so easily, though," Mina said, squaring her shoulders. "There's got to be a loophole. A record of someone else who got out."

"I may actually know someone who could get information on that."

"Someone who got out and lived to tell about it?" Mina shot me a dubious look.

"Well, no. But…" I told them about Eliza, who I hadn't been able to get in touch with again. "And also, my great grandmother —she's a ghost too—is helping me with this case and might could find someone on the other side with some information. Don't take the oath if you can help it. Just in case."

Mina looked tired and resigned, like getting involved in all this had taken its toll.

"Tell me anything else you remember. Anything that could help me trace who did this to Austin," I said.

"There is one thing," Mina said. The way she drew the sentence out and silently communicated with Ben made my scalp tingle. This felt important. "Something Carlie said that's been nagging at me since that night."

I leaned closer. "What?"

Mina looked around us, as if checking for listeners. "When the countdown clicked on and the voice said we had to kill or all be killed, she kept wailing, 'It wasn't supposed to go like this.'"

I remembered Austin relaying the same thing. A thrill

tingled down my spine. "You think she knew what was going down before that night?"

"I mean, it could've been a general why is this my life kind of thing, but yeah, I do."

"And then there was the candelabra," Ben added.

"What about it?"

"When we were cleaning up and planning what to do next, we found it in an odd place," Ben said. "I assumed it was the murder weapon because of the blood, but when the lights came on, we found it at the edge of the room. About halfway between the entrance and the table."

"Could someone have thrown it to hide their guilt?" I asked.

"Possibly. But why?" Ben said.

Why, indeed? To avoid being seen as a killer by their peers? So they could bury it deep inside and convince themselves they did it for the greater good?

I tapped my pen to my lips and thought.

"What was the clean up like? How'd you move Austin and where?"

"The lights stayed off for a good five minutes. Then the voice from the speakers said we'd chosen wisely and passed our ultimate trial. It said we'd all ascend at the ceremony the following week. We had one last task to complete to prove our worth: clean up and prepare the body for the ritual," Ben said.

"When the torches came back on, Nick had this nasty gleam in his eye. I didn't like the dude before, but that cemented my vow never to run into him in a dark alley." Mina shuddered. "Carlie just sat there weeping and carrying on."

"Roman had blood on his sleeves," Ben added. "His eyes looked like he had Halloween contacts on. They were so dilated, they were almost pure black. He kept wringing his hands."

Austin floated back and forth behind them, like he needed to flee from the story.

"What did you two do?" I asked.

"We kind of clung to each other trying to wrap our minds around the fact this was really happening. Then we checked his pulse," Mina said.

Austin looked positively green at the sight of Mina's and Ben's drawn faces.

"I'm sorry. I know this has to be hard to talk about," I said.

Ben sniffed. "It's okay."

After a breather, I realized my lunch break was almost up. "I've got to get back to work, but can I ask you a few more questions first?"

They both nodded in assent.

"Where was everyone positioned when the lights came on?"

Ben sketched everyone's positions on the map of the room he'd started earlier. Roman directly behind Austin's head. Ben on his right and Mina directly next to him. Carlie at his feet.

"And how did you, um, clean up?" I asked.

"Ravenscroft came back in with a body bag and cleaning supplies," Ben said. "They had us bring him through the tunnels but in a different direction than we'd come in. At the end, we went up a sharp incline. We might've been above ground."

Mina shot Ben a look and gave him a curt shake of her head.

"To where? The ritual room?" I asked.

Ben shook his head. "It was a small storage room with some boxes and one of those big chest freezers like hunters use on TV, filled with ice."

I nodded in understanding, feeling thankful I hadn't opted for a snack with my tea because it might have made an emergency exit.

"They had bags packed with fresh clothes for each of us in the room. The place had a tiny bathroom to one side where we washed up and changed. Ravenscroft took all of our dirty clothes to burn."

"They had this all down to a science, huh?" My eyebrows knitted together.

"Or something," Mina said.

"Ravenscroft had this whole congratulatory speech planned for after. He said we should be thankful to each other for doing what was necessary and grateful to Austin for falling so that we may rise. After that, we went our separate ways and were told never to speak of it again."

I shook my head, trying to fathom this senseless death. All for what, greed? Power? A heart's desire?

"If he was supposed to be on ice until the ritual, I still don't understand how he ended up over the balcony of Crumbles."

Ben and Mina exchanged a look I couldn't decipher. They seemed to confer on some silent conundrum.

Mina broke the silence. "That's the question, isn't it?"

Mina and Ben were keeping something from me. I could feel it.

After wrapping up with the two of them, I trekked back to the gift shop. Tonight was Monday, usually a slow night after the weekend rush, so I'd have some time to sort out the new pieces of info our conversation brought to light.

Whatever they were hiding, though, I didn't think it was murder. Neither seemed the type. Hudson, on the other hand, was not so convinced.

"And what did they say about the aftermath?" he asked. He'd waited in the plaza working on his cross-stitch project until I had a head start and had come back to Deveauxs' with me to debrief.

I shared some details we'd discussed at the end of our conversation. "Here's my assessment based on all the info we've collected and a few other things Ben and Mina said. All signs point to this being a rogue task, orchestrated without the sanction of the leadership council. There was some upheaval in the ranks, the higher-ups were not happy, and they wanted a new sacrifice."

"Yikes. One of the existing acolytes?" Hudson asked.

"Not sure, but they aren't counting out the possibility. They also mentioned a meeting scheduled for Tuesday night to talk about their future with the Enclave and kick off a recruiting event. I'm guessing it's one of their vetting parties. And they thought it was at Roman's house."

"Hmmm." Hudson stroked his chin.

"Don't you see what that means?" I asked, bouncing on the balls of my feet.

"I don't follow."

"If it's tomorrow night at Roman's house, this is more evidence he invited me to a vetting party."

Before Hudson could do any nay-saying, the gift shop phone rang.

I held up a finger and grabbed it. "Deveauxs' Historical Haunts, this is Paige. How can I help you?"

"Hey, I'm so glad you answered. My name is Eleanor Doolittle, and I'd like to schedule a tour." I sucked in a breath at the sound of my cousin Eliza's cheeky voice and use of her code name. After trying and failing to reach her on the burner number she left me the other day, I'd worried she might be in big trouble or completely incommunicado for the duration of her investigation. "A private tour is what I'm looking for."

"Uh, sure," I said, playing along. Hudson looked on with a quizzical expression. "When did you have in mind?"

"You still do swamp tours, don't you?" she asked.

"No. We've never done swamp tours. Just ghost, vampire and cemetery. We don't have any boats."

"Oh, don't worry about a boat. I've got that part covered. I just need a guide to accompany me and give me some information. Think you could handle that?"

"Okaaaay. And do you have more information too?"

"Mmm hmm. Are you free Wednesday, say 3pm?"

I checked my schedule. "Yep."

"Good. Meet me at the swamp docks out in Lafitte. And one more thing?"

"Yeah?"

"Remember, they're watching."

✦▲✦▲✦

AFTER I'D FINALLY FINISHED my shift, I checked in with Bridget and Ines to let them know I was heading home. Though we kept different schedules, we still tried to eat dinner together at least a few times a week. Tonight was Ines's turn to cook, and she was making her famous veggie lasagna with zucchini slices stacked where the noodles would normally go.

I was still stewing over Hudson's suspicion of Ben and Mina when I walked in the door. He'd pointed out that I always thought the best of people and shouldn't let a good first impression cloud my judgment without evidence to rule Austin's friends out.

To make matters worse, Magnolia had even taken his side on this point. At least partly, with a directive to use my instincts but always stay open to new information. What the heck did they think I was going to do? I bristled. And there was no way I was dismissing my desire to see the best in people as naiveté. Even with everything that happened with Hudson, even if I got hurt again because of it, I refused to turn cynical.

I toed off my shoes by the front door. The delicious scent of tomato sauce and bubbling ricotta, mozzarella, and Parmesan wafted from the kitchen, taking the edge off my frustration.

"That smells incredible," I called with a groan. Ines loved to cook. It was a treasured pastime she used to do with her grandma before the Alzheimer's had gotten bad this past year.

Ines smiled back at me after checking the oven. She'd tied

her curly brown hair back in a ponytail, and her grandmother's faded apron circled her waist. "Just a few more minutes. I'm going to broil the cheese on the top."

"I'll grab Bridge and Auguste and be right back to set the table."

⋅▲⋅▲⋅▲⋅

A FEW MINUTES LATER, I trotted us downstairs, Auguste in his snuggle sack and his exercise ball tucked under my arm. I'd filled him in on my meet up with Ben and Mina, along with Hudson's and Magnolia's thoughts.

"What do you think, my wise quilly friend?"

"I am famished. I will have much better input after I have had some nourishment."

"Fair enough. I think better on a full stomach too. Apples and bugs?"

"Most excellent."

Then we walked into the dining room.

"Whoa, what is all this?" I gawped and burst into laughter at the sight of a whole bakery's worth of bread overflowing from the biggest basket I'd ever seen on our dining table.

"It's like the miracle of the loaves and fishes in here," Bridget added. She shook the sawdust from her current project out of her hair and set her safety goggles on the counter.

I touched one of the many baguettes and caught sight of at least five other kinds of yeasty goodness: round boules, cranberry orange loaves, sourdough, pretzel bread and—

"Ooh, did you make challah too?" Bridget asked. Ines nodded, and Bridget pulled up a shiny braided loaf. "Think this will keep until the weekend? I can make us some challah French toast Saturday morning."

I tore off a hunk of sourdough and gave Ines a wry smile. "I take it bread making class went well?"

"Obviously," she said.

"Did you make all these in one class?"

"No." She shook her head and brought the cheesy dish out of the oven. "Sam and I only made five loaves, but other people weren't taking theirs home."

"How come?" I asked.

"I don't know. Maybe they were just there for the experience? The couple next to us said they don't eat carbs."

"*You* barely eat carbs," I pointed out.

"I know, but they were just going to throw them away."

Her abject horror at the prospect of so much waste sent my lips twitching into a smile.

"Blasphemy," I said.

"I know. We took the other half to the food bank already, so eat up."

I laughed and maneuvered three plates between the loaves. I got Auguste situated with his dinner on the ground.

I googled whether hedgehogs could eat bread to see if Auguste could share in the bounty, but found that alas, bread was not a recommended part of hedgie eating regimen.

We settled into dinner and conversation, with Ines regaling us about her bread class and Bridget about her latest project.

"And speaking of projects, I finally finished your late birthday present, so I can show you after dinner," Bridget said. Her brown eyes gleamed.

"I can't wait."

All three of us filled with delicious veggies and bread, we lapsed into silence.

"You've been quiet this evening," Bridget said.

"You have." Ines punctuated the thought with a poke of her fork.

"How's the sleuthing going?" Bridget asked.

"And are you finally ready to spill about whatever you've been holding in?" Ines said.

My heart stuttered a beat. I so very much wanted to tell them everything and have them help me make sense of it all. Ghosts. Ghost Grandmothers. Auguste's recent interest in elocution. Hudson. We were each other's sounding boards and confidantes. Would everything change if I sprung the supernatural on them? Talking about any of it felt like a minefield with everything I'd have to leave out.

"It's been intense," I said finally. I gave them as much of the mundane, human-world details as I dared, treading carefully around mentions of my other-worldly helpers and client. Every evaded detail jabbed into me like a million tiny knives. I hated lying to my friends. But then there was something I'd been holding back that I needed to share. Here went nothing.

"And one more thing," I added, knowing this would be a bombshell. "Hudson's back."

THIRTY-FOUR

"He's back?!"

"He's *back* back?"

"Where did you see him?"

"Did he say why he left?"

"That dingus. Do you still want us to leave Legos on his floor?"

After a beat of silence, Ines and Bridget's questions about my disappearing, reappearing ex came at me rapid fire. We took the conversation to the living room, and I sunk into my favorite squashy turquoise chair.

"As it turns out, he left me to run away with the circus and is now a sort of private investigator," I said.

Ines and Bridget shared an incredulous look, and both blinked at me.

Then Ines leaned forward, knocking a mini loaf off the table. "Wait, are you saying Hudson was the PI that was supposed to be your mentor on this case?"

"He didn't know it was me until our meeting."

"Whoa."

"Yeah."

I told them about our awkward reunion at Miss Peacock's and how we'd decided to work together, on this case only, given the circumstances.

"I hope he apologized for totally ghosting all of us four years ago." Bridget folded her arms over her chest.

Auguste made a noise of agreement from his exercise ball.

"He did."

"How are you feeling about all this?" Bridget's voice gentled. "That must've been really hard to see him out of the blue like that."

I flopped my head back on the cushion and sighed. "I don't know. It's so weird being around him again. There are these time warp moments when it's like nothing's changed. But of course, everything's changed. Him being here reminds me how much I doubted and blamed myself for his leaving. It's dredging up all my insecurities."

"Nothing he did was your fault," Ines said.

"You have a big heart. And that's a strength, not a weakness. Don't you ever let anyone tell you otherwise," Bridget added.

I sniffed and gave her a watery smile.

"Did he ever say why he left?" Ines asked.

"He's been elusive about it, but I think it has something to do with this case we're working. Something about the Enclave."

Ines let out a low whistle.

"You think they threatened him, and he booked it?" Bridget asked.

"Maybe. But what I don't get is why he got mixed up with them in the first place."

"And why he didn't tell you about it," Ines added, echoing my next thought.

Auguste scampered his exercise ball up to me, and I picked

him up for a snuggle. Maybe he sensed I needed it. I was such an open book with the people closest to me. It made little sense to me why someone would keep something that big to themselves. Unless we weren't as close as I thought.

"Yeah," I said around the lump in my throat.

But after the last few days and all I'd held back from Bridget and Ines—maybe I could see the other side a little. Maybe there were legit reasons for selective sharing. Not that it erased the nearly four years of pain and wondering.

After sitting in silence, Bridget changed the subject.

"I think it's time for your birthday present." She hopped up and walked to the wall between our twin bookshelves, painted peacock blue with a single painting in a gold picture frame.

The dark cloud over me lifted at the sight of Bridget's face, lit with excitement.

"Ta da." Bridget held her hands out, showroom model style.

I raised an eyebrow at her and studied the wall. No sign of one of Bridget's new gadgets. I walked over, scanning for anything out of the ordinary, but only came up with the same painting of the night sky done in golds and blues that had always been there.

"What am I missing?" I asked.

"Push." Bridget's eyes glittered in anticipation.

"Push what?"

"The wall."

Behind me, Ines bounced on her toes. Clearly, she was in on this too.

I pressed my palms flat against the wall under the painting and pushed.

It *moved*.

To my delight, the entire wall pressed back and clicked onto a secret track.

"Now move it sideways," Bridget instructed. I pushed it to the left and the wall that Bridget had transformed into a sliding door glided away, leaving a pass through to the closet in the extra bedroom.

I stepped inside, squealing in delight. "You made me a secret passageway?"

"I figured you needed a proper mysterious hidey hole."

Bridget beamed, and I pulled her into a hug. "This is the best birthday present ever."

I knelt down and prodded at the mechanism that allowed the door to open. "How does it work? Can you open it from the other side too?"

Bridget demonstrated again how the tracks worked.

"This is genius, Bridge. Your viewers are going to go nuts over this."

"I hope so. Will you pretend to be surprised again for the official video?"

"Of course." A stray hammer lay on the other side of the door. I scooped it up, and something Mina said came back to me. That the weapon had been dropped at an odd place, away from the group and the exit.

But what if it was in front of an exit, after all? Just not an obvious one.

I had to check this out.

I looked from Bridget to Ines. "Who wants to explore a secret underground tunnel with me?"

⋆▲⋆▲⋆▲⋆

OUTFITTED IN MY HIKING BOOTS, yoga pants, and pink moisture-wicking top for our later underground adventures, I gathered up the basket of bread and headed into Declan's precinct to have a little chat and see if I could get him to back me up tomorrow night for my rendezvous with Roman and the others.

"I'll just be a minute," I told Bridget, who'd leaped at the chance to explore secret underground tunnels.

"I'll keep Auguste company in here," she said.

Ines had called dibs on tech duty, and was currently hacking into any CCTV cameras that might catch us outside the entrance to the tunnels. At the front counter, I asked, "Is Officer Durocher here? I need to talk to him about a case."

The man at reception, a grandfatherly type with a fisherman's sweater over his uniform, smiled at me. "Baked goods?" I offered up my stash, and he grabbed a demi loaf before alerting Declan over the intercom.

A few minutes later, Declan strolled up, uniform perfectly pressed, eying me suspiciously all the way.

"I come bearing gifts." I held up my treasure trove of baked goods.

"Good ones too," the gentleman at reception added.

"Is that pretzel bread I smell?" Declan lifted the towel from the basket and breathed in.

"Mmm hmm. There's a challah loaf in there too." I beamed and thrust the basket his way. "Freshly baked. Well, baked last night. Ines took a bread making class and made a whole bakery's worth. I thought, who better to share our abundance with than our favorite local law enforcement officers."

He accepted the bread and tore into a pretzel twist with an appreciative groan. "I appreciate the treats, squirt, but this doesn't mean I can share confidential details about my homicide cases," he said around a mouthful.

"What's this about freshly baked bread?" Officer Crowder, the one who had been so mean to Liz, stepped around the corner. He looked down his nose at me, and his face twisted into a sneer. "Oh, it's you."

Ugh, no baguette for him.

"I know. I know. But can I talk to you outside? Or in your office or something?"

Declan cocked an eyebrow. "Everything okay?"

"It's about some of the names I shared the other night. There's been a development you should know about."

⋆▲⋆▲⋆▲⋆

"YOU DID *WHAT?*" Declan asked when I filled him in on accepting Roman's invitation for the next night and my suspicion it might be an Enclave recruiting event. His eyebrows drew in so much that they seemed poised to shoot daggers at me.

"I said I'd go. It seemed like an excellent opportunity to get more information. See if he'll talk about the Enclave and their illegal activities. Did you run down the other names I gave you?"

"Yes."

"And?"

"They were helpful. Don't change the subject. Dangling yourself as bait for the Enclave is not my idea of staying out of things."

"That's why I came to you," I said. "I thought maybe I could wear a wire, get some information that would help build a case, and you could be there to intervene in case anything untoward happens."

"Anything untoward?" The cleft in Declan's chin dimpled, and a bit of his humor returned.

I nodded and batted my eyelashes, pulling my shoulders back in perfect posture like a demure, pearl-wearing debutante.

Declan shook his head with an exasperated laugh. "Right. You've set up a date with a murder suspect, but wouldn't want to upset your delicate sensibilities. You're something else. All right, fine. But if this turns into me using police resources to spy on a perfectly innocent attempt at a first date or something, we're going to have words."

"Great. And about those suspects..."

THIRTY-FIVE

And that's how I ended up in a secret tunnel underneath the old Ursuline Convent. Which may or may not be surveilled by the Enclave.

"All clear," Ines announced over the phone, and Bridget, Auguste, and I made a run for it.

Bridget had suited up in full Lara Croft gear, in a costume she'd made for her YouTube channel last year. Khaki pants, a tank top, boots. She rounded out the look with a tool belt and its full complement of hiking and exploration materials, including a whip—just in case we had to jump across a pit with spikes or snakes. "Hey it could happen," she said. She'd even braided her hair in the car, waiting for me to talk to Declan.

We didn't stick out or anything.

The three of us high-tailed it to where I thought the door would be, according to Austin's details.

"I've hacked into the cameras, and I'm going to loop the same footage of no one coming or going while you guys get in the door," Ines said.

"Great, and Hudson should be right behind us."

I'd debated whether to call him in on this, especially since there might be some tension between him and Bridget, but ultimately decided it would be better to have backup. There was still a chance that the Enclave had a tail on me.

Even though I'd expected it to be there, the sight of a trap door pull behind an overgrown bush in the shadows sent a thrill through me.

"You want to do the honors?" I asked Bridget.

She slipped her fingerless-gloved hand through the iron circle and pulled. The smell of damp earth wafted up to greet us. My flashlight illuminated a steep set of stairs. How many generations of Enclave members had descended this tunnel? And how many had never come back?

Hudson jogged up in full black, probably far more appropriate for sneaking around. His dimple popped out upon surveying us.

We exchanged hellos, and he gave Bridget a sheepish smile. "Hey Bridget. Nice to see you again."

Bridget's entire demeanor iced. "Hudson."

Oh boy.

When Bridget whipped out the one-word responses, you knew you were in trouble.

I tried to ignore the strain between them and refocus on the task at hand.

"Should we—?" I nodded at the stairway.

"Yeah." Both Hudson and Bridget said at the same time.

Bridget frowned.

The stairs creaked under our weight, and the tunnel below stretched out before us at the bottom. Hudson took the lead, and I put myself between him and Bridget.

"This must go on for miles," I said with wonder in my voice. Hudson's flashlight illuminated the arched stone walls. Some of them crumbled where roots poked their way through, trailing twists of green. My hand brushed the spongy moss that covered the stone bricks, and I shivered. The musty smell of dust and growing things seeped into my pores.

"This reminds me of a crypt," Hudson said.

"How is this even here after Katrina? Wouldn't it have flooded?" Bridget said.

"Perhaps the same magic that gives the Enclave their powers is at work?" Auguste suggested.

"Good call," I said.

"What was that?" Bridget asked.

"Sorry, just talking to myself. Maybe it's the same magic that gives the Enclave its powers."

"Passing my ideas off as your own, I see," Auguste said.

"At least, that's what Auguste thinks." I scratched his head.

He sniffed appreciatively.

"So, I see you've branched out into cosplay," Hudson said to Bridget. In the past, the two had bonded over their shared love of making things.

"Is that a problem?" she shot back.

I elbowed Bridget. I knew she was just being protective of me, but none of us needed the friendly fire with the Enclave potentially on our trail.

"Yes. I've been doing cosplay."

"I've watched some of your videos," Hudson said. "They're really great. My favorite was the Baker Street bookshelf thing."

Bridget thawed a little at this. "You still doing your mosaics?"

"Mostly cross stitch and wood carving lately."

They continued in a tentative, slightly awkward chatter until we came to a door.

It was massive and carved out of what looked like a single slab of stone. About eye-level, a gargoyle knocker with a ring in its mouth stared us down.

Farther in the tunnel, the path forked into multiple paths.

"What's this?" Bridget ran a hand over a circular stone set into the wall flanking the door. Separated into four quadrants, with a gargoyle carved into each, it also had three holes that reminded me of the ones in a bowling ball.

I shrugged. The whole thing had a ceremonial gravitas to it. It almost made me want to do the Nu Omega secret knock we used for ceremonies in college.

Maybe Hudson had the same impulse because he lifted the ring and knocked twice.

The echo jangled my nerves. "I don't think we need to announce ourselves."

To my surprise, the handle turned easily, and the door opened on the first push.

I stepped into the complete darkness of the room within, Hudson close behind. Stone and dust clogged my nostrils. Something skittered in the dark.

"Hang on, I think this gargoyle panel turns," Bridget said. "Let's see what it does."

I tensed and rubbed at the goosebumps on my arms, thinking of all the adventure movies I'd watched. Throwing switches always unleashed terrible things.

"I hope it doesn't release the poison darts or alligators." Though I tried to keep my voice light, it betrayed me by jumping an octave at the end. I gripped my flashlight with trembling hands.

Hudson's hand warmed the small of my back, steadying me. Then, abruptly, he pulled away.

"Sorry. I... muscle memory, I guess," he said.

"It's okay."

A sound from outside clicked, and a ring of torches cast the room in a ghoulish glow.

"Yessss," Bridget exclaimed.

A circular room took shape in the flickering light. Stone

steps led up to a dais at the center. A dark spot at the bottom of the steps caught my attention. All the hairs on the back of my neck stood on end.

"This is it," Hudson said, eyes fixed on the same dark spot.

"This is where Austin died," I said.

Bridget propped the door open with her coil of rope, just in case, and I pulled out Ben's map and spun around until properly oriented.

"If the door is there, then the tablet with the countdown would've been there. And the candlestick would've been dropped there." I approached the wall with a shiver of anticipation.

I wiggled my fingers and pushed the stone, waiting for it to reveal its secrets.

Nothing happened.

I frowned. "I was so sure..."

"We knew this was a possibility," Hudson said. "Austin's friends already tried, and they were highly motivated."

"I know, but they were looking for handles or cracks, not a spring mechanism like in the one Bridget made for me. That requires a different kind of pressure."

Hudson pressed the stones again. "Let's try all the walls, then. Maybe the murderer dropped the candlestick on the way to a door further off."

The three of us tried every section and reconvened. I heaved a defeated sigh. "Dang it. What are we missing?"

"Hmmm," Auguste said from his snuggle sack.

"What?" I whispered.

"It may be nothing, but did you not say it was dark when the terrible deed was done? Perhaps—"

"Yes! The lights were out when everything went down. Bridget, can you do your thing with the light switch again?"

Hudson raised an eyebrow at me.

"It might be a long shot," I said.

His gaze softened, his hazel eyes holding mine. "I have a soft spot for long shots."

The torches snuffed out, plunging us into darkness again.

I clicked my flashlight on and moved back to the section of wall where the candlestick had been dropped.

"On three?" Hudson asked.

I nodded. "One. Two—"

Click.

With a snick, a catch released. The stone wall budged, rock crumbling from its edges. Just like my very own secret hideaway door, this one popped out and, with minimal coaxing, slid open a crack.

Hudson and I shared a wide-eyed look, smiles splitting both of our faces.

I shined my flashlight inside and gasped.

⁘👻⁘👻⁘👻⁘

ANOTHER SECRET ROOM materialized before our eyes.

Ancient and crumbling, this place looked like it was at least a hundred years older than the previous room. Remnants of stone crumbled all around us as we crossed the threshold.

I brushed the dust from my hair and marveled at the tomb-like space. With its central platform ringed by amphitheater style seating, it reminded me of a macabre theater in the round. Four stone walkways emanated from the stage at the center in the shape of an X. My mind conjured images of robed figures chanting in Latin in the candlelight.

"This must be where they hold their rituals," Bridget murmured. "This is so cool."

I turned back to see Hudson's gaze fixed on the stone table

in the middle of the stage. A haunted pallor shrouded his face, like this place was a nightmare made real.

Before I could stop myself, I placed a hand on his arm. "You okay?"

Holding my gaze seemed to snap him out of his stupor, but only for a moment. "Let's just get this over with." His jaw ticked, but he nodded at the path to the altar.

We followed the stone walkway, our footsteps shushing along the ground. I was afraid to look too closely at the waist-high stone slab at the center of it all. Latin words carved rings around another gargoyle symbol at the foot of the altar. "Jus nostrum. Ordo noster," I read.

Bridget whipped out her phone and consulted a translator app. "That means ours by right. Ours by rite."

My stomach swooped.

"These secret society people sound delightful," Bridget said.

At the head of the rectangular slab—*the perfect size for a body*, I noted with a chill—and at the midpoint, runnels were carved into the stone, continuing a downward path to the foot of the stone table and around the dais in circles.

Dark stains marred the grooves of each runnel.

"Is that—?" Bridget peered over, making a face.

"Blood?" I said. "Yeah, I think so."

Hudson had knelt at the foot of the slab. He traced words carved into the stone, his face collapsing.

"What is it?" I asked.

When I crouched beside him, I saw that not more words, but names circled the whole of the platform. "Bill Hoster. Zacharias Stone. Phineas Astor," I read. A year accompanied each name.

"Names of the sacrifices?" I wondered aloud, but what else could they be.

"This Latin part at the beginning of the names means 'for the good of all,'" Bridget said.

"I doubt the people on this stone table thought this was very good," I said.

I studied the pattern of the years that followed the names. Three years, then four, then three again, just like Mina had said and Eliza suspected. I blew out a breath. It was one thing to speculate about secret societies, but another entirely to see written proof of their dark deeds.

Hudson followed the list around the to the more recent ones and crouched down again. His jaw twitched, and pain flashed in his eyes. My gaze flickered to the last name on the list: Clarissa James, with the entry dated four years earlier. The name didn't ring a bell as anyone I'd ever heard Hudson mention. At least, no one I'd known. And I tend to be in everyone's business. "Who—?" I started.

His throat bobbed, but he only stood and said, "We should photograph these. Give them to your police officer."

I studied him for a beat, giving him space to share if he needed to, but he didn't.

"Good idea," I said finally, pulling out my phone. "These will help Eliza with her exposé too."

THIRTY-SIX

The next day at work, I couldn't stop thinking about the way Hudson's face had looked, landing on that final name in the ritual room. It was like that name had broken him. The fate of each of those listed represented a tragedy, but this had the air of something personal. Who was Clarissa, and why had she affected him so much? So much that he'd leave the way he did.

I really hoped to get in a morning yoga session to clear my mind and work through my thoughts, but our late night exploring and the events of the past few days had caught up with me and I'd barely made it to work on time. Plus, I needed to be rested tonight for whatever might go down at Roman's. Hopefully, this would get me some answers or get me closer to them. After this case, I might need to sleep for a week.

I checked in a few more people for a cemetery tour when, speak of the devil, my phone buzzed with a text from Roman.

Can't wait to see you tonight and introduce you to my friends. I've got a bottle of Taittinger with your name on it.

Sounds great, I texted back.

"What's got you so pensive? That's supposed to be my look."

I jumped and fumbled my phone. When I looked up, Austin hovered in front of the display of smudge sticks.

I flicked a glance around. "Besides seeing a ritual sacrifice chamber and possibly being recruited as its next occupant?"

"You found the room?" Austin's fingers flew to his parted lips.

I nodded and caught him up on everything we'd learned last night.

"So, if I was the sacrifice, why not take my body directly there, especially if it was right next door? I'm beginning to think my murderer was not so crafty."

"That's the question, isn't it?" I said. "Maybe it had to be a certain day for the ritual to work, so they had to put you on ice until then."

"I guess that could be," Austin said.

"What I keep getting stuck on today is where did they bring your body out? Did they use the same way that we got in? It seems like carrying you out and then into Crumbles would've caught somebody's notice. I wonder if they took another way out and where those other tunnels lead."

"Should we check it out?" Austin asked.

I bit my thumbnail. "You never used the other tunnels?"

Austin shook his head.

"I'm off in an hour, after I check in the group for the sensory-friendly tour. I might cut it a little close with exploring and getting to Roman's for the party tonight, but we could probably make it."

"Just you and me, or are we calling for back-up?" Austin asked.

I twisted my lips to the side.

"I was going to save my Magnolia and Moisha time for the

party tonight." As impatient as I was to just check it out myself, I also didn't want to get ambushed and end up strapped to the ritual table before I even got a chance to be recruited.

"I'll see if Hudson can meet us too."

•▲•▲•▲•

AN HOUR and some change later, Hudson and I shined our flashlights down the forking paths of the underground tunnel. Austin floated along behind.

The cool damp air below ground provided a welcome relief from the June humidity. My lemon-yellow swing dress stuck to my back.

"Can you see in the dark now that you're a ghost?" I asked.

"I don't know. I never thought to check," Austin said. "Turn off your lights."

We did, and Hudson's arm brushed mine in the dark. Goosebumps trailed down my flesh.

"Okay, that's cool," Austin said. "I can see a little better than before, but not totally. Like night vision goggles."

"Should we split up and cover more ground?" Hudson asked.

My entire body tightened at the suggestion of going it alone.

Austin took one look at me and floated toward the right-hand fork. "How about I take this way and you two see what's down that way? I can cover the ground faster and meet back up with y'all."

I gave him a grateful smile, and Hudson held out a hand for me to take the lead on the left. Ivy grew through the stone walls the farther we got in and soon covered most of the floor.

A few paces in, Hudson pulled me back and swiped a spiderweb I would've face-planted into out of the way.

"Thanks," I said.

"Why don't I go first?" Hudson said.

"To slay all the beasties that await before they can get me?"

"Something like that."

A tension crackled between the two of us ever since he'd touched my back last night. He'd offered the comfort I needed at just the right moment. It put me off guard. I was still trying to get my bearings in this new normal between us.

"I'm glad you called me," Hudson said.

"You mean you're glad I didn't go rogue on this?" I asked, but my tone stayed playful.

"That too." He smiled back at me, full dimpled.

"Do these leaves look trampled here to you?" I shined my light on a muddy section of greenery.

"Yeah, I think you're right. Good eye."

"Thanks."

We walked on in companionable silence, noting other traces of foot traffic through the tunnel.

"I didn't know you read my Grandma Magnolia's books." I'd been ruminating on all the details of her mysteries he'd pulled out during their first meeting at our stakeout. "You never did back when we were together."

Hudson scrubbed the back of his hair, a nervous tick. "I got lonely out on the road. They reminded me of home."

Home. The place it had felt like whenever we were together. An imaginary knife dragged down the center of the scar on my heart.

The image of him the night before, face crumbling at the sight of the name on the altar, flashed through my mind again.

"Hudson, who was Clarissa?"

Hudson sucked in a big breath and released it. "Do you remember me talking about Trenton James?"

"The other fiddle player in your band as a kid?"

He nodded. With all the stage kids thrust into the spotlight fast and furious before they'd even hit puberty, they'd become like family to each other.

"His mom was the art therapist who helped you, right?"

"Yeah." Although Hudson wasn't officially diagnosed with anxiety until later, it often left him devastated as a child performer. Trenton's mom, a child psychologist, worked backstage with Trenton's twin who had similar symptoms. She'd also picked up on Hudson's struggles with anxiety and sensory integration and introduced him to art therapy. Her influence had been profound enough to inspire him to help children the same way as his future career.

"Clarissa was his sister. She was a year older than him."

I blew out a breath.

Whoa. No wonder this had affected him the way it had.

"Trenton called me worried about something she was getting into. She was a thrill seeker, and he thought she was way too trusting. She'd even mentioned the Enclave. When she stopped returning his calls, he asked me to check in on her and help her get out of whatever she'd gotten mixed up in."

"What happened?"

"I asked too many questions. And even then, I was too late."

We trekked in silence, footsteps crunching ivy the only sound.

"I'm so sorry, Hudson."

"It's not your fault."

Although he still sounded defeated, I got the impression saying all this out loud lifted a part of the burden he'd been carrying alone for so long.

"Why didn't you tell me back then? I could've helped, or I don't know, something."

"He made me promise not to get anyone I cared about involved. And good thing too because—"

"Hey, is that a footprint?" Austin returned at that moment,

practically scaring me to death, and pointed to the rounded triangle shape in front of a small square in a rare piece of ground not covered by ivy.

"It looks like the print of a high-heeled shoe," I said. "Maybe Carlie or Mina came this way? Or some other high-heel wearing Enclave member."

"The leaves are mashed down up here too," Hudson said.

I examined the spot he pointed to—an indent about six feet from end to end and a couple of feet wide.

"Maybe whoever carried your body this way needed a rest," Hudson said.

Austin stared at the ground, his features scrunching together.

"What was at the end of the other tunnel?" I asked.

"It came out into a mausoleum inside a cemetery. Couldn't tell which one."

I shivered again.

"Easy access to dispose of sacrifices, I guess," Hudson said.

"Which begs the question again—how did your body get pushed off the balcony at Crumbles? Who stood to gain from that?" I said.

"Enclave people who wanted the rogues that set this up punished for their disobedience?" Austin speculated.

"Or the person who orchestrated it is a psychopath who secretly wanted credit for their crime," Hudson said.

I wasn't so sure. With a glance at the time on my phone, I said, "I'm going to have to head back and get ready for Roman's soirée. Declan wants to meet up beforehand to fit me with a wire."

"Let me float up ahead and see where this one leads," Austin said.

He returned moments later, white as well—a ghost. And shaken too.

"You guys have got to see this."

•♠•♠•♠•

BY THE TIME Hudson and I reached the wooden door where the tunnel ended, both of us were out of breath from jogging to catch up with Austin.

With a shaking hand, I opened it and stepped inside a narrow room. Hudson crowded in behind me. There wasn't much more to it than a pass-through and set of stairs leading to an upper floor.

Muffled voices and street traffic drifted from somewhere beyond.

Hudson leaned his ear to the outer wall. "Is that—?"

"I think we're at street-level again," I said. "Probably still somewhere in the Quarter."

Austin loomed from the top of the stairs, waving us on.

Hudson's arm brushed mine in our clamor up the stairs. A jolt of heat shot through me, further muddying my already confused feelings about him.

A small room with dingy wall paper that looked at least a hundred years old greeted us at the top of the steps.

A coating of dust furred every surface in sight. Not much to see up here besides piles of musty boxes, a single door and—

Hudson lifted the lid of what looked like an industrial freezer. Clusters of ice lined the corners. He sniffed the inside. "Looks fresh. No freezer burn in here."

Discarded plastic bags with *Ice* stamped on them littered the ground. I plucked a receipt from Tiki Tim's, the bar where Austin had worked, out of the detritus. "This yours?"

Austin's features clouded.

"This has to be where they kept you before you went over the balcony," I said. There had to be some other clues here.

I finally registered the familiar scent that wafted up: flour, sugar, butter. I leaped for the door, almost sure of what I'd find beyond.

Sure enough, on the other side, the door to the upstairs bathroom at Crumbles faced me, flanked on either side by the staircase and the balcony Austin had been heaved out of.

"How have I never noticed this door before?" I said.

Austin followed. "Looks like someone wallpapered over it."

"Wait a second. I think I found something else," Hudson said from inside the room. He pulled a metal object from under the freezer.

"What is that?"

He turned the silver links of a charm bracelet around in the beam of his flashlight. "It's one of the only things in the room not covered in dust. I'd say it's recent."

I squinted and made out a scales of justice charm. "Recognize this?" I asked Austin.

If I didn't think Austin could get any paler, I was mistaken. His stricken face flickered. He reached out as though he could touch the bracelet.

"That's Mina's."

THIRTY-SEVEN

"Just because we found her bracelet there doesn't mean she's your murderer," I reminded Austin for the eleventeenth time as I changed into my outfit for the party at Roman's tonight.

I stepped out from behind the screen and adjusted the skirt of my lilac dress, which floated out from my waist. A little bit sweet, a little bit sexy.

Austin flopped onto my bedspread next to Auguste and flung an arm over his face.

"I just can't believe it. I thought I knew her. I thought she was my friend."

"Which is why we're going to find out what really happened." I fluffed my hair and spritzed on some lavender and vanilla perfume.

"Was it all just a lie?"

"Hey." I sat next to him and softened my voice. "I've got the bracelet in my pocket. If Mina's there tonight, and I hope she will be, we can let her know I found this and see how she reacts. Someone could've planted it there. Maybe there's a perfectly reasonable explanation."

⁘▲⁘▲⁘▲⁘

NEXT, we headed to the rendezvous point to meet Hudson and Declan a few blocks away from Roman's home in Lakeview, one of the more affluent neighborhoods in New Orleans. Nerves swarmed my entire body. So much hinged on this meeting tonight. If I played my cards right, this could finally gain me the trust and access to the people who knew what really happened the night of Austin's murder. This could get him justice and clear Liz's name. I pictured my snarky, energetic former professor and how she'd been reduced to a ghost of herself under this suspicion and redoubled my resolve.

Austin remained distraught, so I peppered him with questions to keep his mind occupied.

"Have you ever been to Roman's?" I asked.

The homes grew larger and farther apart the closer we got.

"No. But I hear it's pretty over the top. Old money, but word is he'd been down on his luck recently. The vetting party I went to was at some dude named Caesar's."

"How'd you get invited?"

"My dad. At least, I assumed. Maybe hoped. His last olive branch to me, offering me a chance not to be a total failure."

I winced. Great, I'd unwittingly steered the conversation to another painful place for Austin.

Austin wrung his hands and looked ready to bolt. "I don't think I can see them tonight. I can't see Mina's face if she..." His throat bobbed. "I could really use some pie right now."

"I wish I could get you some." I reached out for him with a sad smile. He couldn't feel it, but I couldn't help wanting to offer comfort.

"Cherry would be nice right now. With some vanilla ice cream."

I smiled.

"Paige?"

"Yeah?"

"Do you think you could do this part on your own? I can meet up with you later."

His help would've been valuable snooping around Roman's and knowing how the parties went down, but I also saw how much anxiety it was causing him. "Of course."

"Thanks for helping me."

Austin's spirit dissipated just as Hudson pulled up in a white pickup truck with a ride share sticker in the window.

He stepped out of the driver's side door looking handsome in his dark washed jeans and cowboy boots. His curls hung wet around his face like he'd just gotten out of the shower, and I caught a whiff of his cedar woods scent.

He smiled up at me, and my insides did funny things. Oh boy.

Something had shifted between us last night when the truth about Clarissa and why Hudson had left came out. Neither time nor the truth had healed all wounds, but some of the toxic parts had been flushed out. Not that I was looking to jump back into a romantic relationship with him, but regardless, his presence still made my stomach fizz. But I felt like we'd laid a foundation where we could have each other's backs as coworkers or friends.

Seeing him tonight also produced a tentative sense of relief.

"Hey," I said, striding over. His hazel eyes looked back at me with reverence despite the worry line between his brows.

"Hey. You look nice," he said.

"Thanks. Got to look the part."

We did the awkward thing—standing there, not sure if we should hug.

"We can still pull back and try another angle if you want to change your mind," Hudson said.

I shook my head. "We'd be missing a prime opportunity."

The crease between his brows deepened.

"Were you hoping I'd changed my mind?"

"Not to be the over-protective mentor, but maybe a little."

"I can handle myself, you know."

"I do know. You're smart and brave and resourceful."

I puffed up at that.

"Doesn't mean I don't worry." I saw the weight of Clarissa's death in that hollow look of his.

I reached out and squeezed his hand, enjoying the feel of his callouses on my palm. "Good thing I've got a whole team looking out for me," I said. "Speaking of—" Declan's police cruiser pulled up to the curb. He held up a finger to signal that he'd be a minute and answered a call.

Magnolia and Moisha joined us at that moment, Magnolia with a chiffon pinch-waisted dress and her always impeccable victory rolls and Moisha with her delightfully over-sized cardigan and trousers.

"Hello, darling. Hello Hudson." Magnolia's gaze moved to our joined hands and the corner of her mouth lifted in an approving smile.

I pulled away and the rest of us exchanged hellos.

"What's the scoop?" Moisha asked.

"We'll head over to Roman's for the recruiting party as soon as Declan's ready. I'll need your help to scope out the place— looking around for the other acolytes and to see if there are any conversations I shouldn't miss. I'm glad you got here when you did. Declan's going to fit me with a recording device, so I won't be able to talk to you much inside without raising suspicions."

Magnolia gave a salute.

"Is Declan your handsome officer friend?" Moisha asked.

Hudson grimaced but recovered quickly.

"That's him over there," I answered rather than stirring the pot, as much as that would have delighted Moisha from the looks of it.

She floated closer to the cruiser. "He *is* handsome. Hello, Officer Durocher. You could cut brie on a chiseled jaw like that."

Magnolia rolled her eyes but smiled, and I barked a laugh.

"How did it go with Carlie at the yoga studio today?" I asked Hudson. "How'd she seem?"

"Oh yes, do tell," Magnolia said.

"I still have a bad feeling about that one," Moisha added.

My eyebrow winged up, and I made a mental note to probe her more about that later.

"She was on edge for sure," Hudson said. "When I saw her through the window, she had this glassy look in her eyes, like she was some place else. Dark circles again too. I don't think she's been sleeping much."

I nodded.

"Then when I came in, she perked up, but in a sort of manic, overly caffeinated way. When I said I was thinking of taking up yoga, she went into" — his eyes darted to mine — "uh, flirtatious mode."

Magnolia nodded sagely. "Lots of batting her eyelashes?"

Red colored Hudson's cheeks, probably at admitting this to my great grandmother. "More like bending over more than strictly necessary."

"Well, well," Magnolia said as though she'd uncovered a new anthropological gem about the kids these days. "It is a new era. Is this a common flirting technique in the modern age? Do you employ this too, Paige?"

My cheeks flamed. "How about we get back to the details of the investigation?"

"You'll fill us in later, right?" Moisha whispered.

I laughed. "Sure."

Hudson and I shared an amused look.

"Anyway, I told her I was there because my therapist said yoga and meditation might be helpful after trauma and asked what she thought," Hudson said.

"Good one," I said. "How did she react?"

"She said, 'Oh yeah, for sure. But there are some things no amount of yoga and meditation can cure.'"

Magnolia and I shared a look.

"Then she zoned out like she was dissociating."

I frowned. "Could be the psychological effects of witnessing a murder."

"Or committing one," Moisha added.

"When I told her that my friend Austin had recommended this place, she shut down. She threw me a towel, told me to enjoy a free class, and booked it behind a locked door."

"Hmmm. I wonder how she'll be tonight," I said.

Moisha's gaze darted away. "Time to wrap up. Here comes Officer Handsome."

Hudson's eyebrows drew together ever so slightly at the sight of Declan.

"I think I detect a hint of jealousy," Magnolia whispered.

I suppressed a smile at her gossipy tone and relish in meddling in my non-existent love life.

Though Declan looked as hot and delicious as one of Liz's pies straight from the oven, not to mention being smart and honorable, he was also less than a year out from his divorce. Not to mention that he had two kids, while I was still figuring everything out. Sure, there were some sparks, and I enjoyed our banter, but we weren't exactly at the same stage.

I eyed Hudson for a moment with his body angled protectively toward me, the square of his jaw and that dimple in the cleft of his chin. Something familiar stirred. Did I *want* him to be jealous?

I shoved that question far to the back of my mind, as it deserved to be.

"Hey, squirt." Declan flashed his dazzling smile, and Moisha fanned herself.

I cracked a grin.

"You ready to go undercover?" he asked.

"Ready as I'll ever be."

"Who's your friend?" Declan had three or four inches on Hudson and looked down at him.

"This is Hudson. Hudson, Declan."

"That's Officer Durocher to you," Declan said, offering a hand to Hudson.

I choked on a laugh.

"Only joking. Declan's fine."

"Good to meet you," Hudson said, and then added, "Thanks for looking out for Paige."

Declan shot me a teasing grin. "She needs all the looking after she can get with what she gets up to."

"Hey!" I gave his arm a playful punch.

"Hey yourself, don't go assaulting an officer before we even get the evening started." Declan pulled a necklace from his pocket and looped it over my head. His fingers brushed my collarbone in the process. Different life circumstances aside, if he kept this up, I might need to fan myself too.

"This is your listening device. And just so you know, I'm sticking my neck out a bit being here. My commanding officer wasn't on board. He said it wasn't a credible lead. Nothing concrete linking Roman to Austin's murder."

Yikes. "Did you go against orders?" My mouth went dry at the thought of Declan getting himself in trouble with his superiors following me out on a limb.

"Not exactly. I think you're onto something here. Let's just hope for both of our sakes you are."

My stomach lurched. The additional pressure settled onto my shoulders like a sack of concrete.

Declan stepped away, and I pulled the necklace up to examine it.

"*This* is the necklace I'm supposed to wear?" I poked at the gaudy, faux black gem with bedazzled edges. The synthetic fiber cord slipped through my fingers.

"What's the matter, doesn't go with your outfit?" Declan smirked.

"I don't think this goes with any outfit."

"It's what we had on hand. Remember the part about sticking my neck out?" Declan said.

I nodded. "It's fine."

"If the sight of it offends you so much, you can tuck it into the top part of your dress."

I exhaled in relief when I had the ugly thing out of sight. "So how does this work?" Despite using Ines's bug just the other day, I wasn't sure they were all created equally or worked in the same ways.

"This is fitted with a receiver that'll pick up any conversations nearby. It's one-way, meaning I can hear everything you say or do, but you can't hear me. It's sound activated, so it'll deactivate if there's dead air."

"What about if I need help? Should I just say so, or do we need a code word?"

Declan shook his head and smiled. "You and your code words."

"What's wrong with code words?"

"Nothing."

Magnolia mused. "You should choose something that you wouldn't bring up in everyday conversation, but could sound natural if you did."

"How about if I say something about my Aunt Posey if I

need immediate help?"

"Do you have an Aunt Posey?"

"No."

"You're something else," Declan said, his grin widening.

Then another thought occurred to me. "Wait a second, you'll hear everything? What if I have to go to the bathroom? Isn't there an off switch?"

"It's not that sophisticated. Just play a song on your phone and set it on top or something," Declan said.

"But then you'll *know* when I'm going."

Declan cracked a smile. "Don't worry, we're all adults here."

I was definitely holding it until the end of the night.

THIRTY-EIGHT

"Now this is what I call a home," Moisha murmured, staring up at Roman's not-so-humble abode.

Through her ghostly body, which swept across the lawn, I took in the white pillars stretching up to the roof. Green as far as the eye could see flanked the path that wound up to his doorway. Magnolia swooped around one of many topiaries.

"Get a load of this pool," she said, hooking her thumb to the right. I veered off the path to follow her to a shallow reflecting pool where water festooned from stone fishes' mouths at orchestrated intervals.

"You couldn't even swim in here," Moisha said. "What good is a pool if you can't take a dip? This is like something out of Jay Gatsby's playbook."

"Yes, very West Egg," Magnolia said. "Or was East Egg the gaudy side?"

I shrugged. "I liked Matilda Mayhew a lot more than Daisy and Gatsby."

Magnolia gave me an indulgent smile. "Yes, well, you do have good taste. Runs in the family," she said.

Then I remembered the awful necklace wire. Ack, I had to watch what I said.

"How much do you think it costs to maintain all this? Just the lawn and pool care is probably more than my mortgage." At least this type of musing aloud would make sense, with Declan listening in.

"It would certainly take a lot to maintain," Magnolia said. "What did you say he does again?"

I pointed to the wire and mouthed, "Entrepreneur."

Magnolia nodded. "Must be a good one. Or living on family money."

An efficiently stylish woman of Asian descent greeted me at the door. She gripped a clipboard with one hand and smoothed her tailored skirt suit with the other. Was she one of the senior Enclave members? She didn't look too much older than me. Thirty-five or forty at the oldest.

"May I have your name, please?" she asked.

"Paige Harrington."

She scanned her list and ran a highlighter over my name. "So glad you could join us tonight. I'm Emily. Cell phone please." She held out a hand.

I frowned. "You need my phone?"

"Standard procedure at these events. Roman or one of our other associates may reveal things of a proprietary nature. We value discretion. Any recordings or photography are strictly prohibited."

The idea of not being able to get a message from Declan or Hudson if things went sour rattled me. "I'd rather keep this with me, thanks. You have my word I won't record or take pictures." I drew a cross over my heart.

Emily stepped forward to block my entrance. "I'm afraid I must insist. Our organization's policy is non negotiable. I assure you we'll take excellent care of any devices you have and see that they're returned to you at the end of the evening."

After the reluctant surrender of my connection to backup, I followed Magnolia and Moisha into the lavish receiving room. Light from the chandeliers twinkled on the polished parquet flooring. Other attendees looked up from their conversations to take my measure. How many were already members and how many were being vetted like I was? My stomach tightened, but I forced my shoulders back and chin high.

"Don't worry, darling. You are every bit as charming and valuable as any of these individuals," Magnolia said.

Meeting her eyes, I felt a pang of gratitude. Rather than the pressure and high expectations I felt from my parents, Magnolia had somehow decided I measured up from the word go. It was a wonderful feeling.

"Paige, so glad you're here." Roman appeared next to me on a breeze of expensive cologne and stole my attention. He leaned in and planted a kiss on each of my cheeks, European style. Tonight, he sported a flawless navy suit and the barest hint of roguish stubble on his light brown cheeks.

"Thanks for the invite. You officially have me intrigued," I said.

"Good." His eyes danced. "I need to grab something from the other room. Have some snacks. Make yourself comfortable. The cave aged gruyere is to die for."

I waited for Moisha to comment on his model-like looks, but she watched him ascend one of the grand staircases that spiraled up to the second floor with a sour expression. "That man thinks he's hot stuff."

"And you disagree?" I asked.

"I know a smooth-talking charlatan when I see one."

"What shall we do first?" Magnolia asked. "How about you

two get the lay of the land, and I'll follow Mr. Smooth to see if he's doing anything incriminating."

I nodded.

I worried that with Magnolia and Moisha tethered to me, they wouldn't be able to explore the way I'd hoped with the size of this place. I'd have to think of an excuse to poke around.

"You get some of that cave raised cheese, and I'll see if I can spot the other suspects," Moisha said.

I gave her another nod. Man, this was weird not to be able to talk back with the recording and all.

"Moscow mule?" A server asked, offering me one of the copper mugs on his tray.

I accepted and filled a small plate with cheese and fruit from the charcuterie spread, scoping out the room as I did so. Next to the grand piano, someone who looked like Carlie from the back turned around. Nope. Not Carlie, and I didn't see any of the others, at least not yet.

A few details piqued my interest. Number one: the crowd gathered was about 90 percent female and attractive. Not all too surprising if Roman was in charge of recruitment, but it did seem odd to me the Enclave didn't want to fill their ranks with more men, given the traditional faction still in control and the makeup of Austin's acolyte class.

Could it be there was only one vacant role to be filled—that of the sacrifice? If it was supposed to have been Carlie or Mina rather than Austin, would the leaders want a replacement of the same gender? Something to think about, anyway.

And detail number two: I'd expected attendees at a party looking for the next group of Enclave elites to be dressed in cocktail attire. Though some were, more than a handful sported designer athleisure wear and gave off more of a soccer mom than a secret society vibe.

A white woman with a lemon-yellow headband and a floral

sheath dress sampled some cheeses. "I guess if nothing else comes of this party, at least we get some good cheese out of it."

I laughed in agreement and imagined Austin drooling over the spread here. "Do you know much about what's going on here tonight?"

She shook her head. "You know Roman. He likes to keep the air of mystery around everything he does." She rolled her eyes. "He gave me some song and dance about an opportunity that I did not want to miss out on."

"Yeah, me too," I said. "Any guesses what the big opportunity is?"

"My bet's on an investment venture." The woman popped an olive in her mouth and flicked a glance behind us like she was self-conscious of being overheard. She bent closer and lowered her voice. "Either that or something to do with that secret society he's always hinting about."

The back of my neck tingled. She'd kept her tone just wry enough to pass it off as a joke if I laughed, but I had a hunch she was fishing for information like I was.

"Wouldn't that be something," I said.

I made a little more conversation, probing for any additional details, before Magnolia popped up next to me.

I nearly choked on a grape and stepped away from the cheese woman.

Magnolia whispered. "Roman went into a room upstairs. He acted very secretive about it all, looking around behind him before he went in. He locked the door when he came out too."

I started to ask her more, but stifled my questions on account of the wire tucked into my cleavage. Thankfully, Moisha joined us in time to hear Magnolia's account and asked for me. "Did you get inside?"

Magnolia shook her head. "I tried, but the tether pulled me back here. It looked like some kind of office or study. Do you think you could make an excuse to go upstairs, so we can check it out?"

I nodded and looked around for Roman. I spotted him near the piano talking to a group of elegant looking women.

"Any sign of the other suspects?" Magnolia asked as we headed his way.

Moisha shook her head. "Not a one."

I frowned. What did that mean?

"Maybe they're having a secret meeting elsewhere in the house before things get rolling?" Moisha continued. "And ladies, if you liked the fancy pool in the front yard, you should see the ones in the back. Mercy me."

Roman met my gaze and excused himself from his conversation.

"Paige, everything okay?"

I rubbed my temples and kept the frown on my face. "Yeah, I've just got a migraine coming on. I took some medicine, but do you have somewhere dark and quiet I could sit for a few minutes while it kicks in?"

Concern creased his brow. "Of course." He rested his hand on the small of my back and led me further into the house on the first level. Shoot.

I stopped walking.

"Do you think I could go somewhere farther away from the crowd? Upstairs maybe?"

His features tightened, but I gave him my best damsel in distress impression, and he crumbled. "Yeah, sure. You want some water or something while you wait?" He snagged a bottle from a mini fridge and offered it to me before leading me up the stairs.

THIRTY-NINE

"You're the best." I admired the carved wood banisters as we looped up the stairs. "These are beautiful."

"My parents had a master wood carver come over from Italy to do them," Roman said. "Their housewarming present to me."

"Wow," I said. "That's a really nice gift. I take it you're following in your parents' footsteps with your business ventures. Did I hear they were in textiles or something?"

Roman's smile faltered the tiniest bit. "Theirs are big footsteps to fill. My parents can be a tad intense."

"Yours too?" I said.

Roman unleashed one of his charming grins. "I knew we'd have much in common."

Magnolia floated ahead and pointed to the door Roman had locked earlier. I slowed in front of it. "That room's a mess. Make sure you don't go in there, or I'll never live down my terrible housekeeping. We'll put you in the home theater."

I followed Roman into the door just before his office. This would do nicely.

He flicked on the lights and dimmed them. In the low light, rows of posh reclining seats in black leather spread out before a theater-sized projection screen. A popcorn machine sat in one corner bookended by two mini fridges, one stocked with snacks and the other with drinks.

"Thank you. This is perfect," I said.

Roman gave me a dazzling smile. "I hope you feel better. I'd hate for you to miss what we have planned. Like I said the other night, you're exactly what I have in mind."

"Wouldn't dream of it. I'm sure I'll be fine in a few."

"This guy." Moisha rolled her eyes again and then floated in front of the giant screen. "Look at me. I'm in the movies."

"We haven't got much time. Let's go check out the study, movie queen," Magnolia said.

They popped through the wall, leaving me to wander the room. Everything here was tidy, not many personal touches or clues to glean, so I settled into a recliner in the middle row and thought about Roman's commentary on his parents.

If this house and his expression earlier were any sign, Roman felt the same pressure to keep up with his wealthy parents and their successful business endeavors as I did with my over-achieving ones.

It made me wonder if all human beings experienced this at some point: never feeling like we were good enough and forever competing with the phantom perfect versions of ourselves.

For me, this manifested in quitting my pursuits before I could fail and constantly bouncing to something new. For Roman, was it bankrupting himself to keep up appearances and relying on his place in the Enclave to deliver on future fortune and power? Even if it meant committing murder to hold on to it?

I leaned forward, and my heel connected with something under the recliner. I bent down and caught the edge of a manila envelope sticking out. It was about half an inch thick with no label on the outside. I grabbed it and glanced at the door before opening it.

My eyes bugged at the contents. Black and white photographs blown up to eight by tens of Austin and Ben looked back at me. In the first few, they were out at a restaurant, then walking down the street in the CBD, close but not holding hands. The next few were grainy and looked like they'd been taken through a window, but their faces were unmistakable. Nothing salacious captured here, just the guys holding hands over bowls of cereal and snuggling on the couch, hair mussed, with TV lights reflected in their faces. All very normal couple things. Then the last set of pictures featured Mina making some kind of exchange in an alley with a man dressed all in black. The angle obscured the man's face.

Had Roman hired a PI to follow his fellow acolytes? To what end? It was also possible that another theater guest could've left these here either by accident or on purpose.

I tipped out the envelope to see if there was anything else left that might identify the owner of the pictures. A single key slid out with a Crumbles keyring attached. The missing key. This would explain how the vandals got in to cause trouble the other day. Had Carlie stolen it or just kept it from when she worked as a barista there? The final item in the envelope was a folded-up piece of paper, which turned out to be a work schedule for the yoga studio with Carlie's shifts highlighted.

A sinking feeling stole over me. Did the last two pieces mean these pictures belonged to Carlie? Was she picking her target to murder? I tried to see the evidence from other angles. Maybe whoever had these pictures taken was tracking Carlie too. She'd cozied up to Nick, at least in the time since the murder. He could easily have nabbed the key and her schedule to keep tabs on her. And if the envelope was here, did that mean that he and Roman were working together to plot and cover up Austin's murder?

Magnolia popped through the wall, with Moisha not far

behind. "One thing's clear. Our boy is up to the top of his multiple swimming pools in debt."

"I'll say," Moisha said. "And he wasn't kidding about that office of his being a mess. Lucky for us, though, with the papers all spread out."

"What did you find?" I asked.

"Piles of late notices," Magnolia reported. "Most notably on his mortgage. He's at least two months behind that I could tell."

"Also, big transactions on his credit card statements to a company called C Limited. Any clue what that is?"

I shook my head and repeated the info they'd shared for Declan's benefit. "He needs this spot in the Enclave to maintain his lifestyle. That's motive to bump off the competition."

Magnolia's expression went pensive. Then she noticed the contents of the envelope in my lap. "What've you got there?"

"Check this out." I detailed the photos and described how I'd found the bakery key and Carlie's schedule for the recording.

"Can you fit those in your purse, darling?" Magnolia asked. "I think your officer friend may find those useful."

I pulled out my clutch and frowned. "Note to self, next under cover mission, bring a bigger purse. Maybe if I rolled it—"

The door creaked open before I could do any rolling.

"Feeling any better? I hope so because we're about to get started," Roman said.

I froze, the evidence of my snooping feeling like a flashing red light in my lap. "Much better, thanks."

With panic in my eyes, I looked to Magnolia for suggestions. How did I get up without Roman seeing me with the envelope?

Magnolia gave me a steadying gaze. I wished I had her poise in the face of danger. "Darling, I believe you lost your earring and need to search for it."

I let out a shaky breath and nodded. "Oh, shoot. I just dropped my earring. Let me find it, and I'm all yours."

Magnolia and Moisha both flashed me a thumbs up.

I bent forward and slid the envelope back to the floor. See, that wasn't so hard. I could do this. Relief flooded me until the atrocious pendant recorder tumbled out of my dress.

My insides clenched.

"Let me help you look." Roman headed my way, and I kicked the envelope under the chair in the nick of time.

"Found it." I palmed the pendant and pretended to refasten my earring.

"Is that yours?" Roman's gaze moved to the necklace cord that protruded from my fist. The bedazzled stone also peeked out. "Doesn't quite look like your style."

See, Declan. I told you!

"It was a gift," I said. "Must have fallen out of my purse while I was looking."

"Not a very good one." Roman smirked.

"Hush." I rose and gave him a flirtatious swat on his arm.

"I'm just saying, stick with me, and I can do much better for you in the present department."

Moisha made gagging noises.

I pressed my lips together to keep from laughing. "I'm sure you would."

⁕▲⁕▲⁕▲⁕

ONCE WE'D all gathered in the living room with floor to ceiling windows that looked out over his impressive back yard, Roman took the proverbial stage.

A hush fell over the crowd, and guests exchanged inquisitive glances. I scanned the room and noted that Mina, Ben, Carlie, and Nick were all still absent. Also, no sign of the others I knew of with Enclave connections, like Hartley and Valerie, the Voodoo doll rep.

Would they present them to us now, so they could mingle and vet us? A tingle of anticipation had me fidgeting with my hands.

Roman cleared his throat. "Thank you all for coming. I've invited you all here because you have that special something about you. That X factor that can't be taught. You've got that tenacity and hunger for something more. And because of that, I'd like to give a select few of you a glimpse of an elite opportunity."

Now we were getting somewhere. I shifted in my seat on the arm of a sofa.

"Are you ready to hear about this once in a lifetime opportunity?"

Murmurs of assent rang out from the crowd.

Roman dimmed the lights and disappeared into the hallway for a second. Was he going to get the others?

Then he stepped back into the room, remote in hand, and the flat screen TV mounted above his fireplace blazed to life.

Wait, was there some kind of video introduction to the Enclave? That didn't seem very on-brand for all their claims of secrecy. I frowned.

The screen filled with calming images of waves crashing on the shore of a white sand beach. White linens floated from a cabana. The scene zoomed in on a table next to a bathtub filled with hibiscus flowers, populated with small brown bottles. Green, leafy plants bordered the scene.

Wait, were those marijuana leaves?

A message flashed across the screen.

Welcome to the elite world of di Rossi Essential Oils, now with CBD!

And that's how I convinced the police to spy on a multilevel marketing pitch.

I trudged back to my car and drove to meet Declan and Hudson, head hung. I'd never live this down.

To make matters worse, Magnolia and Moisha's hour with me was up, so I didn't have the unfaltering support of my allies.

Both men met me on the curb near their vehicles.

I held out the listening device to Declan without daring to look at his face. "Go ahead, say it."

"Say what?" Declan asked. "If I need an in on the next Tupperware crime ring, I know who to call?"

Flames climbed the sides of my neck and cheeks. "I'm sorry, Declan. You put your reputation at work on the line for my hunch, and this is what you got."

"Hey, don't beat yourself up." He put a hand on my shoulder. "Plenty of leads turn out to be dead ends. But like I said before, I may not have much leeway to run down any more in this direction."

"The PI photos could still turn something up," Hudson

added. He didn't look exasperated or overly amused that I'd confused a secret society soiree with an essential oils pitch, only steady and supportive. Just like in the old days. I was grateful for that.

"Can't get my hands on them without a warrant, unfortunately," Declan said. "And as of now, we've got no probable cause to search his house. I can have some PIs I know ask around about who might've taken the pictures, though."

A call squawked in on Declan's radio. "Gotta head out. See you around, squirt."

"YOU GOING to give me the mentor lecture?" I asked Hudson once Declan's cruiser left us alone under the streetlights.

"Nah." The dimple formed in his chin. The lights painted his hair with streaks of gold.

"You're just glad I wasn't on a date with a murderer."

"True. At least not a one-on-one date," Hudson said. He nudged my arm with his elbow and grinned. "Do you think he got many elite oil representatives out of tonight's event?"

"Weirdly, yes. There was a lot of interest. Maybe he'll pull himself out of debt without the Enclave's help after all."

We both sauntered over to his truck and leaned against it, side by side.

Crickets chirped in the background and the tree branches swayed in the breeze.

Cicadas added their screams to the night chorus, and not going to lie, I wanted to scream along with them.

"What do you think happened to the others?" Hudson asked. "Was it a fake meeting Ben and Mina made up to throw you off? Or something else?"

I shrugged and slumped down, the mortification washing

over me again. "Ugh, I'm never going to recover from this," I said.

"Hey, it wasn't a total bust," Hudson said. "You found potentially incriminating financial information and those photos."

"True. But I still made a mess of my one honest police contact."

Hudson gave me a wry smile. "Somehow, I doubt that."

Was it my imagination, or had he veered closer? Our shoulders touched. A floaty feeling mixed in with all the gloom and doom.

He tipped his head back, gaze on the stars. I did the same.

"This reminds me of the night we met," he said. "Locked on that roof outside of your sorority dance. Just us and the warm air and the stars."

I murmured in assent. My emotions were still jumbled where he was concerned. Even the good memories were painted over with a bittersweet brush with what had come after. But just for a moment, I stopped all the fighting and rewriting and just let myself lean into the comfort that he provided now, just like he had back then.

"A lot's changed since then."

He nodded. "You've changed."

I swiveled to look at him. "How so?"

"You seem more sure of yourself. More comfortable in your own skin."

"Really? Because I feel just as confused as ever."

"I don't know if that ever goes away," Hudson said. "Doesn't for me, anyway."

"Do you think you've changed?" I asked.

"I'm sure I have. But some days, even though I traveled around the world, I feel like I've been standing still since the day I left this place."

I knew the feeling. I'd stayed mired in that place of grieving and not knowing why for so long before I finally got on with life.

"Do you think you'll ever go back and finish your degree? Go into art therapy like you wanted," I asked.

"Maybe if I settle back in one place again."

That's right. He was leaving again. As soon as we wrapped this case. I swallowed. Did I want him to go?

"Do you think you ever will?" I asked.

"That depends." He looked over at me, his hazel eyes shining in the moonlight.

My heart skipped a beat with him so close, his breath near enough to graze my cheek.

"On what?"

"On—"

But he didn't get to answer. My phone buzzed, breaking the spell. I shimmied it out of my purse, realizing I hadn't checked it since I retrieved it on the way out of the party.

A notification lit the screen.

The page I'd set up to raise funds to help Liz with repairs at Crumbles had passed $500 in donations already. At least something had gone right tonight. I held up the phone and shared the good news.

He gazed at me with a lopsided grin and a look I couldn't decipher.

"What?" I asked.

He shook his head. "A lot might have changed, but not everything. Was this Liz-sanctioned?"

I shook my head. "She hates asking for help. I figured this was one of those cases I'd rather ask for forgiveness than permission."

"She's lucky to have you. Everyone in your circle is."

I swallowed around the dry lump in my throat.

Was he saying he wanted back into my circle, or was this one more step in our long goodbye?

I cast a hesitant smile back up at him and hitched a thumb at my car. "I should probably go sleep off my humiliation."

He climbed in his truck and waved goodbye.

FORTY-ONE

The next day, I covered for a co-worker for part of the morning shift and tried my best to banish thoughts of the night before. Luckily, we were busy enough with tour bookings and a steady stream of guests that I barely had any downtime, anyway. That, along with Norman's antics composing a sea shanty he hoped would go viral, occupied my mind.

Then finally, at the appointed time, I drove the half an hour trek to the bayou to meet up with Eliza in secret. As I got farther out into the swamplands, I reflected on how far into the weeds I'd gotten with this investigation too, and replayed the memory of that essential oils, *now with CBD!* slideshow and just how far things had gone off the rails last night.

My cheeks burned, and I shrunk back into my seat.

Sure, this case was personal because of Liz and now Austin. Now two people I cared about were directly affected by my ability to continue. For them, I'd see it through, even if I was an embarrassment. But after that? I wasn't as sure as I'd been, even days ago.

Maybe I should consider cutting my losses and moving on in the quest for my calling.

I parked my Prius in the shade of a cypress tree and followed the directions Eliza had given me.

People milled in front of the gift shop, some grabbing a bite to eat before the next tour. That one didn't leave for another hour, according to the notice board.

I walked down the wooden-slatted path of the boat launch in time to see a small airboat headed my way. Wind kicked up from the giant fan in the back of the boat that powered it. A familiar figure with dark hair and pink camo pants and hat waved from the driver's seat as she pulled the boat to a halt in front of me.

Eliza fanned the bodice of her olive tank top and waved me over. "You like our ride?" Eliza said with a show model wave.

"It's perfect."

Eliza's escapades and ability to borrow a swamp boat on a whim were just the distraction I needed after striking out so completely last night. Maybe talking things out with her could give me the clarity I so badly needed.

I hopped on and accepted the yellow ear protection set she handed me. "We'll talk once we get further out," she said.

She started the engine, and I was glad to have the ear muffs to dull the roar as we sped through the swamplands.

Eliza expertly steered us through the tunnels of bald cypress trees festooned with Spanish moss. The late afternoon sun reflected off the murky water, nearly blinding me, but I still caught sight of several gators, their snouts floating just about the surface. A family of raccoons chittered to one another on the right bank.

An egret dive-bombed in front of us, and I yelped and ducked even though it came nowhere near my head. I heard Eliza's laughter ring out, even through the ear protection.

When we'd gotten into the heart of the swamp, Eliza cut the engine and we glided through the water.

She left her post in the driver's seat and sat next to me.

"You said you had more news for me on your investigation?" I said.

Her green eyes twinkled. "Yep-aroo, I do." ~She lounged against the bench seat and relaxed back into her carefree way of talking, now that she was away from the Enclave members. Her transformation the other night had been startling. She was good at this.

"This vetting party they're holding is later tonight," she said. "If this is the party you were invited to, I'd skip it if I were you."

I shook my head and sighed. "Mine ended up being a bust." I filled her in on the great CBD oil scandal of the week.

When I finished, she threw her head back and laughed. "That sounds like something out of my playbook. I'd wrangle you an invitation for tonight's shindig, but in all honesty, it's better that you're not on the guest list. Hartley's already issued the Enclave's version of a BOLO on you."

"I figured he'd be watching me after his threat the other night." When I'd given myself away at my stakeout to save Auguste from the dog. Yet another thing I screwed up. I pushed the thought away and briefed her on everything else that had happened since we last talked.

"They moved the ascension and sacrifice ceremony to this weekend," she said.

I looked away from the wild boar I'd spotted snuffling through the patch of land on our right. "Are they going to bring in an outsider from this vetting party to be the sacrifice or choose someone from the existing group of acolytes?"

"Someone from the existing group. I think it's meant as a punishment to whoever tried to thwart the process."

Yikes. I pictured Ben and then Mina tied to that stone table begging for their lives, and my stomach turned.

"Do you know who it's supposed to be?" I asked.

"Not for certain. Hartley doesn't know. Either that or he's not saying. I've heard the name Carlie tossed around an awful lot in other circles, though."

I blew out a breath. Carlie might've been elitist and unkind to Austin, but I didn't like the idea of anyone subjected to this ritual.

"Do you know who set it all up? The Austin thing?"

Eliza shook her head. "Whoever it is has been really tight-lipped."

"What are you going to do? Are you going to make your move to expose them and stop the ceremony?"

"Ideally. I don't know if I've got enough to go on yet, but I'm working on it. Got any trustworthy friends in local law enforcement? The only officer I know is in the Enclave's pocket."

"Yes, but not one who'd be especially inclined to do me favors after Operation Essential Oils." I studied my shoes. "I could have my own blend—the Peppermint Pariah."

Eliza waved a hand. "Eh, that'll blow over."

"One can dream," I said. "I'll give you his contact info, anyway. Maybe don't mention my name, though."

The thought of Declan and my investigation bloopers reel tanked my mood again. Was that all I'd ever have? A series of false starts instead of a real purpose to build on?

I fixed my gaze on the gators floating near the boat.

"How'd you do it?" I asked after a while.

"Do what? Put up with Hartley and his nationalist blather long enough to get information out of him?"

I snorted. "That too. But I meant, how did you know when you'd found what you were passionate about and decide to run with it? You're so good at the work you're doing. Did you always know undercover journalism was your thing?"

Eliza chuckled. "Heck no. You getting caught up in that 'one true passion' BS?"

I shrugged. "Seems to work for everyone else."

"Listen, I joined the high school paper because of this dork I had a raging crush on. Then I got my first job out of college at the Métairie Star because I had no idea what I wanted to do with my life, so I decided I might as well work with my best friend. She was in the ads department. I wrote my first article filling in for a guy who had emergency dental surgery."

I frowned. "So this didn't feel like destiny from the start?"

Eliza laughed again. "Nah. I stumbled into it and tripped over both my own feet on the way."

"How'd you know it was worth sticking with?"

She gave me a quizzical look. "How can you possibly know what you like or you'll end up being good at until you dig in and give yourself time to learn and grow?"

I leaned back in my seat. "I never really thought of it that way."

The boat finally glided to a stop.

"I don't believe there's some predestined perfect vocation for me. Destiny can kiss my lovely round lady lumps. I'm walking my own path and learning about myself as I go," Eliza said.

"Or in today's case, sailing your own swamp. For a secret meeting with your cousin?"

She cracked a smile. "Yep. This way might be filled with gators, but that's why I brought marshmallows."

She pulled out a sack of mini marshmallows from her pack and tossed a few toward the gators swimming nearby. I'd been baffled the first time I'd seen a guide do this, but apparently it's a common swamp tour thing. One by one, their open snouts broke the water's surface, and they swallowed their treats.

"Give me some of those," I said. I tossed a handful in and considered what Eliza had said.

I couldn't deny that her point of view made sense. I watched the gators' scaly backs swish through the water.

"I guess I just expected if my calling came along, I'd know it because it came naturally. Not that I wouldn't have to work at it, but there would be some kind of natural proclivity to give me a head start."

Now that I'd said it aloud, I understood how it sounded: like I was waiting for a magic bullet or for some superpower to manifest. When maybe I could've spent all that time and effort building skills wherever I was to see what emerged.

"You put too much pressure on yourself, Paige," Eliza said. "Classic oldest/ only child behavior. Roscoe does it too. But you can't expect to be perfect at something out of the gate."

But couldn't I, though?

After a while, Eliza informed me she had more Enclave business and had to head back. The swamp swallowed our secrets and ruminations like big ol' marshmallows.

FORTY-TWO

Driving home from the bayou, I wrestled with my thoughts on passion and the idea of a calling. Just going with it sounded great for a free spirit like Eliza, but for me? Could I really sit back and stumble through all the missteps with no guarantees this path would lead me somewhere worthwhile?

I wasn't so sure.

I also unearthed another uncomfortable truth somewhere between picking up the groceries and gumbo I'd made for Liz and dropping them off before meeting Hudson to debrief.

For the last four years, I'd blamed Hudson and his disappearing act for my curtailed faith in myself. And for shying away from going after what I what I wanted in life.

Sure, his ghosting had done a number on me, but what if it also provided me with a convenient excuse? An excuse to avoid risks, even the kind that could really pay off. I'd been playing it safe, cutting and running every time I got scared I might be less than perfect. I hid behind my ex's disappearance and a can-do attitude.

Maybe because I needed to work things out, maybe because

I just wanted the old familiar comfort we'd shared, I texted Hudson and asked if we could meet up later.

I thought you'd never ask. Tupelo's? he texted back.

My chest warmed as I walked through Liz's door.

"You're a saint. Any updates on finding the killer?" she asked. The hope on her face was so naked and vulnerable that I felt like a monster squashing it.

Her face fell, though she tried to hide it, when I admitted I'd found nothing definite. We turned on an action movie and worked on a puzzle between spoonfuls of gumbo.

"Any more news from the police?"

"Crowder says the results of the fingerprints and DNA should be back tomorrow." She fidgeted with a Kleenex.

Shoot. I needed to hurry. I told her about the pictures and key I thought was Carlie's.

"She was always taking pictures with the food." Liz rolled her eyes. "But she wasn't a bad employee for the most part. At least not until her disappearing act the other day."

"So she just never called and never showed up again after Austin's death? Did she ever return her key?"

"Yep, and nope."

I told her about Carlie working at the yoga studio. She frowned.

"You think she had something to do with the break in and vandalism?"

"Unfortunately, I think she might have."

◆◆◆◆◆

AFTER OUR PUZZLE AND A MOVIE, Liz's eyelids drifted closed. I tucked a blanket over her and left with promises to keep working on the case and check in again soon.

Then, with nerves jangling, I headed to meet my ex-boyfriend.

Tupelo's was one of my favorite quintessential French Quarter bars, always packed to the hilt with locals and tourists alike, faux leather seats and burnt orange walls bursting with live music and cheap drinks. Hudson slid onto the barstool next to mine, the only seat left in the packed establishment.

He smiled over at me and flagged down the bartender. Due to the wall-to-wall humans, personal space was non-existent. Hudson's dark jeans-clad thigh pressed into mine. The person on my other side jostled me, and my arm brushed his. This close, the cedar scent of cologne on his skin overtook the smell of booze and smoke and made me light-headed.

The bartender approached.

"You still like their Long Island iced teas?" Hudson asked with a teasing grin. His golden hair hung into his eyes, and I fought the urge to brush it behind his ear.

I made a face. "I gave up on those after I was of age. How about a Moscow mule?"

He ordered a soda in case I needed a designated driver later, and I studied his square jaw and mischievous hazel eyes for a beat longer than necessary. His smile came easier tonight than it had since his return, like he'd shed some of the burdens he'd been carrying over the past week.

For the first time since his reappearance, I really looked at him without the unshakable conviction he was responsible for the bulk of my insecurities and shortcomings. Without that impenetrable buffer of blame, I no longer had a script for how to act around him. Something about it felt too exposed, too vulnerable.

After some small talk about Austin and the case, my fingers drummed nervously on my copper mug. Condensation trickled down my thumb.

"I have a confession to make," Hudson said.

"Oh yeah?" My pulse hammered in my neck, and I attempted not to look as flustered as I felt. Against my will, my gaze dropped to his lips, and I thought of the way his hand had felt on my back in the tunnel, comforting and warm and right.

Hudson leaned close to my ear to be heard over the music. His stubble grazed my cheek, and the heat of his skin passed to mine. My whole body hummed from the near contact. What was I doing? Did I want him to confess he still had feelings for me? I thought I'd dismissed that notion.

I pulled back, our cheeks brushing along the way, but held his gaze. His eyes dropped to my lips and rose again. Just one more inch and we'd be—

My phone buzzed with a notification. I sucked in a breath and fumbled it from my pocket, the moment broken. Through my flustered state, I felt the blood drain from my face.

"What is it?" Hudson asked, his posture alert and protective in an instant.

I held up the screen.

Paige, it's Ben Park. I didn't know who else to contact. I'm in the hospital. Bad car accident. The meeting we went to was a trap. It wasn't for all the acolytes. They knew we talked. They knew what Mina and I did after. Ran me off the road. Please make sure Mina's okay? I can't reach her. I'm afraid they'll come for you next. Take care, okay?

He also left the hospital name and his room number.

"Come on, I'll drive." Hudson settled our tab and navigated us through the crowd and to his truck in no time. He opened the passenger door for me.

I climbed up into the cab and texted back furiously, telling Ben I was on my way.

"Does he know who ran him down?" Hudson asked.

"I asked, but he hasn't answered. I'll try Mina. And what

does he mean, '*They knew what Mina and I did after*'? After we met or after Austin's murder?"

Hudson shrugged and gunned it all the way to the hospital. My calls to Mina went to voice mail, and she didn't respond to any of my texts. I prayed both Austin's friends would be okay.

"Austin, you might want to join us on this one," I said aloud as Hudson dropped me off at the door to go park.

Austin appeared next to me inside the sliding glass doors. "Ben?" he asked.

I nodded and never wished I could hug him as much as I did at that instant, seeing the look of pain on his face.

After I charmed my way past the nurses' station, saying I was Ben's cousin, I pulled a chair up to Ben's bedside.

"He's sleeping now, but he might stir," the nurse said. Bandages wrapped around his head, and deep bruises marred his cheeks. His shiny dark hair stuck up at all angles. Austin floated next to him and placed a hand over his.

"Ben?" I whispered.

Ben's eyes fluttered open.

"I came as soon as I got your message. How are you feeling?"

"Paige?" His words slurred, and his eyes went glassy.

I nodded. "Austin's here too."

Ben smiled, but winced at the pull on his cheek.

"I'm... not good. You talk to Mina?"

My face fell. "Not yet, but I'll keep trying."

"Where's Aus?" he asked.

"On your other side." I nodded to Austin's grief-stricken face.

Ben looked up at Austin with a sleepy smile. "Thanks for coming. Still looking out for me?"

"Can't have you joining me on the other side too soon, now," Austin said.

Ben's eyes fluttered closed again after I repeated Austin's words. I needed him awake to find out who did this and what his message had meant.

"Ben, in your message, you said they knew what you and Mina did after? What did you mean?" I asked.

"That we stole Austin's body."

"You...what?"

"We got him from the storage room after everybody left and took him out the other tunnel. There's a hidden room upstairs behind the bathrooms. With a freezer. S'connected to the underground tunnels. We pushed him from the balcony the next night. So they couldn't just make him disappear. So he could have justice."

"That explains Mina's heel prints and the bracelet in the secret room we found," I said.

Austin's ethereal body heaved in relief.

"Told you there was a logical explanation."

"You've been to the secret room?" Ben said.

I nodded. "My associate and I found it the other night."

Ben's eyes glazed over again and drifted closed. "Tell Austin we tried to do right by him," he murmured.

Austin leaned closer to Ben.

"He knows," I said.

Ben blinked. "And Mina. Keep Mina safe too, 'kay. Can't let them get her too."

"I'll do everything I can," I promised. "But I need you to tell me about this meeting tonight. Who was there? And are you sure it was them that ran you off the road?"

He nodded emphatically and then winced at the motion. "I'm sure. Recognized the car. Dark red. Saw the face in the rearview." His head lolled to the side. "Brain's getting fuzzy now. I think the morphine's kicking in. I'll just take a nap now."

"Wait, Ben. Who was in the car? Whose car was it?" I pleaded.

"Carlie's.... It was Carlie's..." He trailed off and snored softly.

FORTY-THREE

"What do we do now? We can't just wait around," I said to Hudson as we climbed back into his truck in the hospital parking lot.

"I called Declan while you were in there and told him what happened to Ben."

"You did?" My shoulders slumped in relief. There he went again, knowing what I needed. "Thank goodness. I dreaded that phone call, what with the whole essential oils fiasco."

"I figured." He winked at me. There was that glimmer of our old bond. He'd always been good at intuiting what I needed and helping shoulder my burdens.

"Thanks. I got the impression he wasn't exactly on your list of favorites."

Hudson smirked. "What ever gave you that idea?"

I shrugged, a smile hitching at the corner of my mouth, remembering the protective stance Hudson adopted when Declan showed up. "You told him about Ben, and that it was Carlie who did it?"

I'd texted Hudson with an update while waiting for Ben to wake up again and share any other crucial details. But when an hour had passed, it was clear he needed his sleep to recover, and I called it a night.

Hudson nodded. "He said he'd track Carlie down and check her car for signs of damage."

"Did you tell him Mina might be in danger too? She still hasn't answered any of my texts."

"He's going to check on her too."

I let out a breath and fidgeted with the hem of my dress. My nerves were jittery, and I'd moved past tired, straight into my second adrenaline-fueled wind. We were so close. "Alright, wise mentor, what's our next move?"

Hudson tipped his head against the headrest. "This is one of the hardest parts of the gig. Where we've done all we can and turn it over to the police to finish up and make the arrests."

"But we can't just—what if Carlie's got Mina tied up somewhere?" My stomach dropped at the thought. "Or worse."

"We don't need to add ourselves to the body count if the police are already on it."

I hated how much sense that made. I twisted my lips.

I couldn't stop thinking about the bond that was so clear between Mina, Austin, and Ben. It reminded me of the closeness I shared with Bridget, Ines, and Nat. If there was a killer on the loose after them, I'd stop at nothing to make sure they were safe.

Hudson studied me. "But if it would make you feel better, I'm game for swinging by her place to check on her if you are."

I swallowed around the lump in my throat. "You know I won't let this go, don't you?"

"You, not letting something go?" He gave me a sexy smile.

I smirked and buckled my seatbelt. "Let's do this."

◆❖◆❖◆

INES PULLED up Mina's address for us and thirty minutes later, I knocked on the door of her house, a two-story place in uptown with clean lines and white shutters.

"With the porch lights out, I'd guess she hasn't been home since the meeting this evening," Hudson said.

I peered in the window. "I don't see any lights on inside either. Maybe she went to stay with family or friends if she was worried for her safety."

"Or she could just be out. Maybe Carlie thought scaring Ben would be enough to put Mina off too?"

"Maybe." My voice trailed off. As much as I wanted one of those possibilities to be true, I didn't like this one bit.

We checked her social media and stopped by several places she'd checked in or posted pictures from recently, but no dice. None of the bartenders or wait staff had seen her tonight. Hudson was a trooper, following all of my leads.

"Hey there, sleeping beauty. Maybe we should get you home for some shuteye," Hudson said, shaking me awake before our last stop.

I gasped and wiped the bit of drool from the corner of my mouth. "I'm okay. Have to make sure she's…" I nodded off again and jerked back awake.

Apparently a week of having a corpse drop at your feet, a friend framed for murder, and learning that the supernatural was more natural than I'd ever imagined eventually takes its toll on a girl.

Finally, around midnight, when we'd exhausted our last option and I could hardly keep my eyes open, a text from Mina popped up.

Headed out of town to lie low for a few days. I'm OK. I'll let you know when I'm back.

The breath whooshed out of me with the full force of my relief and exhaustion.

Hudson looked away from the road and raised an eyebrow. "Good news?"

I nodded. "She's okay."

·▲··▲·*·▲·*

I CRANKED the air conditioning all the way up, rolled down my windows, and blasted Taylor Swift to make sure I didn't fall asleep at the wheel. Despite assurances I'd be okay, Hudson followed me home, just in case.

He idled in front of my house and waited until I flashed the porch lights twice. He flashed his headlights twice in return and waved, our old signal. A pang of nostalgia hit me. It was kind of nice having his protectiveness back in my life.

After a quick shower, I fed Auguste and kissed him good-night. I ran my fingers along the spines of my Matilda Mayhew mysteries collection until my chest grew warm and I pulled out the volume I'd landed on once again for guidance, *Matilda Mayhew and the Case of the Devil You Know.*

I flopped down on my bed and fell asleep before I could even soak up its wisdom.

·▲··▲·*·▲·*

THANK heavens I had the next day off because I slept like the dead and didn't crack an eyelid until noon.

Apparently I needed it. I stretched and did a quick sweep of the news to see if Carlie's arrest had been made public (it hadn't) before filling a sleepy and agitated Auguste in on every-thing that had happened since I'd seen him last.

"Sacre blue, ma cher," he said. "No wonder you slept until the middle of the day. But what will you do next? You must confirm that she is in fact the killer, no?"

"Hudson says we should wait for the police to do the dangerous work now."

"Though I am loath to admit it, he has a point," Auguste said.

"I guess I could check in with Declan."

"There's the spirit," Auguste said.

Heat flared up my neck as echoes of mortification from Roman's pyramid scheme washed over me. Ugh. I wanted to face Declan again about as much as I wanted to have one of my naked-in-front-of-my-ghost-tour dreams come true. But to make sure Liz was in the clear, and this thing was really over, I'd bite the bullet.

My heart hammered in my throat the whole time his phone rang.

"Officer Durocher, how can I help you?" Declan answered. Was it my imagination, or did he sound harried, like his coworkers had teased him merciless for the goose chase I'd sent him on?

"Declan, hey. Just wondering if you needed any more bread." I tried to keep my tone light hearted.

He chuckled, which made me feel the tiniest bit better. "All set thanks. If I finished the basket you brought the other night by now, I'd have a sourdough bowl where my abs should be."

I took a deep breath and girded myself to ask the question I really wanted answered, but Declan spoke first.

"I've only got a minute, but I suppose you're calling to follow up on Carlie Lightfoot."

"Did you arrest her? Is Liz's name clear?"

"Carlie's alibi checked out for last night. She was with her brother watching some cooking war show."

A dismayed noise escaped my throat. "Maybe she did that after she ran Ben Park off the road. Did you check her car?"

"Yep. Not a scratch on it. It couldn't have been in the accident your friend described."

"But..."

"I'm sorry, squirt. I've got to get back to it."

Deflated, I relayed the news to Auguste. "Did Ben have it wrong? Maybe the car that ran him off the road just looked like Carlie's?"

"Hmmm." Auguste paced on my bedspread.

"What is it?"

"What precisely did this chap Ben say to you about the car that hit him? And how did you phrase your question to him?"

"I asked him if he recognized the person who hit him and if he knew whose car it had been. He nodded, said it was Carlie's, and then fell asleep again."

"Perhaps he was not yet finished with his sentence when sleep took him."

I sucked in a slow breath. "That's possible. I assumed he meant it was Carlie's car, but it could have been Carlie's boyfriend. Or Carlie's brother."

Why hadn't I thought of this before?

I slipped into my yoga clothes to go test a hunch.

Auguste yawned. "Now, if you'll excuse me, it's past my bedtime."

I tucked a sleepy Auguste into his blanket nest, left him some treats for later tonight, and set off to smoke out a killer.

FORTY-FOUR

Austin joined me in my car on the way to yoga, making me swerve and almost jump a curve.

"Sorry," he said. "Just wanted to check in. Did you find Mina?"

I told him about her text after looking for her all night.

"How's Ben?" I asked.

"Awake more. The doctors are hopeful. His parents have been there a lot. They really care about him."

"That's good," I said. I glanced in the rear-view and saw in his eyes the way Austin both loved the support Ben had from his parents and ached for the absence of it in his own life.

"I went to see my parents," Austin blurted.

"Really? How'd it go?" I asked gently.

Austin looked off into the distance. "I got to the front door, all ready to float right through and face them. But I couldn't make myself go in."

"I'm sorry."

"I just thought after seeing how Ben's parents were with him, maybe—"

I nodded in understanding and sensed that he wanted to

change the subject. "I'm going to pay Carlie a visit. Want to come with?"

Austin shook his head. "I want to get back to Ben."

I told him I'd keep him posted, then parked my car a block from the yoga studio. I shouldered the strap attached to my mat. Was I really going to do this? March up to a potential killer or accomplice and just go do my warrior poses after like nothing off had happened.

Like Magnolia said, I had a knack for reading people. If Carlie had run Ben off the road to silence him for making Austin's murder public, wouldn't I sense her distress if I interacted with her? Still, I wished I'd brought Auguste along for a second opinion. Though I didn't think the studio was hedgehog friendly.

I passed by the auto body shop on the corner where a few guys in coveralls were taking a smoke break, leaving a brick red SUV up in the air, looking like it was flying. I might've kept walking, but the license plate caught my eye.

LTFOOT.

My neck tingled. Could that be short for Lightfoot, as in Carlie Lightfoot, or just a coincidence? Then I remembered Ben had said the car that hit him was red. Did Carlie have a second car? Surely Declan would have checked on that.

I shot a glance at the mechanics and scurried around to the back of the car bays. The front driver's side bumper was twisted and marred with scratches of silver paint.

Perhaps from bashing Ben's car? My sleuthing senses tingled, and I snapped a few pictures.

"Can I help you with something?" One mechanic snuffed out his cigarette and sauntered up to me.

"Oh, sorry, this looked like my friend's car and I was going to text and ask what happened."

"If you're friends with that dude, I'm the one who's sorry," he said.

That dude. Interesting. I made a show of looking at the license plate. "Ah, wrong plate. Definitely not my friend's car. My mistake."

The bells on the door chimed my arrival to the yoga studio a few minutes later. Meditation music floated out along with the smell of incense and sweat. No one manned the reception desk, but raised voices came from the office. One male and one female. I was pretty sure the female voice belonged to Carlie.

I signed in and lingered for a few minutes to see if they'd come out. When they only continued arguing behind closed doors, I gave up and went to class.

Unsurprisingly, it was difficult to relax and get into a meditative state with a possible murderer less than ten feet away. I just kept fixating on how all the pieces of this puzzle fit together.

When I exited class, Carlie stood by the front desk, answering a woman's questions about an upcoming retreat. When she saw me, her sunny, plastered-on smile wavered.

I waved and studied her for a moment. Extra layers of concealer may have camouflaged her dark circles, but couldn't cover the threads of red that shot through her eyes. She looked haggard. Defeated.

Was that because she'd killed someone and hurt another, or because she was keeping secrets for someone else who had? Someone who might still be in her office right now.

Something about the look in her eyes gave me a twinge of sympathy.

I stepped outside and headed back to my car. Before I'd made it back to the auto shop, Carlie came racing after me.

"Oh good, I caught you," she said, out of breath.

"Hey." I assessed her again, but my eyes flicked back to the mechanics, glad to have eyes on the street. "What's up?"

She bit her lip. Her gaze darted back the way she'd come. "You're friends with that cop, right?"

I raised an eyebrow. Not where I thought this was going, but okay.

"What cop is that?"

"The cute one who used to stop in when you and Liz were having your puzzle nights at Crumbles."

"Oh. Yeah, why?"

"I uh, have some information." Carlie tucked a rogue lock of hair behind her ear. I noticed a blotch of purple under her clavicle. Was that a bruise? Perhaps from a car accident?

"About what? Does this have to do with Austin?"

Carlie snuck another glance at the studio. "I have to get back. Can we meet later tonight? I need to find someone trustworthy for this. I could use your advice."

"Yeah, sure. Are you safe?"

She swallowed and gave a curt nod.

"For now."

FORTY-FIVE

Finally, after the longest four hours of my life, my phone buzzed with a text from Carlie. I'd spent most of the afternoon stress-cleaning. Austin had popped in and kept me company for a while, letting me know Ben still hadn't woken up, but the doctors were still hopeful before he headed back to the hospital.

Can you meet me in twenty? Carlie wrote, along with an address where she'd be.

I'll be there.

Auguste was just waking up. Just in case there was any mortal peril, I kissed his little head goodbye and left him in his habitat.

"Let the record show I do not support this plan. At least let me come along to protect you."

"I don't want you to get hurt," I said.

"Nor I you."

"I'm asking Declan and Hudson to meet me there. I'll have backup."

Twenty minutes later, I pulled up to a run-down abandoned house with a frown. The address Carlie had given me was way out in an area ravaged by Hurricane Katrina, and still not fully rehabilitated. Some houses along the lonely streets were still in ruins, water-logged heaps of wood abandoned on their foundations. On a few other lots, pristine new houses had been built, possibly by one of the architecture schools in town, judging by the sleek, modern exteriors. Quiet hung ominously in the air, along with the humidity.

I parked next to the sporty silver car I assumed was Carlie's and checked my phone one more time. No response from Declan yet, but Hudson was on his way and cautioned me not to do anything dangerous before he arrived. Thank goodness, because this place gave me the creeps. I tucked a mini taser into one pocket of my jeans and my phone into another.

Come around back, Carlie texted. *I don't have long before he'll come after me.*

I chewed my lip and glanced around the premises. Street lights flickered to life, but this entire neighborhood was well and truly deserted. There was some evidence of a construction crew with some vehicles parked a few doors down, but it looked like they'd all gone home for the evening.

If this went sideways, no one would hear me scream.

But as much as I wanted to sit tight and wait for Hudson, I got out of the car. I didn't want another person put in danger unnecessarily.

"Carlie?" I called out. The thick night air swallowed my voice.

"On the back porch."

I paused and texted Declan one more time. *If you don't hear from me in an hour, track my phone.*

See, that was sensible.

I also engaged the recording app on my phone and called out for Magnolia and Moisha.

I walked around to the back porch and found Carlie sniffling, leaning against the wrought-iron railing.

"Hey," I whispered. "You alright?"

She laughed without a trace of mirth and shrugged. I almost felt sorry for her. Who was I kidding? I did feel sorry for her. Whatever part she'd played in this had taken its toll.

"I'm glad you reached out."

Quiet, almost imperceptible footsteps came from the other side of the building. I resisted looking behind me, lest I call attention to Hudson's approach.

"I think you know what I need to tell you," Carlie said.

"Is it about Austin Des Jardins' murder?"

"Yes."

I waited, giving her space to lay things out in her own time.

"It wasn't supposed to happen like this." She wiped her nose on the sleeve of her rumpled salmon pink oxford. "I just wanted to set up the fake task, so one of the do-gooders would quit. Then no one would have to get cut."

"Who's we? Were you working with Nick? Roman?"

She shook her head. "But they had to clean up my mess."

Wait, had she been the murderer? Or was it an accident? "Are you saying you took it too far? Or was it an accident in the dark?"

"I didn't take anything too far. I didn't kill Austin, accidentally or on purpose."

She swallowed, and her gaze flicked to someone behind me.

"My brother did."

My stomach dropped to my shoes. I'd been so wrapped up in my reactions to Carlie I'd missed the person now approaching behind me. Rookie mistake, the kind that could get me killed.

My throat bobbed, and I swiveled slowly, all the while praying I'd find Hudson looking back at me and not Carlie's homicidal brother.

Smiling, with all the smugness of a cat that got the primo caviar, stood Hartley. Eliza's mark, head of murder clean-up crew, and I now realized, Carlie Lightfoot's brother. Same straight nose, silky hair, and eyes that vacillated from charming to cold in a hot second.

How had I missed it? Not Carlie's *car*, but Carlie's *brother*. Dark blonde hair shadowed his face. Eyes lit with manic energy, he trained a gun on me.

"Hello, Paige," Hartley Lightfoot said. "We meet again. Let's take a ride, shall we?"

FORTY-SIX

"You." I glared at Hartley Lightfoot with all that I had. "You killed Austin."

Hartley shrugged. "I did what I had to do to save my sister."

"Were you in on this?" My head whipped back to Carlie. She whimpered and mouthed, "I'm sorry."

"Please, like she has the stones to carry out something like this. Her little scheme might've worked if it weren't for the matter of the sacrifice happening this year. But I wasn't at liberty to tell her about that yet. I had to take matters into my own hands."

Details knitted together in my mind. If Hartley was the murderer, that meant he'd been present with the acolytes. "What? No cloak this time, *Ravenscroft?*" I asked, still spitting venom despite the firearm trained on me. I wasn't sure if that made me brave or foolish.

"I see you've used your wiles to extract information on our organization." He motioned Carlie over, and with his free hand, produced a set of plastic zip tie cuffs from his back pocket. "Hold your hands out in front of you," he commanded me. He passed the restraints to Carlie. "Put these on her."

I commandeered Carlie's gaze. "You don't have to be part of this. You can call the police and end this right now."

Her hands shook and for a moment, I could feel the hesitation rolling off of her like a living, breathing thing. Tears tracked down her face. "I'm sorry. He's family. And he saved my life."

I couldn't tell if terror of her brother or loyalty to him drove her actions now. Either way, Hartley Lightfoot held a powerful sway over her. She pulled the restraints tighter, and the hard plastic dug into my skin. That done, she retreated to the railing.

Where was Hudson? Or Declan? Or even Austin or Magnolia and Moisha? I tried calling for them again. Of course, Magnolia and Moisha had other things to do in their afterlife and couldn't be at my beck and call 24/7. But they'd always come when I called them before. I figured time work differently there, and they could attend to their business and pop down when they finished. Why, of all the times that I needed them, was this not the case?

I second-guessed leaving Auguste at home. Maybe he would've had a brilliant idea to get us out of here. Who was going to feed him and take care of him and talk to him if I was gone? I bit my trembling lip and faced Hartley again.

"Why Austin? Did you think you were defending your sister's honor or something because he rejected her?"

"Hardly." Hartley jerked his head towards the street. "Get moving."

I stared him down, but when he pointed the gun at my face, my resolve shriveled. My steps clicked on the wrap-around porch. "If it wasn't a personal vendetta, why not let things run their course and save Carlie if her name came up?"

Hartley scoffed. "Do you know who was in charge of picking the sacrifice this year? The head of the faction actively working to undo our roots and traditions."

"I don't understand. What does that have to do with Austin?"

"You should know how the world works. Just look at this new group of acolytes. Out of six, only two, Carlie and Austin, were not minorities. We're the tokens now, and they can't wait to put us in our place and take everything we've worked so hard for."

I rolled my eyes, biting back a caustic remark on account of the gun trained on the back of my head.

"So that left only two choices for the sacrifice: my sister and Austin. They each had a fifty fifty chance. Except, then Austin started dating that other guy. That put him in a protected class too. So then there was only one choice. Which I confirmed later. I did what I had to do to protect my family."

We descended the front porch steps, and Hartley prodded me to a black sedan with a rental company plate holder parked among the construction vehicles.

Hartley turned to Carlie. "Go back and meet up with Nick. He can give you an alibi, so you won't get wrapped up in this. I've got it under control."

As she retreated, I called out, "Call the police, Carlie. You know it's the right thing to do."

I didn't know if she could be guilted into it with her deranged brother on the loose, but I was running low on options. I knew the odds of my survival would diminish epically if I got in the car with him.

"Where are you taking me?" I demanded. If I could get a location out of him and get the recording to Declan, I might have a fighting chance not to end up at the bottom of Lake Ponchartrain.

"Where I should have taken Austin and dealt with matters straight away."

My stomach curdled like expired milk. Did he mean to

sacrifice me on that altar? My entire body trembled, and I took a step back. I sprinted a few steps, but Hartley tackled me to the ground and clucked his tongue.

I strained for the taser in my back pocket, but with the restraints, it proved futile.

Hartley yanked me to my feet and shoved me against the trunk. He took the taser and tossed it. My vision blurred, and then Hudson's truck came into view next to a backhoe. One last glimmer of hope leaped inside my chest at the sight. Maybe I wouldn't have to take a ride with a murderer after all.

Hartley clicked his key fob, and the trunk latch popped open.

"I've got people tracking my phone," I told him, "and backup coming."

The trunk lifted, and my eyes widened in horror.

Hartley gave a cruel chuckle. "Do you mean *this* backup?"

FORTY-SEVEN

Hudson twisted at the back of Hartley's trunk. An angry lump swelled on his right temple, and Hartley had bound his hands in the same plastic restraints as mine.

"Paige, run!" Even without leverage, he got in a surprisingly good kick to Hartley's stomach.

Hartley swore but locked me in his iron grip and wrestled me into the trunk beside my ex-boyfriend. Before he slammed it shut, he located my phone and smashed it.

My heart sank. There went that back-up plan.

Everything went dark with the lid closed, and Hudson swore up a blue streak. The new car smell of the rental nauseated me in these close quarters.

"Magnolia! Moisha!" I called out. "We could really use your help right now."

"Wait. Not yet. They'll be more helpful when we know where he's taking us."

"I'm pretty sure I know where we're headed—the ritual room. He's going to sacrifice one or both of us in Austin's place."

A strangled sound came from Hudson's mouth, followed by

another string of colorful curses. He kicked the side of the truck so hard it shook.

"Did he take your phone too? Maybe we can get Ines to track us or get ahold of the police."

"He took it. Somewhere between smashing my forehead with a brick and stuffing me in here."

"Son of a—" I stopped. "Are you okay?"

"Still conscious. For the moment, anyway. I'd give my last embroidery floss for an ibuprofen right now, though."

"We'll get out of this." I wasn't sure if I was trying to convince Hudson or myself. "Maybe I can kick out the taillights and wave for help. I've always wanted to do that."

I scootched myself towards the tail light, aiming for more leverage, but it was close quarters in here, with my back curled against Hudson's front like the little spoon.

"Ow!" I yelped when my toe crashed against the inner casing of the light. "I really should've worn tennis shoes for this." Despite the pain, I tried again and again, but nothing budged.

"Easy there. Let me at it. You alright?" Hudson asked.

I let out a frustrated sigh. "Yeah. Better a sore foot than getting sliced and diced when we arrive."

I made myself as small as possible to give Hudson more space to swing his leg. That didn't work either.

"If he takes us to the Ursuline entrance to the tunnels, we'll be close enough to the crowds in the Quarter. We could scream and make a run for it," he said.

"Yeah, good plan," I said. "But what about the gun?"

Hudson let out a sigh that sounded like it held the weight of the world. I dropped the back of my head against Hudson's chest, wanting to reach out for him. The cedar scent of his cologne was like a lifeline through the terror, giving me something to focus on besides not dying. The warmth of his forehead pressed into my hair. He inhaled.

The car veered to the right and accelerated. "I think we're on the freeway," he said.

I nodded. How did we end up here? "Is it always like this?"

"You mean, do we always get a free ride with a murderer?" Hudson said, but the humor rang hollow. Another anguished sound rumbled in this throat and right through me.

After a silent moment, he spoke. "This is my fault."

"No. This is Hartley's fault."

"When we stop near the convent, I'll draw his attention, and you run like your favorite dress is on fire."

"Uh uh. We both get away or neither of us gets away."

"You are the stubbornest woman I've ever met."

"It's at least 40 percent of my charm."

"I'm serious, Paige. I'm the one who got us both roped into this. I failed Clarissa four years ago, but I will not fail you. If there's a chance to get away, I want you to take it. Please, promise me." The rumble of his deep voice in my ear made my throat catch.

I couldn't make that promise.

Maybe he took my silence as assent. "If anything happens to me tonight, there's one more thing I want you to know."

"Hudson—"

"No, let me get this out. This has haunted me for the last four years. Please."

I wanted to protest, tell him to save it for when this was all over, but the way his voice broke on *please* fractured something inside me.

"I know I hurt you when I left. It was cruel, and I hated myself every day for it."

I swallowed around the lump in my throat.

"Clarissa was already gone by then, but I kept asking questions and caught the wrong people's attention. I thought I'd been careful and kept you safe by not telling you. But then the pictures came.

"Of you. In your old apartment, getting dressed. At school. With Bridget and Ines." I felt his head shake behind mine. "They said if I didn't back off and leave town the next day, you'd disappear and no one would ever find you."

My heart squeezed. Oh, Hudson. Of course he left. Of course. But not because he was selfish or for any of the other reasons I'd invented to help myself find closure. Because he was the most selfless person I'd ever known. He'd tried to do the right thing, to help his friend's sister, and the Enclave had blown up his life and everything he had planned.

"I could've handled it if they'd only threatened me. But you?"

I snuggled into him, the best I could do in the circumstances.

"I'm so sorry you went through that," I said. "I'm sorry for everything they took from you."

The car slowed to a stop, and I heard Hartley put it into park.

"Let's get Hartley first," I said. "And then bring all those pompous scumbags down."

FORTY-EIGHT

Hartley opened the trunk with a coil of rope wrapped around his shoulder. He tucked a leather-bound book and a knife into his pocket, all with the gun trained on Hudson and me.

"Get out. Slowly. Any sudden moves and I shoot."

Another blast of fear propelled through me, and my legs turned to jelly. I guess you never really get used to a gun pointed at your face.

I nodded and tried to get my bearings as I swung my legs over the lip of the trunk. The humid night air enveloped me, but not the red beans and rice, sticky booze, and rank standing water smells of the Quarter I'd expected.

No boisterous sounds of voices, either. In fact, not a soul in sight. Only the chirp of crickets and sound of traffic whooshing by. I blinked, my eyes adjusting to the shape of a familiar wall and cemetery gates close to us. The tall wrought iron bars soared into the air below the curved sign with the cemetery name. Though popular tourist destinations during the day, and one of our most popular tour sites, most New Orleans cemeteries were off limits at this hour. This one was no exception, with heavy black chains and a padlock keeping the living out.

"Darn, it's closed. Guess we'll have to use a different secret tunnel entrance," I said, my voice coming out a lot more flippant and confident than I felt.

Hartley rolled his eyes. "Don't be stupid. I have my own way in."

Hudson climbed out behind me while Hartley rifled through the secret compartment inside the trunk.

Hudson's expression went grim as he took in our surroundings. I lifted my restrained hands and brushed the reddening lump on his forehead. With a bittersweet smile, he leaned into my touch until I caught a sore spot and he winced.

"Sorry," I said.

Hartley tucked a pair of bolt cutters under his arm and zeroed the gun back in on us. "Move."

We moved.

He made quick work of the chains and re-wrapped them to cover our tracks before leading us into the night.

This must've been the cemetery that Austin mentioned at the end of the other tunnel. We were miles from the Quarter, though.

The cemeteries in New Orleans had always felt like mythical places to me. With their winding paths of tombs complete with street names and lavish mausoleums filled with generations of New Orleans residents, they felt like miniature cities of the dead. I loved the tours that were part of my Deveauxs' orientation, especially with Norman as the guide.

But tonight, this didn't feel like a place of enchanting historical wonders so much as a preview of where I'd be headed if Hudson and I didn't find some way out of this.

Gnarled old trees curled protectively around the resting

places of their favorite residents, their roots bursting through the paved walkways on some of the streets.

We went down a central aisle, past a stone angel statue and impressive tombs and mausoleums. I knew these streets and their stories. We could make a run for it and hide. But then what? Chances were good Hartley would find us before we could get to other people. And then there was the matter of the gun.

"Do you know that the bodies of the dead basically melt down under the sun and stone inside these?" I said, running my hand along the gate leading to a tomb. "Then when it's time for the next member of the family to go in, they pull out a sack with the diminished remains and just stuff it in a special hole that goes underground."

Hartley made a face, visible in the glow of his flashlight. "That's cheerful."

"And do you know why they're built above ground like this?" I asked.

"I don't particularly care, but I'm sure you'll tell me anyway," Hartley said.

"I will," I said. Talking made me feel like I was at least doing something. "The water table is high here. In some of the early cemeteries, the caskets floated and popped out of the ground like corks after a rainstorm. They tried weighting them down with rocks and drilling holes, but that didn't work out so well and eventually they went to the aboveground system."

Hudson shuddered, probably at that gruesome mental picture.

Hartley made several turns down different streets and stopped at a mausoleum next to a stone pyramid. The stone structure was one of the more ornate on this street, with pillars carved into the corners of and a carved stone gateway in the center. Above the gate, the same gargoyle symbols and Latin phrases that we'd seen in the ritual room were laid out between fleur-de-lis.

Hartley unlocked the gate, which opened into a space lined with rectangular granite plaques, wilted flowers littering the ground. The air felt dank here, like stone and dust and death.

He used the same key to open the door at the back of the structure. I could only guess what awaited us.

I swallowed and shared a tremulous look with Hudson.

This was it. Our last chance. Cross this threshold and the odds someone could reach us in time to help plummeted.

Hudson reached out and squeezed my fingers in his. He leaned his forehead against mine. "We'll find a way."

Hartley stepped out of the path, and a set of stairs that led deep into the belly of the earth took shape.

He gestured with the gun. "After you."

FORTY-NINE

We followed the tunnel deeper and deeper under the city, the damp scent of the crumbling walls seeping into my pores. Soil and dust and the metallic tang of fear.

This was it. I'd be seeing Austin and Magnolia and Moisha on the other side before I knew it.

I squeezed my eyes shut and pushed the thought away, along with the cobwebs that crept into my path. No. There had to be a way. I just had to think.

But I had nothing.

We trekked for what felt like hours in grim silence. Which made sense, given that we were far from the part of the Quarter where the ritual room was located. My feet ached, and the restraints had chafed my wrists raw, but the rest of me had gone numb trying and failing to come up with a viable escape plan. It felt like trying to light a match in the rain, every spark snuffing out before it could catch.

Auguste, please forgive me for leaving you all alone.

I looked over my shoulder to Hudson. "Got any ideas for a Hail Mary here?"

We had to be miles underground by now.

"I wish," he said.

"A little late for that." Hartley's cruel laughter echoed through the tunnel, and the light from his bouncing flashlight blinded me.

I watched Hudson's rage solidify, every muscle coiling tighter in time with Hartley's laughter. Fists clenched, jaw ticking. I sensed his next move before he made it.

He halted. Hartley crashed into him, and Hudson cracked the back of his head into Hartley's nose.

Hartley grunted in pain, the flashlight swinging wildly, making my stomach swoop with vertigo as he reached for his face. Hudson tackled him to the ground.

"Go!" Hudson shouted.

I swiveled back the way we'd come, but hesitated. We were in deep. Even if I ran back that way, how long would it take me to get away from the cemetery to get help? A long time. Forward seemed like the better option. Out the Crumbles or Ursuline Convent exit, where there were plenty of people.

Hudson and Hartley wrestled for control. I kicked Hartley in the back and ran.

I'd only dashed a few yards into the gloom before Hartley said in a voice that chilled my blood, "Freeze or I shoot him."

"Go," Hudson shouted again.

I heard the click of the safety disengaging.

My throat went dry. Slowly, I turned, hands in the air. My insides tied themselves in knots at the sight of the barrel pointed directly at Hudson's temple.

"Don't shoot. I'll do whatever you want," I said.

Hartley shoved Hudson forward. I rooted myself to the spot until they caught up with me. "Don't try *anything* like that again. If you do, I'll shoot her. I don't need both of you, and I have no qualms killing the spare."

⁘▲⁘▲⁘

HUDSON and I walked the rest of the way, close enough to rub shoulders. I think we both needed to soak up the comfort of each other's presence, especially if it was for the last time.

After Hartley unlocked the door, the torches jumped to life, painting the ritual room into a macabre tableau.

Hartley forced Hudson to the ground against the lectern on the dais. He used one length of his rope to secure Hudson in place there with sailor-worthy knots.

"You, on the table." He waved the gun at me. I froze. My gaze flickered to the names on the side of the stone ritual slab.

"I thought the sacrifices had to be members of the Enclave. Otherwise, why not just grab random people from the street and not harm your own," I said.

Hartley's nostrils flared. "You'll take the oath once you're secured."

"What if I refuse?"

"I'm not feeling especially patient right now. Let's not make this any more difficult than it needs to be." He swept the gun in Hudson's direction.

I swallowed. The back of my thighs connected with the table. The cold of the stone seeped into my legs. My hands shook as I hoisted myself up. A chill swept through every part of me.

"Lie down."

I did as instructed, though every fiber of my being screamed not to. Hartley used a tool on his key chain to slice through the plastic zip ties and secured each of my wrists and ankles with rope to the built-in restraints.

Terror snaked through me. I wondered if the previous sacrifices had gone willingly, convinced it was some kind of honor, or if they'd also been taken against their will for this diabolical deal.

"Now, you'll take the oath of the Enclave, acolyte," Hartley said.

He pulled a musty slip of paper from his back pocket. "Repeat after me."

He pointed the gun at Hudson again.

Protests dying on my lips, I repeated.

Hartley exhaled in what looked like relief. "Now the real fun can begin." He yanked the ropes tying my hands to the altar. The coarse material burned against my already chafed wrists.

I bit back a whimper as he withdrew several more items from his pockets and laid them out on a cloth next to the altar.

He growled. "Where's the ritual knife?" Hartley patted his pockets.

"Maybe it fell out during your wrestling match in the tunnel," I said.

He double checked every place on his person and growled. "Don't even think about moving."

He stormed off, and the echo of his footsteps grew fainter.

I let go of all the breath I'd been holding.

Hudson and I waited in a tense silence.

"I really wish we could have a deus ex machina come save us right about now," I said.

"Or even a diabolus ex machina, considering their deal's with the devil," Hudson said.

I cracked a grim smile. Yay for gallows humor.

I tugged at my bonds, but to no avail. I was going to bleed out here, where no one would find me. Unless someone came to save us, which was pretty much out of the question with my phone smashed back at the meetup spot. Come on, deus or diabolus ex machina, I prayed.

I wished I had Magnolia's books to help me now. What would Matilda do?

Just then, an idea shot through me. It was wild and out of left field, but maybe, just maybe, my compulsive re-reading of my great grandmother's mystery novels might save us now.

"Hudson," I hissed.

"Yeah?"

"I have an idea. Did you read Magnolia's book *Matilda Mayhew and the Case of the Devil You Know*?"

"Yeah."

"You think there's any chance it was based on a true story like the others?"

Though I couldn't see his face, I heard the hope in his voice. "You are a genius."

FIFTY

"Austin! Austin! Please, for the love of fully intact arteries, I need your help!"

In the gloom of the ritual room, Austin appeared, and my breath whooshed out in relief. Magnolia and Moisha still hadn't answered my calls, so Austin was my last shot.

He took in the sight of me tied to the table and looked like he might throw up. "Paige, what—?"

I cut him off. "I need you to go find my grandma Magnolia and/or Moisha. Tell them it's an emergency. Ask if they still keep in touch with Betty and her boyfriend and if they do, please beg them to find them and pay me a visit ASAP."

Austin saluted and popped out of existence. *Please let this work.*

Hartley's footfalls grew louder, and the torchlight reflected off the knife in his hand.

My stomach shriveled in on itself. I had no idea how long it would take Magnolia and Moisha to search for the reformed devil and his lady love in the afterlife of all human history. But if there was any chance at all, I willed it to happen now.

Hartley pulled out a worn leather book the size of a journal and flipped through it.

"You gotta get this down as it's happening, Hartley?" Hudson taunted him.

I jumped in too. "Dear Diary, I messed up on my last murder, so today I kidnapped two more innocent people to bump off. I don't understand why nobody likes me."

"Shut up." He added some creative expletives. "I have to do the ceremony right, or I'll have to start all over again. All this work for my sister will be for nothing. I should've just done it right after Austin's death last time."

He raised the knife in one hand and read, first in English and then in Latin.

"You don't have to do this, Hartley." Hudson strained against his bonds. "You can still walk away without our deaths on your conscience."

Hartley's nostrils flared. "Stop. Interrupting."

He inhaled and started again, and Hudson belted out The Devil Went Down to Georgia in a rich baritone.

I couldn't help but laugh at the ridiculousness of it all, despite our situation.

Hartley stamped his foot. "Enough!"

Hudson didn't stop.

Hartley barreled on, louder this time. More Latin I didn't understand. "... Domini."

"I believe that's pronounced dom*i*ni, not *do*mini," an unfamiliar male voice chimed in from Hartley's direction.

"Oh my darling, are you alright?" Magnolia's ghost appeared and cradled my head. My scalp tingled where she stroked my hair.

I slumped against the stone table in relief. "Fine, so far. I'm so glad you're here."

"I would've been here sooner, but there was this mandatory

meeting of the Spirit Council. The big guy doesn't like it when we skip out, but talk about a meeting that could've been a missive."

"Is that—" I twisted my head to the side and caught sight of a feisty red-haired beauty and her beau next to Hartley.

Hartley started and backed away, brandishing the knife. "Who the heck are you?"

Judging by the look on his face and the way he tracked our new arrivals' movements, he could see them too. Maybe ghosts could reveal themselves to humans if they chose.

The elegant gentleman clucked his tongue. He was white, sable-haired, with a bit of grey at the temples, and cut an imposing figure in a grey three-piece suit he made look casual despite its formality. "For an individual so intent on keeping his deal with the devil, you're quite slow to recognize your benefactor."

The next question never made it out of Hartley's mouth. He only stood there, jaw hanging, gaze flicking back and forth between me and the devil.

The devil adjusted his cuff links. "I go by many names, but you may call me Wesley."

Hartley blinked and gaped at me, horrified, like he'd only now seen me for the first time and discovered a wolf in sorority girl's clothing. "Who *are* you?"

The devil strode over to me. "If I don't miss my guess, this must be the delightful and resourceful young Paige. Someone who has cultivated many treasured friendships and connections. And it's those connections that have brought me here today." He touched a finger to my bonds, and they fell away like magic.

My chest expanded with my newfound freedom. I rocketed up and rubbed my sore wrists before I realized Wesley held out his hand, waiting for me to take it. I placed my hand in his, and he pressed a kiss to my knuckles. "Enchante, my clever friend."

"Pleased to meet you too. I read your book. My great-grand-mother's book, I mean. About you and Betty."

"So I hear. I owe a great debt of gratitude to your grand-mother and her friends for persuading me to change my ways."

Magnolia smiled at him. "Give yourself a little credit. You were well on your way before we got ahold of you."

"The ultimate reformed bad boy," Moisha said.

"Do you think you could help my friend there out of his restraints too?" I nodded toward Hudson.

"But of course. And allow me to present my beloved, Betty," he said, waving a hand in the red-head's direction.

"Thank you all for coming," I said to them.

"You people, or whatever you are, are crazy," Hartley said.

Wesley tended to Hudson's bonds and the ones at my ankles. While Wesley was occupied, Hartley shook off his stupor and rushed me, ceremonial knife raised. "You are not going anywhere."

Magnolia threw herself in front of me. But with her being incorporeal, Hartley flew right through her, tackling me back onto the stone table.

Austin tried to pull him off me. But, of course, that didn't work either.

Hartley's weight crushed the air from my lungs. I caught Hartley's wrist just before the dagger plunged into my heart. Sweat poured down my brow. My arm shook, fingers digging into his flesh to fend him off. This could not happen. I'd been saved, only to be thwarted by last-minute vindictiveness. The tip of the knife pressed into my sternum. Blood welled up where it punctured my skin. My wrists throbbed from being tied up, but I pushed with all of my might. I had so much to live for. So many more souls like Austin who'd need my help.

"This is for taking everything from me," Hartley ground out.

Wesley unleashed an invisible force that held Hartley paralyzed. The timbre of the devil's voice would make a trained assassin cower as it reverberated through the room. "Think again, mortal."

With a flick of Wesley's hand, Hartley flew through the air and landed in a heap at the devil's feet.

The knife clattered to the ground next to me. I collapsed back against the stone. Hudson, newly freed, rushed over to cradle me. He scooped the weapon up, along with the gun that had fallen out of Hartley's waistband.

"I don't understand." Hartley fought to his feet, his movements jerky, and his limbs at odd angles. He favored what was surely a broken arm. With a moan, he faced Wesley. "If you're the devil, this was your deal. You give us power beyond our greatest desires, and we give you sacrifices. Why are you helping them?"

Wesley let out a long sigh. "About that—I had a rather troubled youth. Dad thought it would be a good idea to have me look after the bad ones when I was going through my rebellious phase. That didn't go so well. At least, not for me." He put his arm around Betty, who snuggled into his embrace. "During that time, I made some poor choices, including deals like this one." He looked at his feet. "It was a dark couple thousand years.

"But then I met Betty and her friends and saw the error of my ways."

Betty patted his chest, beaming a lovely smile up at him.

Hartley balked.

"I've been on a quest of sorts, to make up for my past misdeeds. And that's why I'm here to set things right. Sort of a Twelve-Thousand Step Program."

Red veins streaked Hartley's eyes as they jumped from place to place. He tried to wipe sweat and grime from his brow and winced at his injury. A pitiful sound wrenched out of him, like the verbal equivalent of stamping his feet. "You can't. You *can't*. A deal's a deal."

Wesley held a hand in the air. "My deal with the Enclave of New Orleans is hereby null and void."

Betty squeezed him to her.

Wesley patted his pockets and frowned. "Have you got the list, my love?"

She handed over a long scroll of parchment and a pen from her handbag. Wesley added a line item for *The Enclave, New Orleans, LA, USA.*

"And here's how this will go," Wesley continued. "The rest of the initiated members will have their minds wiped of all dealings related to this secret society of yours. Any who had a hand in killing innocents will be punished. Lord knows you've gathered enough dirt on one another to facilitate that.

"And as for you, Mr. Lightfoot, I believe you have a confession to deliver." Wesley cocked his head to the side, listening, and grinned at the sound of running from the tunnel. "Ah yes, I believe that's our friendly neighborhood law enforcement now."

A stampede of footsteps grew louder until Declan burst through the doorway in uniform, weapon drawn, followed by an out-of-breath Carlie, and my cousin Eliza.

Hudson looped an arm around my shoulders, and I leaned into the warmth of him. He smelled like cedar and dust and hope. We'd done it. Against all odds, we'd made it through this—not completely unscathed, I'd be racking up the therapy bills—but alive. Carlie flashed me a tentative smile.

I nudged Hudson and nodded in her direction. "She must have been the one to call the cops and lead them here."

"Hey, I had a little hand in that too." Eliza strode over to me and tackled me with a hug so tight I could hardly breathe, her long black hair blinding me. "But yeah, she did."

"If the devil can change his ways, I guess Carlie Lightfoot can too," Hudson said.

Declan cuffed a surly Hartley after his confession, and I filled Eliza in on everything that had transpired this evening. Wesley must have done some of his mind-wiping devil magic already because Declan didn't seem to notice or ask about the ghosts and celestial being in the room.

I turned to Eliza with an apologetic look. "I guess this means you won't get to do your Enclave exposé after all, what with everyone's memories wiped."

Everything she'd worked so hard and risked her life the last few months for, gone in an instant. I could tell how much of a gut punch it was professionally, but she waved it off. "I guess I'll just have to dazzle them with something else. The important thing is you're alive and well."

Wesley and Betty, along with Magnolia, Moisha, and Austin, joined our little crew.

"It was lovely to meet you all and be of service, but we best be getting back," Wesley said.

"Hudson, I almost forgot." Magnolia laid a hand on his shoulder. "Your friend Clarissa sends her best and says thank you for looking out for her. She gave us the names of the ones who were involved with her death, and Wesley here is heading to get their confessions now too."

Hudson's Adam's apple bobbed. He dipped his head in thanks.

"She asked if you'd let her family know that she was all right. Happy."

I squeezed Hudson's arm. The tension drained from his shoulders. "Yes, ma'am. Tell her I'll do that."

This was my life now. Ghosts were real. The devil was making amends. And I'd solved my first ghost PI case.

I leaned into my ex-boyfriend-turned mentor's shoulder and

smiled up at my ghostly mystery squad. I thanked the devil and his lady love profusely for their last-minute save. I didn't know if I believed in the idea of a calling anymore. On further consideration, maybe that was too much pressure to put on any one pursuit. But I knew one thing for sure—even if I didn't get it perfect out of the gate, this ghost PI gig was something I wasn't running away from.

EPILOGUE

The next week, Liz greeted me at the door of the newly repaired Crumbles with a wide smile. The familiar smells of baking bread, buttery, delicious cupcakes, and coffee wafted out.

"Ta da." She waved a hand, showcasing the freshly painted front door and new windows. The color had returned to her cheeks, and the tight worry lines that had imprinted on her face during the investigation had mellowed. She'd cut her hair too, but still kept the streak of grey that framed the side of her face. My former professor looked more relaxed than I'd ever seen her.

"Being cleared of murder charges looks good on you," I said.

Liz smirked—as uncomfortable with compliments as ever—and waved me inside. "Come on. I'll make you your cinnamon latte. Did you hear Carlie's brother just publicly confessed?"

I nodded and grinned at the spring in Liz's step as she bustled behind the counter, grabbing mugs and milk and heading for the espresso machine.

"Murder, trying to frame me for murder. Not to mention your kidnapping and attempted murder," she said.

"I missed the press conference, but I heard about it. I guess he's pleading no contest in exchange for leniency for Carlie."

The espresso machine whirred with the sound of foaming milk. A new barista filled the pastry case with fresh muffins.

"He claimed the devil made him do it," Liz said.

I choked on a laugh and shook my head. *You have no idea.*

I rested a hand on one of the repaired purple chairs I loved so much and turned to admire all the fix-ups. "It looks great in here."

When my gaze snagged on the wall where Liz's sister Laini had lovingly painted her French Quarter mural before she passed, my mouth dropped open.

"Looks great, doesn't it? I think Laini would be proud." Liz dropped two steaming mugs on our usual table and looked up at it.

The last time I'd seen it, the Enclave's graffiti had marred Laini's painstaking artistry. But somehow, the spray paint had been stripped, and they'd restored the bold colors and personal touches to its previous glory.

"Your restoration guy really came through."

"But how? I thought he said parts wouldn't be salvageable."

"Our friend Declan had a hand in the re-detailing. Apparently, he used to do projects like this for his dad's construction company."

I pictured Declan with paint flecks on his cheeks and brush in hand, squinting between a picture of the original and the wall, and grinned. "That man is a good egg."

"He is."

Liz and I sat down, and she caught me up on all she'd been doing since I'd seen her last. It was so nice to see her happy again with a piece of her sister's memory restored and without the burden of a murder investigation hanging over her head.

"So does this mean we're back on for puzzle nights?" I asked, gesturing to the refreshed bakery.

"You know it."

"Good. I have to run, but I got us a new puzzle for next time." I pulled the box out of my bag and slid it to her.

"1000 pieces of baby goats frolicking? I can work with that," Liz said.

When we finished up, Liz walked me to the door and fidgeted awkwardly for a minute before looking up at me. "Thank you. For everything."

Unexpectedly, she threw her arms around me. Once I got over the shock of this new demonstrativeness, I squeezed her back. "Does this mean you're doing the hugging thing now?" I teased.

She shook a finger at me and smiled. "Don't tell anyone. We're not making this a regular thing."

⚜⚜⚜

THE NEXT WEEK, after Ben had been discharged from the hospital and recovered enough to get together, we gathered with Mina in the alumnae garden. The jasmine burst in full bloom for our small wake for Austin.

Hudson came along too, and Auguste in his snuggle sack snoring away.

"You didn't want to let the little guy sleep in his own bed?" Hudson teased.

"He insisted. Wanted to be here to say goodbye to Austin."

And since he hadn't poofed into thin air once Hartley confessed to his murder, Austin was in attendance in person — in spirit? — for his final send off as well.

I suspect he had a spot of unfinished business before he left us for good.

After some joyous remembrances, I led Ben to a secluded area under a willow tree, so I could relay his and Austin's goodbyes.

I left the two alone for some final moments, and Hudson sauntered up to me next to the fountain.

"So, I guess this is goodbye for us too. I said one case, and I'd be out of your hair."

"That was the deal." I peered up at him in the dappled sunlight, a bittersweet smile stretching across my lips.

Maybe it was our recent brush with death, but regardless of what had transpired between us four years ago and my complicated feelings about it, we'd been through a lot together. A lot that almost no one else on the planet would understand. Our relationship may have changed, but I was still glad he'd been by my side on this case.

"About that..." Hudson scratched the back of his head.

My heart skipped a beat.

"I've been thinking."

Silence stretched, shifted, as though he were reconsidering.

"And? Do tell," I prompted.

He looked back at me, a vulnerability I hadn't seen in his hazel eyes in a good long while. "I'll still go if that's what you want or need. But I've been thinking about sticking around. That thing in Savannah seems to be taking a while, and being the only ghost PI in town, you'd have a heavy caseload. Not that you couldn't handle it. You've proven yourself more than capable. Especially with Magnolia and Moisha and Auguste and your police officer in your corner."

I rolled my eyes at the "your police officer" part.

"I could share the load. We could back each other up and consult on each other's cases."

"You don't want to go it alone and call all the shots?" I arched an eyebrow at him.

"If that's what you want, I can call the shots." That charming grin of his spread across his face, and I smacked his shoulder.

"Like heck you will."

We stood there next to the fountain in companionable silence.

"In all seriousness," he said, "working with you has made me realize sometimes letting other people in on the hard things is an asset, not a liability."

"Especially when it comes to dealing with the devil." A smiled tugged at my lips.

"And speaking of," Hudson said, you should probably tell Bridget and Ines about the ghosts before the secret kills you."

"Really? I thought you were firmly anti-spilling the Ghosted secrets."

"It worked for Magnolia. Moisha was an outsider at one time."

"Yes, it did. In fact, that gives me an idea."

I explained, and he nodded his approval.

I elbowed him playfully. "You're coming to all sorts of realizations today. Maybe you should work cases with me more often. You'll be a regular epiphany machine."

Heat crept up my cheeks when I realized what I'd said.

"So, is that a yes to me staying? We could give this friends thing a go."

I looked up at the face of the man who'd been so many things to me. Part of me wanted to bypass the whole friends phase and pick up right where we left off. Especially when he looked at me, all twinkle-eyed and protective. But he had changed and so had I. I wasn't sure I was ready to jump into a romantic relationship again without a lot of thought. But one thing I did know for sure, I wanted Hudson Bennett back in my life.

"Friends. I'd like that," I said. My gaze moved to Austin, where he beckoned me under the tree. I gave Hudson one last mischievous smile and whispered, "But I still get to call the shots."

⁘▲⁘▲⁘▲⁘

AUSTIN WRUNG OUT HIS HANDS, and a furrow creased his so often carefree brow. I thought about how much I was going to miss having him around. He had such a good heart.

"You ready?" I asked.

He sucked in a deep breath. "I think so."

I nodded and waited to follow his lead.

He floated back and forth. "You're the one who's good at going from place to place," he said. He cast a longing look back at Ben. "How do I just move on?"

"Maybe think of it as your next grand adventure. The place where you really get to leave your mark."

The hint of a smile cut through his nerves. "I like that." He rolled his shoulders back. "And for what it's worth, even if you give up on the idea of a calling, I think you can help a lot of people doing this Ghosted gig. And it seems to make you happy."

"It does." I looked at my new friend, trying to memorize his features. "You wouldn't think so, what with the kidnapping and near-death experiences, but yeah."

He punched my shoulder, but it only tingled when his fist went right through.

"Thanks for sticking with me. And for helping me find the confidence to carry on, even when I was ready to run."

"I wish I'd known you better before it was time to move on," Austin said.

"The feeling is mutual, my friend."

"Oh, did I tell you I finally went to see my parents?" Austin bit his lip.

My eyes widened. "Good for you."

"I figured if you could call the devil and face down my killer, I could face my parents."

"And?"

"They were still my parents. Bickering about investments and the social pariahs of the week." He rolled his eyes, but the lightness in his mannerisms spoke volumes. "My dad played videos of me as a kid the night he was there. He snuck off to his study after my mom went to bed and watched them for hours. He may not have loved me the way I wanted, but I think he loved me in the way he knew how."

My heart swelled to hear he'd made peace with his family before moving on.

"One more thing. Do you think you could call Magnolia and Moisha to come with me?" Austin asked sheepishly.

"Austin has requested your escort services," I said to my great grandmother and Moisha when they arrived.

Magnolia grinned. "It would be my honor."

Moisha linked her arm through his.

I leaned forward and dropped a kiss on Austin's ghostly cheek, surprised to find him more solid than he'd ever been. Both of our eyes went wide, and I pulled him in for a hug.

"Thank you. For everything." He squeezed me fiercely, and I fought the tears forming in my eyes.

"Until it's my time," I said.

"Until then."

"Oh, and Magnolia and Moisha, if it's not too much trouble, could you come back to my house and see me in a few hours? There's someone I'd like you to meet."

⚜✦⚜✦⚜

AFTER MAKING sure both Bridget and Ines were free for dinner, I set to work preparing shrimp and grits, my entire body buzzing with nerves.

"Why are you so nervous?" Ines asked with a skeptical raise of her brow.

I released a big whoosh of breath. "Because I have something important to tell you. Or rather, show you."

"You didn't get back together with Hudson, did you?" Ines said. She looked up from her computer to eye the place settings on the table.

"No. I did not get back together with Hudson. But he is staying in town. I just want to wait for Bridget."

Ines groaned. "I hate secrets. Just tell me. Promise I'll act surprised when she gets here."

I pulled the cast-iron skillet of shrimp off the burner. "I can only do this once."

Bridget breezed in, arms full of mail, just as Magnolia and Moisha appeared my living room and admired some of Bridget's creations by the fireplace.

"Can you get Nat on the video call?" I asked Ines.

"On it."

A few seconds later, Nat's cheery face popped on the screen at what looked like a British pub.

My heart galloped. I was really doing this.

Before I chickened out, I waved Magnolia and Moisha over.

Ines's brows furrowed. "Who are you waving at?"

"I know this is going to sound completely out there, but just go with me on this." I wiped my sweaty palms on my yellow skirt.

"I didn't know how to tell you, so I thought I'd show you instead. Remember the two older ladies I told you were mentoring me on Austin's case?"

"Yes." Ines and Bridget exchanged puzzled glances.

"Well, there's someone I'd like you to meet. Two someones, actually."

Magnolia floated into the kitchen in all her dolled up 1940s glam glory. "This is my great grandmother, Magnolia Castile."

"Nice to meet you," Magnolia said.

Ines's fork clattered to the table.

After Hartley could see them in the tomb, I confirmed my hunch with Magnolia that ghosts could reveal themselves to humans if they chose.

"And this is her best friend, Moisha Mosher-Harter." Moisha swished in, her hair freshly pin-curled, with her slacks and cardigan and waved at my friends.

Bridget's brown eyes went wide as dinner plates. She blinked and shook her head, as though to clear it.

"Wait, but aren't they, er, no longer alive?" Nat said from the screen.

"Technically, that's correct," Magnolia said. "You could say we're here in spirit."

"This one and the jokes," Moisha said.

"Magnolia, Moisha, I'd like you to meet my very best friends. That's Bridget in the blue dress, and Ines over here with the curly hair. And that's Natalie on the computer screen. Remember, I told you she was over in England working on that regency vampire TV show?"

All three of my friends blinked back at me in stunned silence. I checked rational Ines to make sure she wouldn't faint at the sight of a house full of ghosts. But besides the shock, she seemed to be doing okay.

"I'm so pleased to meet all of you. I know you're very important to my Paige," Magnolia said.

"Same here," Moisha added.

"But you're—there's no such thing," Ines whispered.

"It's okay, we ghosts aren't particularly concerned whether or not the living believe in us," Moisha said.

"Now" — Magnolia floated into the kitchen and took the chair between Bridget and Ines—"which of you is the technological genius and which of you is responsible for that exquisite contraption in the living room?"

Bridget and Ines both sat up straighter.

I held my breath for the beat of silence that passed.

The room erupted in warm chatter as my best friends got to know my crime-solving great grandma and Moisha. I served up the shrimp and grits along with some drinks. I made Ines's a double to compensate for the truth I'd dropped on her, and my heart glowed with relief. Two important pieces of my life connected, and no more secrets.

Well, maybe a few.

Before we knew it, Magnolia and Moisha's allotted hour drew to a close. Magnolia glanced up at the clock. "It's been delightful to meet all of you, but I'm afraid it's time for us to go."

"Aww, do you have to?" Bridget said.

Magnolia favored her with an indulgent smile. "We'll see each other again soon, I'm sure. This one's going to be in high demand on the ghost circuit, mark my words." She squeezed my shoulder.

After a round of goodbyes, I walked to the living room with Magnolia and Moisha.

"You did well, my darling," Magnolia said. "You did right by many people in the way you solved this case."

My eyes welled with tears.

"Couldn't have done it without you two," I said.

"Darn right." Moisha's eyes twinkled with mirth. "You did good, kiddo."

I hugged them both, and just as they flitted out of existence, my new phone buzzed with a notification.

I walked back to the kitchen to join my friends again.

"Is it a new case?" Ines's eyes glittered.

I held up the screen for her, Bridget, and Nat to see.

Next to the Ghosted Icon, a message lit up: *You've been Ghosted. Click to see new matches.*

"I call background research," Ines said.

"I call props and engineering support," Bridget said.

"I might actually get to help on the next one too," Nat said. "I'll be in town for a bit soon."

A grin spread across my face.

Bridget cleared her throat, and we all turned her direction. She folded and unfolded her hands. I raised an eyebrow.

"Speaking of otherworldly beings," Bridget said, "this would probably be a good time to tell y'all something else."

Ines, Nat, and I exchanged quizzical glances.

"Are you sure Ines's heart can take it?" I teased.

Bridget pushed Ines's drink closer to her, and her gaze swept to all of us. "I may need your help investigating something else. You know that blind date I had the other night? I'm about 90% sure he's a vampire."

✦✦✦

THANK you so much for reading!

If you'd like to keep up with what's next for Paige and the gang, along with other book news, sneak peeks, crafting attempts, and behind the scenes stuff, please sign up for my newsletter here: https://view.flodesk.com/pages/60f20392d2b5fd7ee54a013d . I've also got some cute Ghosted themed printable reading trackers just for subscribers.

IF YOU ENJOYED ONCE GHOSTED, Twice Shy, please consider telling a cozy mystery loving friend or leaving a review on your favorite retailer's website. Every time you leave a review, Auguste gets a treat.

ACKNOWLEDGMENTS

Thank you to everyone who sprinkled their magic dust on this book from concept to final edits. Like Paige, I owe much of my success to my community of friends, family members, and fellow writers and readers. I truly wouldn't be me without you. I'm so grateful to have found my people.

Thank you to Jennie Booth, Tamara/Tara Lush, Amanda Trejbrowski, and Gina Mitchican for being my earliest test readers in the midst of the pandemic when I was fighting through brain fog, depression, and uncertainty while coaxing this little ember of an idea to life. Your enthusiasm and words of encouragement kept me going until THE END.

Love and gratitude to my Binderhaus ladies: Amanda, Deb, Gina, Jen, Jena, Jocelyn, Louise, Thien-Kim, and Tamara, who provide endless support, inspiration, and serve as my sounding boards. Hopefully we can hot tub plot tub again soon.

This book is also a love letter to my enduring college friendships. Abby, Marissa, and Michele, especially, as well as our other sorority sisters and dorm mates, I don't know how I would've survived my 20s without you. (And thank goodness all of our shenanigans were not preserved forever on social media, amirite?) I hope you enjoy the AGD Easter eggs.

A huge thanks also to my beta readers and editors for your eagle eyes and valuable input. Jocelyn, Jennie, Jen, Tamara, Amanda, Gina, you are gold. Gwen Hayes, thank you for your helpful edit.

And to my family, nothing I write (or do, for that matter) would be possible without you. Mom, you started my love of stories. Mom, Jon, Dad, all my siblings and siblings-in-law, nephews, and parents-in-law, who now live next door, you are the best. Paul and my boys Archer and Fisher, you are what keeps me going. Thanks for your generous spirits, love, laughter, and support.

Last, but certainly not least, thank *you* for reading. With a million+ books in the world, thanks for taking a chance on this one and spending your time with Paige and the gang.

ABOUT THE AUTHOR

Jessica Arden writes cozy mysteries, and quirky contemporary romance, usually with a supernatural twist. She's stomped grapes in her native California, hiked 350 miles on an ancient pilgrimage route in Spain, had breakfast with a coatimundi in Costa Rica, and spent the night in a monastery. But no matter where life takes her, her true north will always be with her husband and two energetic boys.

When she's not writing, you can find Jessica teaching college English classes, doing designing projects, making crafts (she's currently obsessed with vinyl and stickers), and dreaming of eating chips and salsa in a restaurant again.

www.ingramcontent.com/pod-product-compliance
Lightning Source LLC
Chambersburg PA
CBHW051215190726
48288CB00006B/1962